CONFES

OF A CLEANER

BY

BOG BRUSH BARRY

It's Time To Come Clean

Written by

Matt Bird

This is not based on a True Story; this is a True Story.

To all you unsung heroes out there who undertake cleaning, and supermarket trolley pushers for that matter, you have my heartfelt respect.

CONTENTS

ABOUT THE AUTHOR

After the success of his first book, *Baby Pigeon*, based on his online dating experience – Matt Bird is back, sharing his words of wisdom on the cleaning industry, an industry he knows inside and out.

Matt Bird – a unique, funny, hard-working and successful 40-odd-year-old (anyone would think he wrote this.)

He has run a successful cleaning business for 20-odd years in a small rural town in Devon. It's a special place. Let's just say the marriage counselling service here isn't called Relate, it's called RELATED, and the £3 supermarket meal deal comes with a two-litre bottle of cider as a drinks option.

Let's just say that over the years he has employed the good, the bad, and the stupid, and dealt with customers you would not believe.

He who laughs last, laughs longest…

INTRODUCTION

Once Upon a Grime

So, before I start, let's get a few confessions out of the way first…

Have I ever walked out of a restaurant without paying?

YES! Twice! In my defence one of those times it was an accident and I did go back and pay; the 2nd time, however…

Have I ever had anything shoved up my bum?

YES! Twice! And both experiences were not enjoyable. Let's just say having colonic irrigation during a hosepipe ban was not my best move.

What's the most random thing you do?

I quite often have Alpen – I have the no added sugar one for breakfast but end up putting sugar on it; work that out!

Have I ever been to court?

YES! Eh-hem! THREE TIMES! *Hangs head*. Please note, it was all for the same offence!

Have I ever broken the law?

Well, I suppose that is obvious since I have been to court. Buuuuut, I will tell you more about that later in the book.

For now, I just want to be fair; all of us have broken the law at some point, haven't we? It's just some of us have not been caught. Does this relate to cleaning? Maybe… Buuuuuut, I never set out purposely to break the law. However, I can say I like to just bend them slightly.

1

Have I done things I regret?

Absolutely! I confess to some of these things in this book too... Just some, though. I think it's reasonable that other regrets will accompany me to the grave.

Have I run a successful cleaning company for 20 years?

YES! It has been educational, amazing, and astonishing. Some of the stories... well! I can't wait to tell them to you.

Will this book shock you?

Most of you, yes! For those of you who know me, you might have heard some of these tales. In fact, a few of you might have even been there at the time.

So let us begin: It is an interesting fact that the average woman cleans for around 12,896 hours in her lifetime, whereas men spend a diminutive 6,448 hours doing chores. In fact, 20% of men say they never clean at all, so I'm guessing a few of those who answered the survey included putting up a shelf in their cleaning hours.

Well, I didn't conduct that survey, so I don't know if it is accurate. But one thing I do know is that I have done around 500,000 cleaning hours in my lifetime.

And they say men who do more housework get more sex! I can assure you that part is not true!

There is a stigma attached to my line of work. It's an industry which is looked down on by most, laughed at by others, and totally ignored by some. However, we are not the lowest of the low, as some people seem to think, and most of us are certainly not stupid or uneducated. Well, to be fair, I was thick as shit at school – I think my biggest achievement was that I got a signed Rusty Lee picture as she liked my risotto recipe. Oh, and I caught nits, but there's more than one way to get a-head. Lack of school success does not mean lack of success in life, and it also doesn't mean you are stupid. Fundamentally, it has always annoyed me when people feel the need to look down on my chosen career path as a cleaner.

I say chosen career path, however, the reality is that it's a path I fell into out of necessity. My GCSE grades meant options were limited when I left school. Let's just say Oxford and Cambridge were not as exactly fighting over me. A strange thing is, when growing up my mum heard fish was good for the brain, so she fed me lots of seafood. Well, what a crock of crap that was! Plus, you never see a mackerel on Mastermind, do you?

Talking of Mum, she was great by the way! Of course I would say this, what with being her son, however, she smothered me in more than just love. When I was a child one of my earliest memories was banging my head on the brick fireplace and her putting butter on my head! Still to this day, I remember walking around with a lump of yellow stuff, *I can't believe it was butter*, smothered on me and I still don't know why. They say Mum knows best, however I'm not sure this is true judging by her butter uses. Additionally, my head injury might explain things a bit. Plus, it is strange but true, I don't like butter or margarine on anything since this childhood trauma!

I think I had at least one thing going for me as a kid; I learnt to swim before I could walk. For example, I learned to make opportunities for myself, and fake it to make it. But also, I was really good at swimming too. This was only because I shared the bed with my two brothers, and they used to piss the bed, so I spent most of the night treading water! Dad would always ask us what position in the bed we'd like to sleep in, and I always opted for the shallow end! Anyway, even though I was good at swimming, I was still thick as shit, and it doesn't help that my accent makes me sound like I should qualify for some form of special needs status too. There is something about the West Country accent; it sounds as though Worzel Gummidge gave us voice training. I might not sound exotic, but this is the sound of being uneducated and not paying attention at school. And I'm not being as rude as you think – I am damn proud of my achievements and want to highlight how it takes all shapes and sizes to create a successful society. One thing I did leave education with, though, was common sense; I've noticed common sense is so rare these days it should be considered a superpower! Why is it that the most intelligent people I come across have no common sense whatsoever?

Well, I guess without stupid people in the world we would have no one to laugh at – unless we subscribe to social judgement and laugh at cleaners and trolley pushers (please don't). My book is a way to push back and let us cleaners have a little laugh at you; although I spend a lot of time poking fun at ourselves too, exposing our dirty secrets from the inside. I suppose lots of things about work are funny, like when you get people who don't obviously fit their jobs, like a fat receptionist at the gym or a squeamish doctor who can't stand the sight of blood, or a fussy chef… or an ugly stripper.

I guess the seed was planted in my head at an early age that I probably wouldn't aspire to much. I was in the remedial unit class at school, let's just say in the school nativity play they couldn't find three wise men let alone virgin. Being in the remedial unit at school meant we were always under constant supervision and constantly underestimated. There are a few times that stuck with me and I learned from – some of which clearly inspired my work choices years later. There was this time when our regular teacher was off, and we had a supply teacher. Drug-Head Darren's face lit up when he heard this, until he realised it wasn't that sort of supply teacher. We called her Henry's Cat, and I still have no idea why to this day. Anyway, I think she hated kids.

"Children should be seen and not heard!" she shouted at us firmly. This was her mantra for teaching. I'm not sure she'd ever win Supply Teacher of the Year with that attitude. Anyway, repeating her favourite expectation to us again, she gave each of us a high-viz bib to wear, a black bag, and a litter-picker tool.

"Today's project for our special class is about the environment!" she announced, her beady eyes gleeful in our misery.

We had to walk around the school grounds picking up litter under her watchful eye, while the rest of our year group were released from the school grounds to enjoy orienteering. They didn't trust us to tie up our own shoelaces, let alone give us maps and compasses.

"Whoever brings back the most rubbish will win a special prize!" she roared. "You have two hours!"

Never one to miss out on being top of the remi-class, I targeted the areas of the school ground I knew there was always rubbish. I headed off happy with my strategy to all the hot-spots, including behind the bike sheds, or as the kids used to call it: The D.F.S. area (Designated Fingering Section – teens are gross, right?). I was smarter than I looked, on a roll, and whistling while I worked. Certain I would win, I hurried to pick up all the debris: packets of Monster Munch, Dib-Dab wrappers, old cans of Lilt, empty cans of Panda Pops; you know, the old-skool treats.

I had quite a sweat on, to be fair; it was certainly a case of betty swallocks. I even felt some groin juice trickling down my legs.

As I've gotten older, I've come to learn that not everybody who wears high-viz actually works that hard. You always see groups of men stood around in high-viz doing jack shit! Have you ever wondered who Jack Shit actually was? Well, I was once told a story that he was a German bloke called Schitt. He married a posh lady called Noe Sherlock, who became Noe Schitt-Sherlock. They then had five kids as they didn't believe in contraception. They called their kids Holie, Loda, Fulla and twins Deep and Dip. I know it sounds like I know Jack Schitt, however I can assure you I don't know Jack Schitt... But I was always taught that if you don't know the answer, baffle them with bull-schitt!

Anyway, back to the high-viz... You know the type of bloke: they stand around in groups as if some of them are being paid to watch the work being done. Anyway, back to the story. I was pretty confident I was going to win Henry Cat's prize. The two hours were nearly up so I headed back. I felt like Santa carrying the black bag over my shoulder back to the classroom. It didn't bother me that older kids were looking out of their classroom windows, banging on the glass, shouting, "Spacker!" at me. I was up for the Litter-Picker-of-the-Day award – or so I thought. So, their jeers slid off me like butter off Teflon (or my forehead, but whatever).

Once in the classroom, I sat smugly with my bag of overflowing rubbish, confident the award was also in the bag. Moments later, my confidence deflated faster than a piñata in the shape of Donald Trump at Stormy Daniels' birthday party. One of the other kids entered the room with his swag and a swagger.

"Are you chewing gum?" Henry's Cat asked as he entered.

"No! I'm Peter Skidloads!" he replied, cool as a cucumber from the fridge. This kid was actually not as stupid as he looked or sounded. With all the strength and style he could muster, he flaunted his way into the room with TWO overflowing bags of rubbish! The teacher was thrilled! We all celebrated and cheered well done to him.

However, I smelt a rat. Not literally; he hadn't accidentally dragged in some rodents too. Don't get me wrong, Peter was thick as shit and quite often stunk of piss – but every now and then he had moments of lucid glory! I swear there was a genius living his head, but only part-time – like his skull was their holiday home. I know everyone has the right to be stupid, however Peter really did abuse the privilege. I remember us doing Letter of the Day at school and the teacher said to Peter, "Today's letter is 'L'. Tell the class something you're not very good at beginning with the letter 'L'."

He replied, "Spelling."

There was another occasion he was asked to name five animals that live in the Arctic. He replied, "Two polar bears and three seals."

But this day was his day; Peter was the winner. And his strategy deserved credit. He wanted to win, but he also didn't want to do the work – who could win by working fairly when you were up against kids like me sweating away?

So, when the teacher wasn't looking, he took the black bags out of the already full school bins.

That day I learned to never underestimate the power of a remi-unit kid.

Peter's approach was a stroke of evil genius; they also say

what goes around comes around. His cheeky-hack meant he both won and lost that day. The treat Henry's Cat promised turned out to be a booby-prize; the winner had to look after the class pet during the school holiday. Our class pet was a stick insect called Woody. Though it might not have been too onerous a task; I have suspicions it was just an old twig stuck in an enclosure. Even so, I'm still glad I didn't win. Coming in second doesn't always mean you are the first loser. Anyway, moving on.

After leaving education, I spent several years stacking shelves at a local supermarket, which I guess exceeded the expectations of my teacher who probably thought I'd end up working in a supermarket but pushing trollies. I mean, they've always got a special on. I was fortunate to land my dream job working in radio. For a while, I juggled both jobs – part-time day shifts for the radio station and night shifts at the supermarket. Then, as if by fate, I lost my job at the supermarket.

I'm a bit limited in what I can say on the subject. Let's just say it didn't end well and I had to take them to a tribunal – which I won. Okay, I will say something about it. On one particular night shift, I was key holder for the store, and I let a member of staff into the building when they weren't on shift. In hindsight, I should never have let him in as it should have dawned on me to question who wants to be in a supermarket at night when they are not working. He claimed he had left something in his locker! Anyway, I let him in. Then, a conversation took place where I was informed that a case of cigarettes was hidden in the warehouse instead of being in the normal secure area. I was offered money if I turned a blind eye to them being removed from the store.

This is the bit of the story that has never been contested, however, the next part was the problem.

I went into the warehouse to the exact area where I was told these cigarettes were hidden. Looking up, I saw a camera pointing directly at them, so I knew a manager was aware they were hidden. I then took these cigarettes and moved them to the secure area. I then told the member of staff I let in to leave the store, which he promptly did.

The next morning, I informed one of the managers that during my night shift I had come across the cigarettes and moved them to the secure area. I didn't inform him about the staff member who dropped in during the night. So, to cut a long story short, the managers responded quickly and replayed the security cameras to see what happened. Everything then unfolded horribly; suddenly, I lost my job as they assumed I was in on this scam! Now, if I had lost my job for letting a member of staff in outside of working hours, I would have accepted it. However, being sacked for attempted theft was unjust and infuriating – I wasn't going to stand for that!

Fate can be a funny thing. The strange thing is, the day after I lost my job at the supermarket, a full-time position came up at the radio station. I basically blagged myself the job; what I lacked in education I made up for in confidence. I had bags of it, like a toddler walking around naked with his pants on his head. However, there is a true downside to doing the jobs you love in life, and that is they don't necessarily pay well. So, I knew eventually I would have to find a way to supplement my wages. Anyway, I have digressed. Where was I? Oh, yes…

The supermarket case ended up a tribunal in Bristol. The judge was brilliant! In summing up, he gave the analogy: if the defendant was driving down the motorway at 90 miles per hour and saw a police car on the bridge a mile away, can you prove that by the time he gets to the bridge he would be still doing 90 miles per hour?

I got a pay-off and an existential kick up the ass. It's just funny how life goes; if I hadn't lost my job at the supermarket I would probably still be working there now. My life would have turned out so differently. I guess sometimes fate plays a part in our journey of life. It also goes to show you can work your ass off for a company, but it often means jack schitt. I never fully got the promotions I should have while working there; they always seem to promote the idiots who never really did any work. I guess it's true, skilled workers are hard to find, that's why idiots get promoted to management.

Now, let's get back to cleaning and how this idea began to grow. Inspiration can take the oddest forms, and my inspiration came in the form of a balding man in leather. One day while in my studio by the office, I met our new station cleaner. He was called Nick, and he looked like a 70s porn star complete with handlebar moustache. To be honest, he wasn't the greatest cleaner, however, he did just enough so that nobody would ever complain. I imagine if they did complain, he wouldn't have taken it lightly; I had visions of him getting his wanger out and bashing them around the head.

Funnily enough, Nick the Cleaner became a local celebrity while working at the radio station, and we would often get him to do a feature on our shows as he was game for anything – and I mean anything! We ran a competition once called 'Stomach of Steel', which was one of my suggestions for features that made it to air. I also suggested 'Name the Beaver' and my boss nearly had a heart attack. In my defence, it was genuine – a local wildlife place had two baby beavers and wanted to name them, so get your mind out of the gutter! And when it was National Apple Day, I wanted to play a game I called 'What's in Zid-her!' Again, my boss didn't see the funny side.

Anyway, back to 'Stomach of Steel'. This is a game where listeners would phone up and suggest things for Nick to eat. Oh, the hilarity! And potential 999 moments! One morning, someone suggested Nick eat cat food. Now, the beauty of radio back then was that nobody could see what you were doing. Pre vlogs, web-shows and social media, we were limited to just live audio. This meant we could effectively make it sound like he was eating cat food, snot, vomit – anything really – when actually he was eating something far more appetising. However, without intending to feed the stigma that all cleaners are thick as shit, Nick hadn't noticed that we could have swapped his cat food for a delicious burger. On this particular morning, we opened up a genuine tin of cat food, and he took a spoonful and ate it! I think we gagged and retched more than he did! However, it did make great radio. Too much? You've read nothing yet!

Nick was full of wisdom, and he told me that cleaning is one of very few jobs where you get paid per job and not necessarily by the hour. Take the cleaning of the radio station – he was paid for three hours per day. Generally, he did his job outside of normal working hours, and most days his work was complete in an hour, and he still pocketed the rest of the cash. This is when I had my lightbulb moment – this would be the perfect work for me outside of my radio hours. I always like to live by the adage, work smarter and not harder.

So that's how I got into cleaning.

I have since given up radio – well, to be fair, I was more

pushed out the door. However, the less said about that the better. A gagging order prevents me from saying too much, but I got a pay-off from them too. Let's just say they are all Heart! And they still pretty much play the same songs every hour to this day.

So, this story ends up with the fact that I have run a successful cleaning business for nearly 20 years. I started off all those years ago in my hometown, which is a special place. I don't want to be rude about it, but the marriage counselling service there isn't called Relate, it's called Related. And the £3 meal deal in the local Tescos has a two-litre bottle of cider as a drink option. The town itself is lovely; unfortunately it's the people that let it down. We're not very cultured; having said that, a Turkish barbershop has recently opened up. Anyway, when I started cleaning, I basically took on anything and everything from cleaning public toilets to celebrity houses. I've since gone full circle from starting off as a one-man band to employing 20 staff at one point. Now, I am back to just me and one other, and I like it that way.

I've made my money, bought a string of houses along the way, and invested wisely. I have a wealth of experience, a few regrets, and a heap of hilarious stories. But I'm pretty much done and dusted, like a mantelpiece in a show home. One thing I learnt early on, in society cleaners are treated like dirt. It's ironic really, since we scrub your dirt away. It's a sad truth but to be a cleaner you need incredibly thick skin – and not just to keep out the germs, as we have gloves for that. I for one hold cleaners in high regard. It's an honest job; it's a dirty job; but someone has to do it.

So, I've decided to fight back, write a book, and literally dish the dirt! This book is for all you people who have ever looked down upon me and treated me like something you trod in. You might have laughed at me, but I'm about to have the final laugh! Oh, and for all you unsung heroes out there who undertake cleaning, and all you supermarket trolley pushers for that matter, you have my heartfelt respect.

Over the past 20 years, I have seen it all! Whoever says nothing surprises them should become a cleaner. There have been surreal moments, like finding £2,000 in cash under a bed, finding a dead goat in a public toilet, and finding used condoms lying around an old biddy's house – to me, I thought her bits would look like a dried Weetabix, and that her wild shagging days were done. I was evidently wrong. I'm guessing I underestimated her sexual power... and the power of lube – by the gallon. I have seen clients using a toilet brush as a microphone with bog-water dripping down their hand, and a celebrity getting out of the shower. And I had to call the RSPCA when I found two dead cats in a hoarder's house. Even more shockingly, when I told the house owner what I had found, her reply was, "Oh... I thought I hadn't seen them for a while." But more on all these later.

Some stories are shocking, other stories are funny, some are so disturbing I still wonder how I didn't end up in therapy. Saying that, I still can't listen to the 'On the Wings of Love' song due to my experiences, but more about that later. However, all the stories are true. Identities have been changed to protect the innocent – and to avoid unnecessary legal proceedings. Otherwise, I have maintained the honest integrity of each confession, no matter how painful or squeamish.

So, from being a remi-unit reject to a cleaning company magnate, this is my story. This is *The Confessions of a Cleaner.*

CHAPTER 1

Getting My Equipment Out

Let me take you back right to the very beginning. The great thing about starting a cleaning company is the start-up costs are low and pretty much anyone can do it. It's a savvy business, and success is attainable.

My first cleaning job was at an estate agents. I landed the job as my girlfriend at the time did it but wanted to quit, so I took it off her hands. If I'm honest, she also inspired and pushed me, opening my eyes to the potential of earning extra cash. This gig was actually cleaning for another firm, and I was paid £15 per visit. It basically took me an hour and half and back then that was good money – especially for a young whipper-snapper like me.

Ever curious and shrewd, I got to thinking… If I'm being paid £15, I wonder what the cleaning company are charging? Granted, the firm supplied all the cleaning materials and equipment – well, at first! But that is another story I will return to in a minute. Then, one day while cleaning a desk, I came across an invoice from the cleaning company. I wasn't snooping exactly, but I wasn't exactly avoiding finding things out either. And what I found out got me stirred even more. The company were charging them £30 per visit – every time I cleaned, they were doubling the cash. So, I reasoned, they were getting the same money as me, and all they had to do was send an invoice each month. They didn't even supply the materials anymore, as it turned out once I had used all their cleaning materials, I had to buy my own. They never got round to dropping any more off!

So, wily and confident, I thought I needed to set up a proper business so I could cash in. After all, everyone is an opportunist if they have an opportunity. I most certainly was.

Firstly, I was aware I needed to sound bigger than I was. Working in radio, I had learnt a few advertising tricks along the way. The name of the company came easy; I called it Marbles Southwest with the slogan, 'You'll be lost without us'. I had a big pair of balls on me, so I wanted my company to be confident. Plus, if you lose your marbles in life you are snookered. Marbles had a meaning. The full story is for another day; however, I will give you the quick lowdown on it. Prior to getting into radio, I set up a jingles company with my friend Rob and we also used the name Marbles. It actually stood for **M**att **A**nd **R**ob's **B**rilliant **L**ittle **E**nterprising **S**cheme.

Before settling on Marbles, I toyed with a few other names which I thought might draw attention. Names like Bog-Brush Barry, or Cillet-Matt, Bang and the Work is Done made me chuckle, but I also thought they sounded a little cheap and tacky. I wanted to sound professional and for it to be an easy name to remember. So, Marbles it was! By the adding the word Southwest I made it sound like Marbles had regional divisions. In reality, I was a young bloke with no GCSEs, a hoover, a duster, a clapped-out car, and not a ruddy clue about cleaning.

There are other funny cleaning company names and slogans I have come across over the years. Some of my favourite named competitors include:

- Twinkle Time: We will make your place shine!

- The Cleaning Whizzard: Let me pop around with my wand! (This made me laugh, but I also thought it sounded a bit odd.)

- Maid in Heaven

- Dust Bunnies

- Lean Mean Clean Machine

- Let us hurt your dirt (I'm not sure if the owners were gay or not, but there's something about this name that makes me think so).

- Two Girls and a Bucket (I'm glad they said and a bucket and not with a bucket).

- J. Edgar Hoover Cleaners (I actually think this one is genius – I love it!).

- Rent-a-Maid (This one sounds like an escort service, as does the next one).

- Maid 2 Order

- Partners in Grime

- (And last but definitely not least) Neat, Sweet, and Discreet Cleaning Service

I assure you these are all genuine company names – though I am not privy to whether they conduct any specialist work for the discerning customer...

At one stage I did toy with the idea of employing all Asian ladies as I could have then called the business 'Maid in China'. Although in many ways, I wish my name was Freddie as I could have called my business, 'Another One Fights the Dust'.

I do love a good pun.

If you ever need to name a business, my best advice is to just be original as you can, then you will always stand out. Radio advertising also taught me you should never name a company using your first name. Matt the Cleaner didn't have a good ring to it; plus, naming a business after yourself emphasises you are a one-man band – even if you aren't. Richard Branson always says, "If you want to stand out from the crowd, give them a reason not to forget you." The name Marbles really worked for me.

The next thing was to let potential customers know I was there. So, I designed a few flyers; well, when I say I designed a few flyers, I really mean I had flyers designed. While at the radio station, I got friendly with one of the office staff. She was few years older than me but a childless Milf, if there is ever such a thing. I guess she would be a Wilf – 'A woman I'd like to f*ck'. Or are they cougars? To be fair, there are a lot of Wilfs around – older ladies are getting hotter and hotter. Anyhow, I gave her a bit of flannel and complimented her on her appearance. Who am I kidding? In return for doing the flyers for me, I gave her dick. It was a simple transaction and it worked for both parties, both of us getting what we wanted from our arrangement.

I ended up giving her a bit more dick than I first planned as she kept changing the design of the flyers. I would say she clearly got more out of it than I did, but it was a small price to pay. After all, if you want success in life you have to make a few sacrifices along the way. And anyway, while I was grinding her, I just thought about someone else. And if you are shocked by that, believe me, every bloke does it – and no doubt women do too. Sometimes we lie back and think of England – or in my case a former neighbour who apparently gives the best blow-jobs in town – not that I ever got to experience this for myself. But I must confess she took up a lot of my teenage fantasies, especially as she used to sunbathe in the front garden in the skimpiest bikini ever. Talk about separating the meat and dairy section! She was rare for a woman from the 80s since having a big bush was all the rage – I was surprised her meat section didn't have a big hairy bush poking out the sides of her skimpy bikini pants. Back then, ladies had hanging baskets, rockeries, and all sorts growing down there. Let's just say they were pleasantly wild… Anyway, moving on!

Once the flyers were sorted, I invested in some equipment. I bought a Henry hoover, a couple of dusters, a polish and a thing called a multi-purpose spray.

I basically had all the gear and still no idea what I was doing, pretty much like the time I lost my virginity to this rather dumpy girl in a Yellow Metro – she gave me the phrase no bloke ever wants to hear: "You're cute, but you're nowhere near the hole!" I just thought, *Ruddy Hell, love, there's too much choice down here!* They do say it takes a long time to understand a woman's hidden treasure. I had no chance of finding it under her rolls of fat – and that's my excuse anyway. The joke of it was she claimed to have an eating dis-order, I thought No-Schitt Sherlock , looks like you can't stop eating.

Anyhow, where was I? Oh yes! I loaded the equipment into my maroon-coloured, clapped-out Vauxhall Cavalier. It was complete with the exhaust hanging off and questionable paintwork, as was the trend at the time for young men desperate to be free and mobile. Then, certain of my imminent success, I headed off to some local business parks to drop off some flyers to advertise my work. Oh! I knew the phone would be off the hook!

I pulled up outside one office, exhaust popping and rattling, my engine clattering to a halt. The receptionist must have heard me coming as I could see her peering over her desk as I got out of the car. I never realised my car sounded as loud as it did or considered the impression it might make. I walked in, smiled at her, and she sneered back. She never really gave me the time of day – she had no interest in what I was saying. At the time, I just assumed she was either a lesbian for not succumbing to my charms, or just having a rough day. It didn't occur to me that turning up in a clapped-out car, and looking rough as rats wearing shorts and t-shirt, might have been the turn-off. I went to the next unit and pretty much had the same response. This time it was a bloke on reception, so my wiles were never going to work, but I thought reason might. The penny still hadn't dropped; I told you I was thick as shit. Every single place I went to just didn't seem interested in my services.

The leaflets might have looked professional; however, I gave off the appearance of a cowboy cleaner. I think they were surprised I didn't turn up on a horse! I might have been a slow learner when I was young, but I was a hard worker, and persistent. So, I eventually learnt a valuable lesson from that day. It's true that nothing succeeds without the appearance of success. So I went home, confidence knocked, dusted myself down, and thought, *Next time I'll put on my suit.* To be fair, to that point it only came out for weddings and funerals, so this was a decent opportunity to look smart. I also resolved to try a different business park. Heading out once more, I parked up on the outskirts of the business park and went in on foot. I finally realised there was no point looking the part and turning up in a council-estate limo. I might not have minded about my car, but the weight of everyone's judgements still weighed heavy on my confidence.

It should have been a reassuring vehicle – it had a fish logo on the back, which is a religious symbol and apparently a sign of trustworthiness!

I walked around every single unit that day, dropping off flyers and speaking to receptionists. They treated me very differently: every single place I went to listened to what I had to say. Don't get me wrong – I blagged all of it! But, by the end of the day I had picked up two cleaning contracts. I was thrilled and my confidence reinflated.

Both of these contracts were Key Jobs, which is the Holy Grail of cleaning work. You see, as Nick the Cleaner had taught me, Key Jobs are the ones where you conduct the work when all the staff have gone home. You can then whizz in, clean and leave, and they have no idea how long you spent on site. Any cleaning firm or cleaner who says they have done their allocated time on a Key Job are liars as it just doesn't happen – you get the job done as quickly as you can.

In the early days, I made the mistake of quoting work by the hour. However, as I got more experienced, I changed the wording to price per visit. That way, if there were come-backs, I could just turn around to the client and say they paid per job and not per hour. As I learnt over time, some firms would check the alarm systems to see how long cleaners were spending on sites. It was a game of cat and mouse – them looking for value for money, and me trying to maximise income and efficiency. Checking the alarm system was the most common tactic firms used back then to get rid of crap cleaners or they brought in tick sheets which cleaners had to sign to make them accountable. For the record, tick sheets don't work at all and cleaners will just tick the sheet regardless if they have done all the daily, weekly tasks on the list.

Thankfully, I never made out that I did the work myself, which was another stroke of genius on my part. Then, if and when I got complaints about crap cleaning or staff not doing the allotted time, I would pretend to remove that cleaner from that contract and spend a little extra time on site so I didn't lose the business. Clients were normally well-impressed with my swift action; however, it was a total blag. The only person I was ever having words with was myself. But it worked a treat.

I'm not saying it was plain sailing to start off with; it was bloody hard work! I was juggling a job I loved in radio and working unsociable hours cleaning. Time off for rest or socialising just didn't happen. There's this myth that in order to run a business you must enjoy what you are doing; that if you are in it purely for the money it will never work – well, what a crock of crap that is! I was running my cleaning company purely for the money, and I was slogging my guts out to earn it. Did I enjoy it? Did I heck! Looking back, there were fun times, and good times – but I can't say hand on my heart that I enjoyed it. It was all about the money for me: the more I earnt, the more I wanted. Stupid thing is , I only really enjoyed cleaning after 20 odd years when it wasn't about the money anymore.

But there are lessons to be found in success as well as in our failures. Even though it paid off financially for me, it took me an age to realise money is not the key to happiness. Granted, I am lucky as I can now retire despite still being relatively young. But there are things I missed out on. Love, connections, and all the fluffy stuff are things I did not prioritise – somewhat to my loss.

But boy! I was ruthless when I was younger! There's a

saying that if the competition is drowning, shove a hosepipe in their mouth and finish them off. I wholeheartedly embraced this approach. My first estate agent job, when I was working for that first cleaning firm, was one place I unleashed my ruthless streak. One day, I just happened to be in the office cleaning when the office manager was on site. It was the first time I had met him, and I was determined to make the meeting count.

Using a manner that suggested I was looking out for him, I mentioned the cleaning firm were not supplying the cleaners with materials and remarked on this lack of professionalism. I then offered to undertake the cleaning for him for £25 per visit. As you know, I already knew that this was cheaper than what he was paying, but to cover my tracks, I casually dropped in, "I imagine it's more than you are paying, but I would like to buy the proper materials in order to do the job properly."

I must have had an honest face back then. Lo and behold, he said, "It's good to find a cleaner who cares. Actually, it's cheaper than what I am paying." Then and there, he gave me the contract. Bang! And the job was done!

It is fair to say when I first started out, I didn't have a clue what I was doing. Cleaning to me was just emptying bins, spraying a bit of air freshener in the air, and whizzing the hoover around. The nuanced methods of cleaning surfaces was far beyond me. I once got asked if I did French polishing; I just thought that was speaking French while doing it. I can't remember my reply, but if it had been nowadays I'm sure I'd have ended up on a Reddit thread being laughed at. I didn't even know that when you sweep floors, you need to sweep away from you and not towards you. And as for cleaning under a sofa, the whole idea of it baffled me. I just thought it was something you lay on.

Little by little I learned my trade and eventually I became an expert in cleaning. Now, I can laugh at customers who have no idea what they are doing, as if I have been the paragon of shiny surfaces all my life. But sometimes, not knowing what to do inspires you to think of innovative and creative solutions.

I remember when I first started out, one client asked me to remove the mould from her conservatory. I tried wiping it, scrubbing it, bleaching it… Nothing seemed to get the mould off. I was exasperated. In the end I popped into WH Smiths, bought some Tipp-Ex, and painted over the mould! The funny thing was, as I was panicking about how my client might react, the lady returned home from work and thought I was a miracle worker! She said she had never seen it so clean! Tipp-Ex says mistakes happen, but choosing it that day was a sensation! Thankfully, she didn't look too closely at my work.

It's only right to confess, back in the early days I was a right scammer when it came to cleaning. One such scam was improvised when I was cleaning a big country house on my own. The owner had popped home unexpectedly between tending to her horses. I was used to not seeing anyone; it was rare that we ever saw the lady of the house. However, that particular day I had so much work on and I wanted to make a hasty exit. Her arrival was about to throw my plans out of sync. I was supposed to be at her house for three hours, so when I saw her heading towards the house, I needed to scam fast! I ran upstairs with the hoover and left it running, then I ran back downstairs and continued casually cleaning the kitchen area. She came in and we exchanged pleasantries. She then commented, "Oh! There are two of you here today?"

She had heard the hoover and assumed there was a colleague about the house – just as I wanted. I confidently replied, "Yep – we'll be done shortly."

Happily, she didn't go upstairs and check. Instead, she grabbed a drink from the kitchen and left again. Tracks covered. Scam level Genius: complete, and I was not at all in over my head.

CHAPTER 2

Don't Stress, Let Us Handle Your Mess

Over the years, things have changed, and I'm not sure all changes are for the best. For one thing, you can no longer tell staff exactly what you're thinking just in case you upset them or offend them. Apparently, each day you have to ask them how they are feeling, and ask if there is anything you can do to help them. I yearn for the days when I could say, "Christ, you're shit today!" Or, "Speed up or I'll sack you!" I ask you, what's wrong with that? This snowflake generation would never have survived back in my day. Maybe if we tell them the brain is an app, they might start using it.

It can't be just me who thinks this? We live in a society where everyone is afraid to speak their minds, and we have to second guess reactions to everything.

My supermarket days, back in the early 90s, provided so many good experiences for life, and a lot of what I learnt back then I used in my cleaning business. Stuff like sorting staff schedules, strategies to ensure staff were productive, managing budgets and even how to map out time and resources – all these things came in useful to me. But inevitably there were new problems and new learning curves.

Back in those days, staff management was different. Can you remember those days when safe sex meant pulling your bed away from the wall, or sticking a cushion behind the head board? Anyway, back then we used to have chiller-chats. I mean – flip me! Basically, if you had an issue with a member of staff you would take them into the fridge, close the door, and have it out with them. I guess it was a form of torture – I think political prisoners have received less stress than freezing your butt off while being informed how shit you are. When I first started off, I was on the receiving end of a few of these chiller-chats. However, these experiences put me in a good stead.

The store manager at the time was ruthless yet everyone respected him. When he moved to a different store, I soon followed him. People said I brown-nosed him to get a promotion, but that wasn't the case at all. I just couldn't work with the store manager who replaced him; he was a complete idiot who got moved from store to store because he couldn't keep his willy in his pants. Even when he was working at my local store, he was having an affair with another department manager. I think she was called Penny Pants-Down, and she looked like someone who worked in a health food shop. Flip me! Have you seen the people who work in health food shops? Don't they look like munters? They're all shrivelled and dry; none of them look healthy!

Where was I? Oh yes! So, I ended up working in Taunton Safeways, and I learned another lesson. It was safe to say the store manager was sent there to sort things out. At the time, the staff who worked there didn't give a shit. When I joined the management team there, I couldn't get over why the managers only worked 8 hours per day. When I was in my home town store, we all worked at least 12 hours a day and never dared to go home before the store manager left. We were too scared to. But then, looking back, I was the stupid one – I was only paid 8 hours a day so the amount of free labour I gave over my period there is scary.

I learned lots of things about how to manage people, and what kind of manager I was while working for this company. I was the grocery manager for a while, which meant I oversaw all the shelf-filling and warehouse deliveries. I monitored how much staff would shelf-fill per hour; back then, staff were expected to unload 26 cases an hour. To be fair, Steven Hawkins could have achieved this. However, one particular lady who worked for me was as fat as a house and would barely make 15 cases per hour. I used to be on her back all the time to speed up. I probably bullied her a bit too much. She soon left. On reflection, I could have spoken to her better. But I think if one member of the team is not pulling their weight, none of them do. On the flip side, the ones who do pull their weight normally get asked to pull for two.

I'm not proud of the way I treated her. But unknown to me she had given me the nickname 'Pampers' because I was always on her ass and full of shit, which made me laugh. Apparently, she hasn't worked since, so perhaps she wasn't really cut out for working anyway. Mind you, she was a big girl so I imagine the main thing stopping her from working is her front door.

There was another time a young kid came into the warehouse and dumped an empty pallet just inside the door. I asked him politely to move it as it was clogging up the entrance. He didn't do it. So I pinned him up against the cardboard bailer machine! You could never get away with man management like that these days; perhaps for the best. The kid's father came into the store and had a go at me. I had a disciplinary for it, however it was only a verbal one. The kid in question got moved to another department. I am not proud of how I treated people back then, but I am glad I have learned from it. I guess I just wanted to succeed in life, and had no limits to my determination to get there.

I actually believed all those bullshit business slogans back then which we were fed at meetings. Slogans like: 'there's no I in team', or 'teamwork makes the dream work', which I must admit makes me gag a little when I hear them these days. Oh! And my favourite cringy one was 'The 7 Ps: Proper Planning and Practice Prevents Piss Poor Performance'. I think the only slogan I ever really take note of these days is BOSS which stands for 'Built On Self Success'.

As a manager, one of the tricky things to handle well is staff sickness. It's a minefield! Thankfully, I didn't suffer too many problems with staff going off sick while managing my cleaning business. This was mostly because if they ever did phone in sick, I would pop around and visit them to see if they really were ill. Funnily enough, one girl who had phoned in lost credibility. As I pulled up to her house to see if she was okay, she was loading her car up with the hoover, and heading off to do her private cleaning job! Amazingly, within the space of two hours since she called me, where she claimed to be sooo ill she could barely get out of bed, she had bounced back! Apparently, she felt so much better by then she thought she could still fit in her private cleaning job!

I've had one or two employees over the years off sick. When they call you and put on the sick voice, it's a strangely awkward conversation – you know the voice – I think even genuinely sick people struggle with this voice; how do you express your suffering in sound without wailing? I've even had parents phoning me telling me their daughter wouldn't be in due to sickness. Since the invention of mobile phones, the sick voice is rarely used as people now find it acceptable to send a text saying they are not coming into work. The stupid thing is, when calling in with the sick voice, people go into great detail about what is wrong with them to express their discomfort, but they end up involved in the kind of personal conversation nobody ever wants to be a part of. They say things like, "Oh, I can't even speak!" Well, I think you can since you called me. Another one is, "It's coming out both ends, vomiting, diarrhoea…" Errrr, I'm not sure I need to know about your anal leakage, to be honest. But I soon learnt the more details they gave me, the more suspicious I became about whether they were genuinely ill.

But some absence reasons are truly mad. I had a lady call me once and say she couldn't work because her daughter's hamster had died. I mean, I always thought of hamsters as pets of convenience – they tend to only survive a couple of years by which stage the child's fascination with them has waned. But perhaps I was wrong. This woman said her daughter's hamster Hammy (a truly original name) had passed away and they were devastated. She was letting her six-year-old daughter not go school as she was heartbroken, and she had to stay home to care for her. So they had a day of mourning for Hammy. And there was me thinking having pets of convenience like rodents and goldfish was a way of teaching kids the importance of life and death. I suppose that's exactly what happened.

Animal-related absences turn out to be relatively common too, among other bizarre reasons. I read a story once where somebody had phoned in sick because their dog was depressed. Others I heard were: not being able to work because their goldfish was sick, and even someone who was too upset to work when Jack Duckworth died on Corrie! Another one that stood out for me was someone who read in their horoscope that it didn't look like a good day for working, so couldn't come in.

There are some personal issues that have taught me things that leave me feeling embarrassed about my former actions. One occasion a lady had phoned in sick due to lady issues, as some of them referred to it. I assumed they meant period pains. Back when I first set out, I was unsympathetic and uneducated, and used to say, "Can't you just stick a pipe up or put a pad in or something?" Or, "Don't worry about getting blood on the van seat." Yes, I know – I was a bit of a knob back then. I've also learnt over the years that ladies keep an emergency Lillet in their handbags and know full well how to look after their periods.

One cleaner was really open about when she was on which I found odd. "Got the painters in!" she would tell us! The same lady once said to another member of staff, "Why you so grumpy? Is your period late?" Then in the next breath, "I shouldn't have thought you have slept with anyone so don't worry!" To be fair, this cleaner came across like the Virgin Mary whereas 'The Period Proclaimer' always smelt of TCP and by all accounts she had had more pricks than Kerplunk. Part of me thought she used TCP to clean her vagina… Especially after she once slept with a Big Issue vendor. Which reminds me, there was also a local prostitute in Bridgwater known as 'Tenna Lady' – apparently she was pretty cheap, but moving on.

Some staff absence reasons are seriously funny, and others are completely tragic. I shouldn't laugh, but the best one I had was when a guy called me and said he couldn't work because his wife had run off with another woman! It turned out this was genuine, so I told him to take as much time as he needed.

The opposite sometimes happens too. There have been various staff who have turned up for work, but they were not physically fit for the job in hand. Occasionally, this is because the illness is self-inflicted. One of the excuses I heard was, "My drink got spiked!" I thought, yeah right! Your drink was spiked by your wallet constantly being used at the bar!

Another time, a great turn of phrase I heard in response to the dreaded hangover was, "My head is banging; I'm like woodpecker with a migraine!" I know it's smug to say, but my response is always: maybe if you didn't drink last night you wouldn't be in this condition!

Talking of booze, like for all firms, our Christmas party is a big deal. It is like Marmite: everyone either dreads the do or they absolutely love it. We have had some corkers of parties over the years, all memorable and some for the wrong reasons. Looking back, having a snow machine at my house party was not a good idea. One girl fell over, who actually didn't work for me. She was in a bit of pain, and tried to sit out of the fun to rest her foot. One of my staff members tried to grab her to dance, and she said she couldn't as she was in too much discomfort. That didn't go down well. The girl was heckled for not joining in, and people called her a miserable cow! One staff member went on… and on, although bear in mind she was drunk too. She was saying things like, "Look at her, miserable cow, doesn't want to dance!"

Anyway, it turned out she had broken her toes in five places. It was one of the worst toe-breaks the doctor had seen, apparently. The funny thing was the next day she said,

"Don't worry, Matt, I won't sue you for compensation!" I laughed; it is sad that we live in a compensation culture now!

Most parties would end up in drunken games; Bush, Bog, Booze was a pretty memorable game. To play it, everyone is given an envelope containing one of these words. If you had booze you had to do a shot; if you had bush you'd have to eat something horrible in the style of the famous bush-tucker trial; if you had bog you had to phone a number which we had removed from a public toilet wall. Basically, this was a collection of funny one-liners and filthy requests we had collected from public loos we had cleaned. It was a large collection of pervs generally looking for cock or to be Rogered. This game was hilarious! Obviously, we would block the caller ID before calling, and to do this from a landline, you just have to put 141 before dialling the number. Well, the bog card was drawn at this one party, and a bloke had to call a randomly selected number from the pack. Some weirdo answered and said he couldn't talk as his wife was present. But he had written on the wall in a public toilet that he was looking for a discreet cock. He must have been a man still in his closet. But stupidly, or drunkenly, the bloke didn't dial 141 beforehand, so my number wasn't concealed. For days afterwards, this weirdo kept calling my landline. I had to disconnect the line in the end. I suppose that's no great loss; nobody uses landlines these days anyway.

Christmas parties are synonymous with Secret Santa gifts. I often think this is normally a load of old tosh, however, not within our company. Most companies give a low limit, such as £5, to help everyone to be involved, but then it means gifts are dull and wasteful. Then, to join in, you have to pick a name out of a hat, and buy a gift for that person no matter how little you know them. We went about things a different way; our Secret Santas were brutal. A deaf lady was given ear-muffs; another cleaner was given a tin of tuna after someone claimed her minge was a bit fishy; another got a cheese grater as he was an old guy and the buyer thought he needed it to clean his dick. The gifts were intensely offensive. DS Boy (I will explain this nickname later) was given a cabbage; another cleaner was given incontinence pads because she pissed her pants once. But all these things are given within a framework of trust. Having the ability to laugh at yourself was part and parcel of working for my cleaning company. Every offence given was also paid back in full – and there were no hierarchical limitations on humour.

Nowadays, everything has to be PC. People are afraid to say and do anything in case it offends. I'm thankful that all this nonsense came in after my heyday as I'm pretty sure I would have been taken to an employment tribunal on numerous occasions. I get that the world has changed, and I also get the TV show Fingermouse would never have been commissioned in this current age. Do you remember the show? The main concept was fingering a mouse... Anyway, the world is a crazy place. I hear that kids are not allowed to sing Bah Bah Black Sheep anymore in schools and black boards are now referred to as chalk boards. I love something Ricky Gervais once said: "Just because you're offended, doesn't mean you're right." I mean, being offended by symbolic resonance just means there's no limit to what things could mean. Where does it stop? Can it get to the point when we are at the laundrette and having to worry about separating white and coloured loads just in case we are seen!

The sad truth about life is that everyone and anyone can

be offended by something someone says without offence being intended. I was having a conversation with this snobby cow of a client and in conversation I asked her how her kids were doing at school. She replied, "They are children, not kids... kids are baby goats."

Then there was the lady with the double-barrelled name. I called her Jenny when I first met her. She said, "My Roddy would turn in his grave if he heard you call me that. It's Jenny Ingram-Cook."

Another posh lady once said to me, "I've bought you a new toilet brush you can use."

I replied, "Thank you. I'll stick to using loo roll, thanks." Now, I thought this was funny, she, on the other hand, didn't see the joke.

"You're paid to work, not make fun," she snarled. To be fair, she was high maintenance as a client. She once kicked off that her kettle handle wasn't facing the right way, so I didn't take the loo brush incident to heart.

I guess humour is subjective and not everyone will find me funny, like an older gentleman who once stopped me while walking along the local canal, who did not appreciate my attitude. He asked if I knew what type of fish was floating on the surface. I replied, "A dead one."

I've employed all types of people over the years: white people, black people, Eastern Europeans, busy people and lazy people, thin people and fat people. I just thought, *Stick a harness on her and we'll get a good day's work out of her!* And people who were as thick as shit. Did I treat them any differently because of their colour, race or religion or fatness? Of course I didn't! I aimed to offend everyone with my humour, and I encouraged facetious, rude joking in return! Cleaning is a dirty job, and you need gallows humour to survive. As long as they could do the job, why would I want to single anyone out?

At the end of the day, we are all the same, and a good staff member is literally worth their weight in gold. Sometimes more. And as a cleaner, I know first-hand we all poo the same. Mind you, saying that, some people don't poo every day which I find odd. Don't they have tummy ache? I am as regular as clockwork, dropping 2.5 logs every single day. I have a little confession though: when no one is home I poo with the toilet door open.

CHAPTER 3

Staff – The Key to Cleanliness

Many years ago, when I first set up the cleaning company, back when Cif was called Jif, I learned how important staff are to success. To be fair, times were good back then – pancakes haven't tasted the same since. And swimming pools had verruca pools you had to stand in before swimming – whatever happened to them? Plus, the dentist would always give you a lollipop if you were a good boy or girl – no wonder at one stage my teeth looked like cheesy Wotsits.

Anyway, back then, a lot of workplaces would employ an old lady who undertook the cleaning. Typically, this old lady would have been there since 1892 and would always wear a pinny or an apron. You know the sort of old lady; she is the type who hung plates on walls. Her generation cared about their professionalism and skills and had morals. But these women have all since died, and what's left is a load of redundant pinnies and people who don't see cleaning as a proper job. But it is a proper job, and I always expect decent graft from my staff. But the wearing of a pinny was optional.

It became evident quite early on, employing family members was not the best way to grow my business. It's not just that your other employees think they get special treatment – it's also that they expect to get special treatment! Jokes aside, if you want your business to be successful, you have to treat it as such, and not make do with people you know who are easily available.

If I am honest, employing staff is probably the hardest part of running a business. This is a lesson I learned gradually. In the beginning, when I had work coming out of my earholes, I decided to place an advert in a local paper to try and recruit staff. Now, in hindsight, I should have foreseen trouble unfolding. When you advertise a job at minimum wage you are going to attract all sorts of people – and I mean all sorts. I had sooooo many nutters contact me looking for work, from the stupid to the frightening!

One bloke phoned me and said, "Just checking you definitely don't do CRB checks."

Another said, "I got sacked from my last job because Sue in payroll was a slag."

And one dopehead said, "Is it okay to smoke weed while I work?"

What's the saying? Pay peanuts, you get monkeys. Another person informed me he only wanted a job until he won the lottery then he would tell me to "F*ck Off" – I soon learnt that to get decent staff you had to pay more.

Over time, I also found – like in any workplace – it's all about the people. This is where the effort has to be. Once you start employing people, you become like a counsellor to them, a guide, and a friend. I also learnt over the years, when you are interviewing for staff, if they start using phrases like: I love cleaning, or I almost have OCD, it is typically a load of bullocks! People who say these things are the worst ones! I guess it is a bit like when people say, "I'm not normally one to complain," you know they are the ones who will complain the most. Anyway, back to my staff...

Some staff were certainly better than others; some only lasted a few days, others were with me for years; I guess as long as they were making me money I really didn't care. However, I did lead by example; I never ask a cleaner to do a job I wouldn't do myself. I wasn't a desktop company owner; I was very much hands on. I think staff respected me for this. There is definitely one thing for sure – they worked harder knowing I was always around working too.

People, and staff, come in all shapes and sizes – and with different levels of IQ. I am sure you can all think of at least one colleague from your workplace who isn't the full shilling. However, I seem to have been blessed with an entire village of idiots who have worked for me at one time or another.

Some of the people I employed made me wonder how they even tie their own shoelaces unaided. Let's just say, if aliens ever invaded and the only thing they ate were brains… my staff would be safe. Once, I even had an Elvis impersonator who said he was looking for something to tide him over until his singing took off. I mean, it sounds plausible if you like that kind of thing. Then, I heard him sing. I'm not Simon Cowell, but it's safe to say he didn't have the X Factor! I find extensive lack of self-awareness a sure sign of nuttiness. When someone is that bad at singing but they believe they are good, well, delusional is the term that comes to mind. I had more chance of fingering a whale than he did of getting a recording contract. Mind you, saying that, I did once get with a larger girl. It was a touch-and-go situation. Well, her fanny had the suction of a Dyson and I nearly lost my arm up her. Hopefully I was in the right hole, but I am not completely certain. I think that's the reason they put support bases on butt-plugs, so they don't get lost in the

Bermuda Triangle, aka The Black Hole...

Now, where was I?

I remember employing one bloke who didn't get off to the best start, to put it mildly. I once passed him a job which involved collecting a carpet machine from my garage and heading to the client's place in Torquay to clean. He got all the way to Exeter before phoning me to tell me he had forgotten the carpet machine.

If that wasn't ridiculous enough, the same cleaner was sent to do an urgent job at the leisure centre in our hometown. After 30 minutes, the leisure centre phoned me moaning that I had promised them the cleaner would be there within 10 minutes – reiterating the urgent status of the work. Confused, I phoned my cleaner to find out what had happened. It turned out he had driven to the wrong leisure centre... in a town 20 miles away!

Despite this start, this chap worked for me for seven years! When he started, he told me he just wanted to do the job until he found something better – yet, at that stage he proved he couldn't even keep up with this job. Thankfully, he turned out to be a good guy. Back then, he had recently had the snip, so I put his memory lapses down to this. After all, they do say men's brains are in their pants. I really think this explains a lot – especially where this particular cleaner was concerned.

But I must confess I have also suffered from listening to the wrong brain at times too. One of the mistakes I made was mixing business and pleasure in the early days. I suppose there is an old adage about this, but I succumbed to temptation. I employed a girl for a short time who I completely fancied the pants off. The downside, predictably, was that she was a crap cleaner, and the rest of the staff got annoyed when I made allowances for her. I guess in business, men need to listen to their head-brain and not their pants-brain. As my dad says, "If you can control your urges, you can control the world."

I had another girl who spent more time on the toilet than actually cleaning. We were driving out to a job out in the sticks, and she was desperate for a wee so she begged for me to pull over so she could pee. So I pulled into a layby. Ironically it said 'No Dumping', but I guess a piss was allowed. Anyway, skipping forward, she managed to piss all down her pants and leggings!

When she got back in the van, she looked sheepish and soggy. Without thinking, I asked her why her leggings were wet, and she was obviously embarrassed. She reckoned that while she was crouched down a wasp flew towards her fanny – so she shuffled and ended up with piss all over herself!

To make things worse, when we got to the client's house, the client asked her the same question! Defending her honour, I quickly replied she dropped a drink on herself in the van. I say I was defending her honour – but I couldn't really say a wasp was flying towards her fanny and she pissed herself, could I?

If you think that is bad, I had a bloke who worked for me who did sooooo much worse! We were working in Torquay on the morning in question, and we were cleaning a communal area in a block of flats. It was quite early, around 8:30am, when the incident occurred. The job was straight forward; we simply had to sweep and mop the staircases and landings. Anyway, there were no toilets in the shared areas at this particular job, and my cleaner got caught short – too short.

Without knowing what had happened, I merrily returned to the van, and noticed what appeared to be curry splattered all over the floor around near the passenger door. It seemed like a rough block of flats, so I said to the cleaner, "Look at that! Some dirty git has thrown a curry out the window!"

He turned to me, awkwardly shrugging his shoulders, and said, "No, I needed a shit…"

To make matters even worse, he was totally exposed! He tried to hide behind the van for privacy, but the emergency pooping position he selected turned out to be compromised – his decision making must have been shattered by diarrhoea sweats. Concealed from the front by the van, but he gave a full pooping-moon to the security camera which was pointing directly at the spot. Not surprisingly, shortly after this incident we lost that contract. I still don't know if it was bum related, but I have a suspicion the two things are connected.

And the stories related to excretions go on! And it often wasn't even my staff at fault! Clients can get funny if you use the toilets in their houses – and I understand there are boundaries. I mean, so many staff don't poo at their own work places, but it is normal to need the loo throughout the day. I remember an incident that involved a black girl who worked for me – and in fairness, aside from this memory I'm about to share, she was probably one of the best cleaners I have ever employed. But still… This one day, we had to do a deep clean on a lady's house; let's just say she lived in a tiny hamlet, and it was a little behind the times. When I turned up with my staff member, the black girl asked to use her toilet. The client frostily responded, "If you really must, but you should have gone before you left home."

Anyway, we didn't think anything of it at the time; we

cleaned her house, she appeared to be happy, and then we left. That night, the customer phoned me and said our cleaning was great, but she was not happy a black girl had used her toilet. I was gobsmacked! You know when people say the customer is always right? Well, that is not always true! 'The customer is always right' is half a sentence; it should be followed by 'if the customer is reasonable, not an idiot and not a racist'. I politely pointed out that, at the end of the day, we are all the same regardless of skin colour. She didn't accept my point and we never undertook work for her again. See what I mean? God knows what she would have said if I had told her one of my staff was gay. I'm pretty sure she would have said something like, "What, a bottom explorer? Not in my house!" The work is rarely the issue; people are the problem.

Talking of taking the piss, one of my staff has a daughter who got drunk and during the night got out of bed, walked onto the landing and mistook a laundry basket for a toilet. She sat on it and urinated everywhere. The parents were not happy, but we've all been there when drunk and gone to the toilet somewhere we shouldn't. The funny thing is the next day they moved the laundry basket into their daughter's bedroom and said, "There you go. You have an en suite now."

I suppose that isn't as bad as a friend I know who stayed at his girlfriend's parents' house, got drunk and during the night he couldn't find the toilet. He ended up going for a poo in a wardrobe! Funny enough, the relationship didn't last long after this experience, but it did bring a whole new meaning to a shitty relationship.

I had another member of staff who took six goes to pass her driving test! She didn't mention this in her interview; nor did she mention that she wouldn't drive on motorways – so to get to any long-distance jobs, she would always take the B roads. "Straight roads do not make skilful drivers," was always her argument. However, it soon became apparent that windy roads don't guarantee any skill development either! My insurance premiums went through the roof – she had sooooo many accidents while driving my vans. She once hit a TREE! And she defended herself by saying the tree moved! Funnily enough, I didn't put this on the insurance claim form. However, I once heard that someone wrote on their claim form, "I was going to work at 7am this morning. I drove out of my drive straight into a bus. The bus was 5 minutes early that day." Some people are stupid.

Anyway, this cleaner had accidents aplenty. She once hit an Indian woman while driving. Luckily, no one was badly hurt, but by God did I have earache from the Indian woman over the phone. The sad thing is, I didn't have a ruddy clue what she was saying. I'm no racist, however, I have some hearing issues, which are especially true when people have strong accents. (I am embarrassed by this fact since my own accent is thicker than I am.) I find it so hard, like when you are put through to a call centre and they are based in India, and everyone speaks in a different lingo. It's made even worse when most of the call centre staff are given English names, and they introduce themselves with, "Hello, my name is Harry!" It's so obvious that isn't true.

So, back to Driving Miss Daisy: she was probably the second-best cleaner I ever employed despite her lack of driving skills. We did have a few run-ins over the years, but I reminded her, like I do all my staff, I rescued her from the gutter and gave her a career. Sounds harsh, but she did try and scam me a few times. There was a time when she claimed she needed more hours to do a certain job, so I gave her more hours. She had booked down to work until 3pm, so I was a little surprised when I drove past her walking her dog at 1:30pm. Prior to her scamming, you could not fault her honesty. She once found some money in a client's pocket and gave it back. I don't mean she started touching him up on a job – she was paid to clean this man's house, and part of her role was to do the ironing. While doing this one day, she found £20 in a pocket, so she left it with a note on the side before leaving. The next day, I got a phone call from the customer informing me of what she had done and he wanted to give her half the money as a thank you. £10 for her honesty! See, sometimes honesty does pay! See, sometimes honesty does pay! I'd never tell her this however out of all my staff I've employed I enjoyed working with her the most and was gutted when she left the company.

Driving seems to be central to a few of my staff issues; I once had a couple of cleaners who decided to drive through flood water and got stuck. When they were finally rescued, they were sat on the roof of the van, and they appeared on the local news. The worst thing is, I didn't even get any free advertising out of it! The vans were all sign-written, however, the flood water was so deep, my company name couldn't be seen! Though, bobbing around in a flood is probably not the best recommendation for a cleaning company.

I once employed a member of staff who was superstitious to the point of distraction. I'm not really superstitious at all so I don't always know these old beliefs; I'm more just super-tidy. I mean, if I break a mirror my first thought isn't, *OMG I now have seven years' bad luck*. I'm more likely to think, *Ruddy hell! I better clear up this mess before someone stands on it!* Anyway, this staff member would salute or count to ten every time we drove past a magpie. On a bad day she would do a combination of both! And don't get me started on how she acted if we ever saw a black cat crossing the road! She would suddenly, and without any warning, yell, "Bad Luck!" Often, I wouldn't have even noticed the cat was crossing the road. Luckily, she wasn't working the day a cleaner broke a mirror at someone's house! But I have more stories about damage limitation later in the book!

Often, the most outstanding memories with staff are somewhat unrelated to the cleaning. For example, one morning one of my staff came to work smiling like a Cheshire cat. This was strange as he was going through a tough time; his wife had left him, they had become saddled with debt, and he was basically just having a shit time. So, I wanted to know what had caused this giddy joy. When I inquired what was with his big grin, he replied, "Mate, I had my first blow job in years last night!" He had started seeing a girl and their relationship was in the early stages, and apparently his ex-wife didn't like playing the trumpet, as it were. The funny thing unfolded as he continued to describe his evening. He said it had been soooo long since he last had a blowey, he didn't know what to do.

I said, "What do you mean, not sure what to do?" His confession surprised me. What on Earth was he talking about? Did he think he was going to cook a three-course dinner while being sucked off?

He replied, "Well, you know… I didn't know what noises to make, and do I move while she was down there?" He still sounded uncertain.

I asked, "What did you do?" Imagining all sorts of awkwardness.

He replied, "I just lay there and didn't move. But then, after a while I did move, but I didn't make any noises as I had forgotten what noises to make."

I inquired, "How did you move?"

He replied, "Do you remember those red, plastic, fortune-telling fish you used to get at Christmas in crackers?" Well, it turned out he moved like that, curling up and tossing around. I thought, flip me! She must have thought he was disabled or having some kind of spack-attack.

One day a member of my staff confided in me that he was having a few problems weeing. When I say he was having a few problems, I don't mean he couldn't go; it was more to the point he couldn't stop going! At the time, my dad had prostate cancer, so I encouraged him to get checked out at the doctors. He wasn't an old chap. He was in his early 40s; but age is not the point, and it is always better to be safe than sorry.

So, he went to the doctors and explained the situation: he was weeing sometimes five to six times every hour. The doctor said he needed to run some tests, and as most of you know, the prostate is situated up the bum hole. The doctor advised him he might feel a little pain during the examination; with that, the doctor shoved his finger up his anus. The first thing my worker said, "Fecking hell, Doctor! You could have used your little finger!" It made me laugh! But on a serious note, if you are having problems down below don't be afraid to get checked out – it might just save your life. As it happened, there was nothing seriously wrong with him; he just had some kind of bladder infection.

Other personal issues can get in the way sometimes with

staff management. Over the years, I've unwittingly employed a few alcoholics. Some were really seriously so – one bloke always wanted to finish his shift at 11am each day to be free for when the pubs opened. Otherwise, he got the shakes. I have never been a big drinker – I find drinking two litres of water a day a struggle so God knows how he managed to drink that much in spirits every day.

What made me laugh though was his cavalier approach to rules. He once got pulled over by the police when he was driving. The officer said to him, "I have a feeling you've been drinking."

He replied, "Thank God for that! I thought the steering had gone!"

He subsequently, and unsurprisingly, lost his licence for 12 months. Despite this, I kept him on; he might not have warranted a cleaner of the year award; however, he was loyal and would always start whatever time of day I wanted. I wish he'd cleaned himself up though – he smelled like a dog with no tongue, like a pair of dirty bollocks!

There was an odd occasion when he had to do an afternoon shift, and this would mean him turning up AFTER a morning visit to the pub. Christ! He ruddy stunk of it! He attempted a level of strategy to hide his issues. For example, he always tried to disguise his breath by eating a pickled onion. Weirdly, the thing is he was a better cleaner after he had been drinking! What is it they say? Everyone has a hidden talent they don't know about until the shots are poured. Well his hidden talent was cleaning. He even used to think that by drinking apple cider he was getting one of his five-a-day!

Did you know that in 1971 the government guideline regarding healthy weekly alcohol intake was 56 units! These days it's 14 units which is about five pints per week. I know everyone lies when they go to the doctor and they get asked how many units of alcohol they drink each week, but drinking responsibly in his case meant not spilling it.

Then there was another lady who I employed, who was deaf as a post but unknown to me had a secret vodka obsession. I never noticed or realised in the whole time she worked for me; she was a ruddy good cleaner, and her habit didn't seem to impact her at all – or at least, she hid it well. In alcohol's defence, she did some crazy stuff even when she was sober. Do you remember the van I mentioned that was stuck in a flood? Well, she was there at the time!

One of the most bizarre things I have come across during my time as a cleaner was with a staff member of another company. She was like a member of Extinction Rebellion, and she only used eco-friendly products, and this probably explains what happened next. I promise, I really do think let everyone keep each to their own, however, I can't help but notice habits that seem unexplainable or comedic to me. And this woman, well, she kept three crystals in her bra as apparently they brought her luck and had healing powers. When she told me this, I didn't believe her one bit. So to prove it, she turned her back, reached into her bra, and took out three crystals. One of these crystals was huge – like a huge lump of coal. I wondered out loud whether it was uncomfortable having them in her bra all day. She assured me she just got used to it. She said, "A little bit of healing pain does you good!" *Stuff that,* I thought. I mean, I've heard of ladies putting things in their bras to make their boobs look bigger, but not putting in things that make their boobs look bumpy and deformed! I thought, *Flip me!* Imagine if you pulled her on a night out and took her home, undid her clothes and had rocks tumble out onto your feet. You would think she had robbed a jewellery shop on the way home.

It's a big risk when you become an employer as you can lose faith in people. I've had staff who have been with me for years, we've built a strong relationship and become friends, and I totally trust them when they tell me that they don't like doing a certain job as the customer is rude. Then, after I cancel the contract, I find out they are doing the job outside of their cleaning work with me. I guess it's karma; I shafted the first company I cleaned for by nicking their contract, now my own staff were doing it to me. I guess there is no loyalty in any line of work these days.

So, obviously, not all staff worked out well. I once employed an Eastern European woman who said she loved cleaning. Sadly, I had to sack her after a few weeks; let's just say she wasn't good at Russian; she was definitely more Slow-Vac. I'm always told Eastern Europeans are good workers, however the one I employed was a bloody nightmare! Although, the situation was not helped by the fact she couldn't speak the lingo. Personally, I think if you can't speak the lingo you shouldn't be in this country working – and I think this is true for a lot of jobs. I'm all for giving people a chance, however the ones that come over just for our healthcare system and our very generous benefits system can sod off as far as I'm concerned. Not that she was one of these – she intended to do the right thing. In fact, she was just too thorough! I know, I know – that sounds like a good thing, but hear me out. She just didn't understand the concept that we had limited time at our workplaces. I recall one situation: she was doing a two-hour shift in an office block. In the allotted time, she had only managed to clean the ladies' toilets. I tried to explain to her that we had been paid to clean the whole office area in that time, including the kitchen, offices, and toilets. She replied, "No! Too dirty. Not enough time!" She was just so slow and thorough, I asked her to speed up, she would reply, "No! Not understand!"

The joke of it was after I let her go she went to Citizen's Advice to report me for sacking her. I gave her a one-week trial, paid her for work completed, however, she told them they I got rid of her because she was Polish which was rubbish. I got rid of her as she couldn't do the work – simple!

I employed one girl who was stunning but was as thick as a brick. She didn't even know what date Christmas Day was on. One year it just happened to fall on a Friday and when I told her this she said, "As long as it's not the 13th." And her spelling in her text messages was shocking – I needed a translator to convert her messages. She told us once that her partner was working away so they had indulged in a bit of sexting. All was going well when they were just sending rude pictures to each other. Then her partner asked her to send a dirty message about what she wanted to do to him. She replied, "I want to suck your duck."

After that, the saucy moment passed – and I don't mean hoisin.

I once employed a cleaner who was very likeable and initially seemed to be quite educated, but she seemingly struggled to grasp the most obvious of things. I gave her a regular job; all she had to do was turn up and clean this workplace once a week for a total of three hours per shift. She started off great, then after a month I got a call from the manager. They asked if my cleaner was okay as they hadn't seen her for three weeks! I was more than a bit concerned, as I am sure you can imagine. So, I phoned her and asked if she was okay, and inquired why she hadn't been doing her cleaning work. She responded by saying she had been busy! "Don't worry!" she assured me. "I'll go three times this week to make up for it!" She just didn't grasp the concept they required a cleaner every week! So, I sacked her.

I always think it is funny in life when people cause their own problems, then cry and act like they are the victims.

Another staff archetype that can cause hassle is the team gossip. We had one of those. God! She was a nightmare! It's been my experience that when you hear people gossip to you in life, they will be gossiping about you when you turn your back. She caused so many problems as gossip destroys trust. I had to be very selective whatever I told her about other staff, and customers for that matter. For example, I told her one day we were off to clean a celebrity's house. I emphasised we had to be discreet and we would probably have to sign a confidentiality agreement. Within seconds of me informing her of this, she decided to post it on Facebook! Thankfully, she removed the post, but not until after I was informed by a member of staff what she had done.

It's strange how people act around famous people. After spending years in radio, I kind of got used to meeting the odd celebrity. At the end of the day, we are all the same: we all poo the same, some are just more famous for doing it. I just act the same as I always do, but some people are starstruck. When we met this celebrity for the first time, the gossip-cleaner decided to curtsey! I've never laughed so much in my life! The celebrity wasn't royalty; just a singer who had sold millions of records.

I have employed the good, the bad, and the ugly. Oh! And I also employed a bloke whose wife ran off with another lady after 30 years of marriage! I think he took it well though. He said, "Well, no point her going with another man once you have had the best." That said, he did end up going through a rough patch which sadly resulted in me sacking him. I had tried to be supportive; he had lost his wife, house and business, and was declared bankrupt. However, support can only be stretched so far. He stole from a customer, and that was a no-no. We cleaned a pub and the owner made me aware that things were going missing on the days this chap was working. The managers set a trap and caught him in the act. I begged them not to go to the police in exchange for us paying back everything he stole. I certainly didn't want a thieving member of staff broadcasted about in the press. It is disappointing, but there are times in life when you reach out and give someone a chance and they let you down. However bad I felt for him in his circumstances, after that I didn't have a choice.

Despite giving staff all PPE, even before COVID, some would choose not to wear anything. This has always worried and surprised me; I employed this one bloke who never wore gloves while cleaning public toilets – I mean, I can't understand how this didn't freak him out. It certainly freaked me out. To make matters even worse, I have seen him clean public toilets, then eat his sandwich without washing his hands. How he never got food poisoning is beyond me! Or an STD… on his face! I remember one day the other staff played a practical joke on him and put toilet urinal blocks in his lunch box; I bet he still ate all his food that day. He might have even eaten the urinal blocks too!

When employing people, I found I ended up developing

some habits and routines. Some of these gave us joy and entertainment. I've found lots of workplaces have nicknames for staff, and we were no different. Giving staff nicknames was a good way of forming team spirit, however I must admit some of them were a bit too close to the knuckle. This was especially true for staff who stayed for a substantial period of time, and their names were often intended to be offensive. One of the most un-PC names was DS Boy; he wasn't obsessed with the Nintendo console – he looked like he had Down Syndrome.

But some names were just fun. We employed a former hospital porter for a few months who assured us he was experienced and hard-working. He was known as Dr Do-Little – I mean, need I say more? Then there was this girl we called Bubbles as she would always have snot bubbles coming out of her nose. We also used to have this cleaner called Steve – which incidentally was not his real name – though I don't actually know why we called him Steve, and it wasn't his only nickname – I will tell you his other one in a moment. He didn't last long with us; he really didn't grasp simple things and he was soooooo lazy. He was in his mid-50s, and his inability to learn anything was shocking. I'm not saying he was thick at school, however, by the time he got through registration, it was break time. This is a man who was so lazy he even married a pregnant woman. One problem with managing staff is that if you have one person not pulling their weight it brings down the morale of the rest of the team and they start questioning, why's he getting the same pay as us when we do twice as much? I heard a theory years ago that you should always give a lazy person the hardest job because they will find the easiest way of doing it. I'm not sure if this is true or not; what I do know is that TWAT-ALIGHT didn't last long. We could have punned on his lazy stupidity, but instead we called him this as he had a funny-shaped head, like a satellite.

There was another lady I employed for a few months; she was quite a big lady who had the biggest hands I have ever seen on a lady. They were not the sort of hands you would want tugging you off as it would make your willy look so small, and every bloke loves the helmet sticking out over the top... Anyway... We called her Minke after the whale. However, it would have been more appropriate to call her Sick-Note Minke as she was always off sick. She didn't last long. For some reason, she never seemed to wear a bra while cleaning. I'm not sure what it is with larger ladies; they either wear wrong sized bras or none at all. Don't get me wrong, I like a good old wind-stiffened nipple like most men but Christ! Those puppies were barking alright and they had big brown noses... Moving on!

Other staff nicknames included 'Gobble' and it wasn't because her body was shaped like a turkey. We had one guy called 'Hermanator' which was a cross between Herman Munster and the Terminator. Probably the funniest staff nicknames I've come across over the years were in a warehouse where they employed two brothers they called 'Soup' and 'Stew'. Let's just say soup wasn't as thick as stew. There was building site where a big black man worked on security who always stunk, so they gave him the name 'B.O. Baracus' which was genius. And the Scottish bloke called Dean who loved 70s music was given the name 'Abba Dean'.

Even the royal family give each other nicknames. Apparently Prince Phillip referred to the Queen as 'Sausage', and Prince William used to refer to her as 'Gary'. I'm assuming that's because he couldn't say Granny at the time and not because the Queen really is a bloke with a big Sausage!

I do have a confession to make; I gave all of my ex-girlfriends nicknames as well which included 'Tufty Spuds' as she had a little tufty bit as pubes and would lie there during sex like a stunned gazelle. I said to her once, you can move as well! And there was also 'Nagatha Christie' because she constantly nagged me. Then there was Crocodile Vagina; and no, her fanny didn't have teeth, it was because she was always snappy. To be fair, I'm sure they all refer to me as 'The Twat', or perhaps worse...

Staff, girlfriends, and others alike, they all gave as good as they got. I once said to a member of staff who was moaning a bit too much, "Flip me! Do you live in Nagsville?"

Without even thinking, she replied, "Yes. It's just around the corner from Twatsville where you live." It made me laugh.

I think the funniest nickname I was ever given by someone was 'Isaiah'. I have a lazy eye which goes off when I'm tired so it looks like one eye is higher than the other. Or as my best friend says, one eye off to the shops, the other is coming home with the change.

So I've employed: men, women, young people, old people, people from different ethnicities and speaking different languages; there have been stupid people, bad drivers, a deaf person, a lady that smelt of TCP, a person we nicknamed 'Terry' as in chocolate orange as he really should have been sectioned. Oh! And I mustn't forget the gossip. It's been an adventure – and one I never expected to be so challenging.

CHAPTER 4

Look Who's Talking Poo!

So cleaning is a dirty job. Honestly, some of the things we have seen would make your whole foot curl, and not just your toes. Your eyes and nose would want to close up forever. It is a sad thing, but having worked as a cleaner, nothing ever shocks me anymore – I really have seen some of the worst things imaginable.

Without a grime-smear of doubt, one of the worst jobs I have ever attended was for a council tenant who was a hoarder. You can normally tell the state of a house by the colour of the net curtains; these just happened to be a dirty orange, almost brown colour. Not that you could see them from outside. She lived in a ground-floor flat, and we felt dreadful for all her neighbours in the block, for as soon as we opened the door to the block of flats, the smell hit us like a sledgehammer made of rotting vomit. She took living in a shit-hole to a whole new level.

We put on our disposable boiler suits; they looked like hazmat suits – only tougher! We looked like we were out on day release from a Victorian asylum! We stuck on our face masks and doubled up on gloves, unwilling to trust just one layer of protection. Then, we were ready for action!

We knew it was going to be bad, we just didn't anticipate how bad. We knocked on the flat door and a rodent-looking woman opened it slowly. She must have been in her 30s, fat as a house. Well, she was literally as wide as her flat; her hips touched both sides of the hallway, and there were greasy scuff marks down the walls at hip height. And when she turned around it looked like she had raw crumpets stuck in her leggings as her cellulite was well bad. And don't get me started on her visible panty line; it was enough to make me want to vomit.

"I take it you're here to clean?" she crowed. "It's not that bad…" she grunted defensively. "I made a start on it."

Looking around, I wasn't exactly sure where she had made a start, and my imagination burned with impossible thoughts about how much worse it could have been; to be fair it looked like a good impression of a landfill site.

It was HORRENDOUS! Rubbish hummed and teetered at waist height in every single room. I still don't know how she slept as there was no space for a bed or sofa anywhere in the whole place. You could not see any floor whatsoever; we found ourselves wading through the rubbish to get into each room, stumbling on unidentified objects in the carpet of debris.

The only room you could get into was the bathroom, which led us to believe she must have slept on the shitter. However, despite the space, it wasn't a clement experience being in there. For some reason, she used the bathtub to store all, and I mean all, her used sanitary pads. It was rank! The strongest of face masks couldn't protect us from this war-zone of poor hygiene. God only knows what her Fanny must have looked like , judging by the discharge on the pads I can only assume something like a diseased badger.

Elsewhere in the flat were other hazards; for example, we discovered half-eaten tins of cat food alive with maggots. We didn't even see a cat, but at that point we didn't think anything of it. Perhaps the poor little pet had escaped to cleaner pastures! There were hosts of flies buzzing all over the place; she had created an entire ecosystem for them to thrive in.

I had WTF moments several times that day, and probably could have benefitted from some PTSD counselling after. The joke of it was she didn't see what all the fuss was about. She could not understand why she was being threatened with eviction. It's such an odd thing how the wrong people in life teach you the right lessons, and I learned a few in that flat – and not just about the depths of human depravity. She taught me that even though every man dreams of having a dirty missus, we should all be careful what we wish for...

Our remit that day was to clean and clear. It took three of us the best part of a morning just to bag up the rubbish and finally see floor space. I took the cleaner who pisses a lot and the cleaner who shat himself to tackle that nightmare. So, in that strange little dustbin of a home, there was just the three of us and the tenant scurrying around in the background. They do say one in four people are mentally unbalanced, but on this day, I would say the stats were the other way round! (You can test this statistic yourself – just think of three of your closest friends – if they appear okay, you know you're the one). Believe me, with the four of us in the flat, it was so unbelievably bizarre, I genuinely felt normal.

But I haven't even told you the most disturbing thing yet! It's honestly so horrific it is hard to type it out. The most alarming part for us happened when we were clearing the lounge. Underneath all the rubbish we found the remains of two dead cats – and they were mummified! I was fuming; I am a cat lover so I was immediately distressed by the discovery. But even if I wasn't a kitty fan, it would still have been shocking. No animal deserves that demise! When I spoke to the tenant regarding our find, expecting some sort of emotional response, she replied, "I thought I hadn't seen them for a while."

After the job was complete, I stepped outside the house, took off all my PPE, peeled a used sanitary pad off the base of my shoe… Damn those adhesive flaps, they are a bugger to get off! And then I took in several gulps of fresh air. I then called the relevant authorities. The person should never be allowed to keep animals ever; she couldn't even look after herself, let alone anyone or anything else. As upsetting as it is, you can't help anyone who doesn't see an issue with their actions. So, it was of no surprise to me a few months later to find out she had been evicted and we were being sent in again to do a final clean up.

Yet this kind of experience isn't as rare as you would like to believe. While many of you tidy a bit before a cleaner arrives, scared we will judge you for letting some junk mail pile up, or that you have stacked your recycling by the back door for a few days as it was raining outside – honestly, to that, the only response I can offer is, you know nothing. Another lady we cleaned for, who I'm sure was a lot smarter than she acted, demonstrated such a lack of hygiene awareness, I'm surprised she didn't reintroduce typhoid to her village. It's safe to say she didn't believe in using soap – ever!

My firm was paid to go and clean her place on a weekly basis. Now, you might be thinking we should be more sympathetic as clearly these people have some serious needs to get to this point. But this lady's sanitation behaviour defied logic – she functioned normally in many ways, such as she had passed her driving test and was legally allowed to drive, however, for some reason, when she went to the loo, she couldn't flush any paper down. Instead, she threw it on the floor and left it to pile up.

So, once a week, we had to go in and pick up all the tissue from the floor. It was covered in poo and all the other juices that come out of a woman's body. And, to make matters worse (if that is possible) another habit of hers was to leave her dirty underwear all around the flat. We had to pick it all up, remove the stuck-on panty liners and put it all in the wash basket. And the contents of those pads would quite often look like she had discharged chunky vegetable soup and we are talking Heinz, not the cheap watery imitation brands. To get through it, we sang the song 'On the Wings of Love', changing the lyrics to be about cleaning up after a hoarder. I still can't listen to it now as it brings back too many painful memories. I always wonder, how does this kind of thing become your normal? Not the discharge, but I mean the way she lived.

I realise some people must have issues flushing a toilet. And I don't mean the childish kind where the noise and rush of water make you feel vulnerable to being flushed away too, or like you might be attacked by the mythical loo-monster, or bitten on the bum by gremlins. I wonder if toilet issues are a sub-genre in mental health care? Like, does it come under OCD, or actually the opposite of OCD? Are there treatment plans? Or are toilet issues one of the final taboos, a frontier not yet admittable in public?

Looking back, I think perhaps loos are at the centre of a lot of shit. I have friends who have confessed to flushing their dead goldfish down the toilet before. Also, when I was a kid, I had a cousin who clearly wasn't right in the head. At about 8 years old, not only did she once hit her brother on the head with a hammer, she also tried to flush her pet rabbit down the toilet! Her defence was she thought it needed a bath!

I guess we have become lazy and needy as a society; we want everything to be easy, and to be possible immediately. It won't be long when we will be saying, "Alexa – flush the toilet!" (Actually, I bet that already exists.)

The number of places we have cleaned over the years, from public toilets to posh solicitors' offices, which have suffered from someone who just doesn't use the loo politely. There are frequently dirty protests, people who just don't seem to want to clear away their mess such as accidentally dropped used paper, and you always find a toilet which has a floater bobbing about. Is it really that hard to flush a toilet!? I get that sometimes one flush isn't enough, but as the saying goes, if at first you don't succeed, flush, and flush, and flush again! We have all experienced this at some point in our lives: the unsinkable floater. No matter how many times you flush the toilet, it just won't go down. It stays there living rent free. The amount of times we have gone to offices, including posh ones, and found floaters waiting for us, it just goes to show we all shit the same.

One particular time I remember cleaning at an office and in their toilets there was a humungous turd. It was so big, and so floaty, it could have been used as a life raft for a sinking boat. I flushed the toilet so many times, I think I caused a hosepipe ban in the local area. It just wouldn't go down; it was so stubborn. I even tried breaking it up with the bog brush, and that didn't work either. I used the old trick of plunging the loo with a mop. That didn't work either. In fact, it made matters worse as the bloody mop head came off and fell into the pan. In the end, I had to face up to the dilemma and accept the only way out was to remove the shit by hand. I put on my extra-long gloves, you know the ones farmers use to shove their hands up a cow's rear end, and grabbed the giant turd. Panicking slightly that I had a stranger's shit in my hand, I threw it out the window – which backed onto grass and happened to be at the top of a three-storey building. I didn't hear anyone scream, apart from the anguish in my soul, so I choose to believe nothing bad came out of that unpleasant moment. But the funny thing for my imagination is, if it did land on anyone, they would have been mighty shocked. What would they think? The only conclusion I can think of would be assuming that ruddy Big Bird from Sesame Street had flown over and dropped a log!

There's also nothing worse than when you are at a friend's house and you're caught short and find your log won't flush away. No matter how many flushes you give it, it bobs back up to the surface, taunting you. I have heard so many horror stories of people panicking in this situation, and then acting like I did in that office loo, picking up their shit in their hand and throwing it out of the window, only for it to land in some awkward place, making matters worse. I once heard of a woman in this situation at a posh wedding. After launching her poop out of the window, she returned to the orangery and to the speeches taking place. She then found out her poop had landed squarely – and noisily – on the glass orangery roof.

I've had to deal with my fair share of crap over the years; for God knows how long, we had a phantom logger in a public toilet block we looked after. He would basically turn up and shit in the doorway of a cubicle. You do find in most public toilets lots of people don't like using the seats. Instead, they will place toilet paper around the seat and then sit down. People can be so cautious. But, oh no! Not this bloke! He thought it was acceptable to drop his pants and shit in the cubicle doorway! At first, we thought it was a bloke bringing in a dog with him, however, it became apparent it was human poo. Why anyone would shit in a doorway is beyond me. We never did find out his identity despite doing random checks on the toilets each day. Staff were always reluctant to clean it off the floor, however, I adopted an easy strategy. Two bits of cardboard either side normally removed most of it – and of course I wore gloves as well. However, do you remember the cleaner I told you about who never used gloves? He used to just mop it and the shit would spread everywhere, making extra work for himself!

Public toilets are weird places – and the posters are weird too. What a strange place to advertise things. I also never see the point of the posters which ask, 'Please do not flush paper towels down the toilet. Please use the bin provided.' Some idiot always sticks them in the toilet, as if inspired by the challenge to see if the poster is lying. Then, they run away to avoid blame for blocking the loo! In fact, toilet signs in general are pretty pointless, aren't they? Many years ago, pretty much every household would have a sign which said, 'If you sprinkle when you tinkle, be a sweet and wipe the seat.' Again, this sign was pointless, other than for giving you something to read while sitting there. So many times, the seat would still be wet. People just take the piss – or perhaps I should say, give it generously, splashing it around unwantedly.

People have such peculiar and specific pooping habits. Clearly freaked out by stories like the one above, I have spoken to people who claim to never poo at other people's houses or at workplaces, EVER! This baffles me; doesn't this cause tummy ache? Surely, if you have got to go, you have got to go! Some people spend hours on the toilet, and sit and think, then there are others who shit and stink!

Pooping habits are fascinating – but perhaps that's just for us cleaners. I confess, I often find myself wondering how blind people wipe their bums; how do they know when their bum is completely clean? I don't know about you, but after wiping, I always spend a bit of time checking the toilet paper before dropping it in the bowl; you know, just to make sure the final wipe is a clean wipe. Normally, I use 6 to 8 sheets for each wipe, which is pretty much a tree a year just to wipe my bum. So, returning to blind people, maybe this is where a dog comes in handy. Get your mind out of the gutter, even my sense of humour is not that sick! I don't mean to lick their bums clean; I mean to bark if they need more wipes. After all, if you don't wipe you get clunkers, which nobody wants in their bum hair!

Anyway, let's carry on with gruesome pooping stories. I went to a house party once where somebody had blocked the toilet. They had tried to rectify the problem, however, every time they flushed, the water would come up over the bowl and onto the floor, leaving an unsettling flood. To make matters worse, they had used the home-owner's towels to mop up the water… and didn't mention it to anyone, leaving the scene of the crime for another unsuspecting guest to find.

And I still don't get why people don't close the lid after flushing; it is scientifically proven that poo particles fly around everywhere when you flush – landing on everything including your toothbrush! Sorry, I feel like I have gone on a mini toilet rant. Wow! I really do have a lot to say about our relationship with the humble bathroom throne. It is true what they say, you can judge a shit-hole by the turds that run through it. Right, back to the worst jobs ever...

You will always find you can normally charge a premium for the jobs nobody wants to do; this includes things like picking up shitty toilet paper and removing mummified cats from properties. Funnily enough, most people don't have the stomach for it. But while some of these stories are comical or even grotesque, others are tragic. Over the years, we have been to countless properties where the owners have sadly passed away, but they have been left for weeks on end as nobody knew they had died – and I find this so sad. I wonder, is it a problem of this day and age? When I was a kid, everybody knew their neighbours. An elderly person, no matter how alone or unsociable, would have been missed if they didn't come out for a gossip over the garden fence or to moan about the length of someone's lawn. I suppose that could be just Devon life though. These days, nobody really knows anyone in their street anymore.

In truth, it is quite a morbid job undertaking this line of work. If you overthink things too much when you are cleaning these places, you wouldn't be able to do it. Cleaners need thick skin plus a strong gag reflex. Some of the worse ones we have had to clean up have been drug-related where they have overdosed. This is made especially tragic when they are still young, having lost out on a full life. It's so sad, and hard to get back to office banter after a day on a job like this.

But on the flip side of this coin, and especially noticeable when you are a cleaner, there are some drug addicts who use public toilets to shoot up and then place their used needles on top of the toilet doors, which is unbelievably selfish – and another horrific job to have to clean.

We had to undertake an awful job in a small village in Devon. An elderly couple lived there, both alcoholics, and sadly the husband had passed away in the property. We were asked by the local authority to clean the place to make it a safe and clean environment for the wife to stay living there. It was evident they liked their drink too much, and they had clearly lost control of their home. Their bungalow had become a cack-hole! I wouldn't have even let a pig live there, let alone humans!

When we attended the bungalow, I got chatting to the widow she looked weathered, as though she should belong in a field. She must have been in her 70s, and she had burn marks on her arm. It transpires she had been mentally and physically abused by her alcoholic husband pretty much all her life. Her husband used to stub his cigarette butts out on her arm, among other forms of abuse he committed. She told us her tale, and it was shocking.

It's so sad that people never know what goes on behind closed doors; and it's sad this is left to be picked up by a stranger paid to clean up the property after a tragedy. So many people only see what they want to see. When we pulled up that day, one of the neighbours said, "Good luck with cleaning that place, they are a horrible couple," and he was glad the man had snuffed it.

After talking to the widow, she said that she never used to drink, and didn't fall into alcoholism for years. However, her husband's abuse drove her to it, as it was a way of numbing the pain and making her life bearable. Imagine spending 50 years of your life married to an alcoholic who beats and abuses you. She tolerated it all her life. Her husband pretty much controlled everything – he controlled who she could talk to and see; he controlled the purse strings, cut off her contact with friends, neighbours and family, and tormented her into submission. After she told me all of this, I felt happy for her that her husband was dead – a bit like the neighbour. I hoped this gave her some freedom. However, I couldn't help but feel so sorry for this lady. After 50 years of this life, would she know how to live a different one? Plus, she must have been attached to him, and even missed him – he was her only companion after all. It was all clearly too much for her to handle, as she was drinking when we arrived at 9am.

In a cruel twist of fate, while cleaning behind a bedroom cupboard we found a wallet with a wadful of cash in it. Her husband had hidden it and she had no idea it was there. There was over two thousand pounds in it. The smile on her face was enormous when we gave the wallet to her – it was a priceless moment! This lady had lived hand to mouth all her life and had never seen so much money before.

The cruel twist was that within two weeks she was also dead. She had used the money to buy spirits and other alcoholic drinks, and basically drank herself to death. Isn't it ironic, as Alanis Morissette said in her song, 'The old man, turned ninety-eight / He won the lottery, and died the next day'. Sometimes life is just too unfair and unfathomable to understand.

Tragedy is part and parcel of the cleaning profession. Another particularly bad job we encountered had a sad ending. We were called to a bungalow where there had been a fire in the loft space; our job was to clear all the remaining items from the loft, and clean the toilet area, so the workmen could undertake the necessary building work to put the place back together.

An old man with dementia had lived there, and his grandson would visit him every day. The neighbours all thought what a lovely grandson he was, however, unknown to them he had an ulterior motive for visiting. I am not sure of his name, however, for the purpose of this story we will call him Smackhead Steve. Up inside his grandad's loft, he had set up a greenhouse – and I'm not saying he kept tomato plants up there either. He had set up a cannabis plant factory. One day, one of the heat lamps caught fire, and effectively damaged the bungalow to the extent it was no longer liveable. Smackhead Steve got banged up in jail, as he deserved. But his poor grandad was made homeless and ended up living in sheltered accommodation.

We had to clear the entire loft, including the insulation, as it was all smoke damaged. Have you ever handled loft insulation? Even with gloves and masks on, it's not a very nice job to do. It's super itchy. Plus, with years of dust, and lots of post-fire soot and grime flying everywhere, it was close to impossible to endure. We had to take it in twenty-minute-long shifts, ensuring we had plenty of time to rest and get some fresh air. The atmosphere was so dense and fuggy. Despite wearing all the PPE, it was awful.

Some jobs can be bad, not because of the condition of the place, but more to do with the customer. And unlike what you might be thinking, it would appear the posher they are, the more anal and unpleasant they are. Plus, the ones that had money would always plead poverty and take ages to pay your invoices.

We were asked to undertake a clean at a manor house; this posh lady had visitors coming to stay so wanted to make sure the west wing, as she called it, was clean. To me, it was an annexe, but whatever.

I find it strange that people only properly clean their houses when guests are coming; it's similar to buying new clothes to impress strangers on holiday. Why not have it all nice for yourself?

And, as another aside, I've never understood why there are certain phrases and words only posh people use – when did these words get divided up among the classes? I mean, the amount times she used the words 'jolly', 'marvellous', 'ghastly' and 'beastly' was terribly dreadful. She said in her posh plummy voice, "I'm rather afraid to say, this area needs a jolly good clean. It's in a terrible state – so if you can clean this, it would be splendid."

The house wasn't too bad, but we were paid to do a thorough job, so it took a fair amount of time. After we had cleaned, and bear in mind, we cleaned from top to bottom, she wanted to walk us through the wing and inspect our work – and this is never a good thing. We were confident we had done a good job, but when customers want to walk through and check the work, you know they're looking for fault. And here's what we had not done right:

1. Apparently the kettle was not left at the correct angle; the way we had left it was ghastly.

2. The toilet paper wasn't left with a folded triangle point. She said, "How are my guests going to feel when they see the way you left it?" Granted, I can be a bit of a heathen about this as I've never understood the argument about which way the toilet paper should hang – I just don't care whether it's

over or under the holder; on the holder is the correct way. But to fold in it in a triangular point seems rather odd to me!

As always, I had a smart-arsed comment to follow. I said, "Well, I'm sure they will still be able to wipe their ass with it." My customer services skills were not so refined in the early years.

3. Additionally, I had moved the fruit bowl and the bananas were no longer facing in a southerly position (honestly). Everything she complained about was stuff being at the wrong angles. I wondered if she had some form of OCD, or I had seriously missed some crucial household information.

The inspection seem to last a lifetime. She ran her finger along every surface; if she found the slightest bit of dust, she would look at me in disgust. I was half expecting some hidden camera crew to pop out and say, "We got you!" But they never did. This was actually happening. Some people are unreal…

One of the main differences I've noticed between rich and poor people is that rich people have small TVs and loads of books everywhere, whereas poor people have huge TVs and not a book in sight. The west wing of the house almost looked like a library. Oh, and apparently one of the books was not in its rightful place – and again, I got blamed for moving it. There were hundreds of books – how she noticed one I will never know. Perhaps it was the key to her secret basement…

As we were walking round, she asked why I had opened the windows. I said I wanted to air the place and let in the lovely fresh air. Then, she moaned about some beastly smell, which just happened to be the jasmine flowers growing outside her windows. She said it smelt horrible, shut the windows, and sprayed some air freshener around. Happier, she said, "That smells better!" As if she had removed some crime from her home. I looked at the can; it just happened to be jasmine air freshener!

That day I vowed never to return to the west wing. She informed us in the morning that she struggled to keep cleaners. By the end of the day, I thought, *No shit, Sherlock. I can't think why!* It just goes to show even posh people can be stupid – and lack complete self-awareness.

Another horrible old lady we cleaned for was the complete opposite end of the spectrum. She was well old – I guess you could call her ancient, but not justified!

She lived in a grotty bungalow and had the most disgusting habits. I guess she was a bit like Mrs Twit from Roald Dahl's classic children's book. She would sit in the same chair day in, day out, splashing around in her own piss, watching TV, and generally being angry. Granted, she had a carers pop in twice a day to help her out of bed, help her wash, and get her food. However, she was a miserable old cow and never appreciated anything. She was waiting to die, and almost angry with the world that she was waking up each day. I know this also sounds sad, and you probably think I'm being harsh. But honestly, sometimes anger and bitterness corrodes the soul – even if you do feel sorry for her.

However, while watching TV, she would cough up phlegm and spit it on the floor. This wasn't a mobility issue – she had tissues and a bin beside her, she was capable of using her hands, and had all her mental faculties. After she spat on the floor, she would bark at us to come over and clean it up. She was vile and spoke to us like we were dirt. We were there to help her, and make a difference to her surroundings, but all she was concerned about was that she couldn't hear the TV when we were cleaning – despite the TV being on full blast! I think the whole bloody neighbourhood could hear it. It was the same volume every time we arrived – full blast!

OCD-Man, as he shall flippantly be known purely to protect identities, was another nutter I worked for only once. I never returned, and never will. In fairness, I think he probably had some mental disorder for real, and I don't mean to mock their suffering – however, I honestly thought I was never leaving his house that day. It was truly scary.

I turned up to clean and knocked on the door as cheerful as ever. He put the chain on and unlocked the door, peering through the narrow gap. Realising who I was, he asked me to take my shoes off, which I do as a matter of course in anybody's house. As soon as I entered the house, he asked if I would mind just running a wet wipe over the base of my socks and hands. *Okay,* I thought, *this is a little odd but let's just go with it.* It turns out the bloke was extremely obsessive about his entire home and didn't like any of his surfaces being touched. God knows why he got us in to clean the house.

I then told him I planned to start at the top of the house and work my way down, etc. This is obviously a normal cleaning strategy. When walking up the stairs, my trouser leg brushed against the side of the staircase.

"Stop!" he shouted! "Wet wipe needed! Your leg brushed the wall as you walked past! It's now contaminated!"

He followed me around every room of the house, watching intently. It seemed to be the longest two hours of my life; there is nothing worse when you are a tradesman than someone watching over you when you work. It is made even worse when you are dealing with a customer who clearly has issues. After each room he wanted to wipe the hoover wheels with wet wipes as he was worried about cross contamination from room to room. He did leave me alone for about five minutes but then like a premature ejaculation, he would just come out of nowhere.

After I had been into each room, he would wipe the door handle and shut the door. When I had done my time, I took my gloves off placed them in his bin. Then, I made the biggest mistake of my life. I went to open the front door and touched his door handle with my bare hands! God! He had some sort of panic attack! I had to wait ten minutes to leave because he wanted to wipe the handle first and leave it just to make sure any bacteria was killed before he let me out! That day, I thought stupid people were put on this planet to test my anger management skills. How I stayed cool and calm is beyond me; perhaps the evident distress he was experiencing, and the terror created by the oddness of the encounter, meant I defaulted to patience. You learn something from every job and person in life, and that day I learned that bacteria on a door handle take a long time to die when wet-wiped.

For a while we undertook a lot of site-work. When I say site-work, I don't mean we were cleaning tools and wheelbarrows. It was basically cleaning the welfare and public areas of building sites; quite often, this included the portacabins. These toilets were rank to clean. The workers would come off the building site, covered in mud, to use the facilities. It was a pointless task as within five minutes of cleaning these areas looked shit again! And, as you might already have guessed, some builders are complete animals. They would not think twice about shitting in a toilet that was clearly already blocked. Happily, they would pile a shit on top of someone else's shit. We would come in and find literal shit mountains waiting for us.

The signing-in book at these sites always cracked me up. Most of the labourers are self-employed so they would habitually sign in an hour before they actually arrived. One builder had a go at me for signing in at the correct time, which meant he couldn't scam any extra time that day. I signed in for 7:30am, which was the time I started. Enraged, he said he normally signed in for 7am but couldn't do that as I had already signed in for 7:30am! How unreasonable of me! You can see why some sites go over budget. It just goes to show, it's not always the cleaning that makes this job hard.

CHAPTER 5

Sex and the Cillit Bang

Did you know teachers are the people who have the most affairs? The list is fascinating – doctors and politicians feature pretty highly too. But cleaners don't even appear in the top thirty professions of common cheaters. I guess it makes sense; nobody wants to shag a cleaner, do they? And no one ever puts on their dating profile they're looking for a tall, dark, handsome scrubber!

The article made me smile. You see, dating a cleaner does have its benefits; we are not likely to cheat on you. The fact no one wants us is not the point.

It's safe to say running any kind of business causes stress and impacts on your personal life. Everything is made even worse if you run a business in the unsociable hours. Hence, I'm in my forties and I have never been married or had kids. This fact is one major regret of mine. Stupidly, I just thought money would buy happiness; however, it didn't. A painful thing is, every time I go to weddings, I hear old people say, "Don't worry, your time will come; you'll be next."

I sometimes feel like I need to do the same back to them when I see them at funerals; perhaps I should poke them back saying, "You're next; won't be long…" Anyway…

Most relationships I entered into either ended because I didn't make time for my partner, or when I did, I was so knackered I was lethargic and grumpy. However, I guess being single is like a vacuum cleaner: it sucks. So, I tried repeatedly to keep girlfriends. One former girlfriend used to like having sex late at night, which is probably the norm for lots of people, but when you have been up since 1am, trying to perform at 11pm is a struggle. I failed to raise a smile let alone anything else! Once, to make her happy, I ended up taking some Viagra, which was unknown to her. It's safe to say they worked… just a bit too well! When she sat on me, she said it was like sitting on a toilet brush holder! I had an erection well into the next day; the ruddy thing wouldn't go down! My girlfriend joked it felt like I had an Eiffel Tower in my pants; she'd never seen it soooooo big! She even started talking French afterwards… and walking a bit funny the next day! And no, not because I took her up the bum – in my eyes, bums are for poo, and poo only. The biggest problem I found with taking Viagra is that your head and willy are in different places. Mentally, you might not feel like sex, however, your willy tells a different story. Argh, you know when you are not in the right zone, but here my body was betraying me. My girlfriend thought I was loving the moment due to how big and hard I was; the truth was something different.

At the heart of the problem, while I was trying to keep her happy, I was running myself into the ground. We were in different places, and the knock-on effect was harmful.

And fellas, if you are having problems getting a boner, go and see a doctor. It's more common than you think. Please don't do what I did and try to solve it all alone; make sure you tell your girlfriend.

Another funny moment was when an ex commented on my manhood. She said I was like a donkey. I thought I'd take that. It turns out she meant I smelt like one and was not hung like one!

Being a cleaner has brought about some interesting sexual encounters – some for me, but mostly I'm talking about the sex lives of my clients – the weird and the wonderful. This experience has left me with some interesting observations on the carnal nature of mankind.

I'm pretty confident in saying, in any line of work, men tend to go the extra mile if there is a looker present. Take the gym for example; if there are some hot girls in the gym, men will lift a slightly heavier weight to impress them, or grunt a little louder.

However, it has not really worked out for me. Cleaning in people's homes can put you in odd and intimate positions with clients. Mostly, it is easy to maintain boundaries, but occasionally things get trickier. There have been a few times I have tried to be impressive when working at customers' houses; the owners have been ruddy stunning, and I put on my Charlie-Charmhead routine. However, they just saw me as a cleaner, and didn't really give me the time of day; sometimes they obviously looked down on me. But then, they didn't book me to come round and flatter their egos either.

Saying that, on a night out once I got talking to a lady in my local Wetherspoons; classy, I know. She claimed to be a sex addict. I jokingly said I could help her on that front. She turned and retorted, "I'm not having sex with you!" I thought, *Christ! I've cured her addiction!* I didn't even tell her I was a cleaner either.

It's really hard when you find a client attractive. On the one hand, you desperately want to flirt. On the other hand, you are there to do a job. One lady I used to clean for was a total fantasy, really attractive and very comfortable with her sexuality – but she didn't notice me in the slightest. I was just someone who cleaned her house once a week and picked up the used condoms from under her bed. One particular day, she was getting ready to go out, and she walked through her house in just her underwear. She was a tanned lady; to be fair it looked like she'd been given a coat of Cuprinol. Oh, I felt so embarrassed! I tried to be a gentleman and not look. I was so uncomfortable! Who am I kidding, my eyes almost popped out of my head like fish out of water.

She then called me up to her bedroom. God! It's safe to say I had trouser movement; I started to have chest pains! Was she inviting me up to talk about my work? Was she still in her underwear… or less? Why did she want me in her room? I have never moved so fast in my life! I almost tripped over the hoover cable! I was totally overcome! I peeled off my disposable gloves while running up the stairs. In porn, obviously the source of all reality, horny women always go for the hired help, and I suddenly wondered whether I was going to be offered a bit of action. This beautiful and sexy woman had succumbed to my polishing skills! I had all these thoughts and countless more buzzing through my head. My heart was pounding, and my feet felt clumsy on the stairs.

But I needn't have worried. When I got to her bedroom doorway, she asked me to zip up the back of her dress as she was meeting her husband at work for some business lunch. While I was there, she asked me to pick up some tissue paper which was on the bedroom floor near the bed. I cringed, but I did it anyway. I had already taken my gloves off so felt exposed (ironic, I know). So, there's a moral to this story: always wear protection – even if you are not going to get any action!

There have been a few times where things have got a little weird. Once, I actually got propositioned on a job by the client. I was undertaking a job in a village near to my home. It was around February time, not that the weather is relevant to the story. The lady had phoned me a few days earlier and booked us to clean her lounge carpet. When I turned up, her husband was just leaving for work, and we exchanged polite conversation. All was normal to this point.

I entered the house and started setting up. The lady then came down the stairs in just her dressing gown. She was a good-looking lady, especially considering she was sporting the 'just got out of bed' look. She showed me the area she wanted cleaning and told me she was off for a shower. Again, this is all regular for a home cleaning job.

I finished setting up my machine, and started cleaning the carpet. After I had completed the lounge, the lady reappeared showered and dressed. She was transformed into an elegant lady. We then started chatting away and she seemed really nice – but also overtly flirtatious. She kept making suggestive comments about the size of my hose, jesting at my cleaning equipment. She was about 15 years older than me, but I'd be lying if I said I didn't fancy her, and I found this banter fun. She then told me there was stain on her bedroom carpet and asked if while I was there to have a look at it. During the conversation, she asked if I ever considered hoovering in my pants. I laughed it off and said my balls never got that dusty!

Then, we went up to her bedroom. She said it felt strange having another man in her bedroom with his equipment out! "This carpet has a deep shag pile," she said with a smile on her face, I laughed it off, however, the flirtier her remarks became, the more uncomfortable I felt. I know it sounds odd, and most blokes would have probably jumped at the chance of jumping her bones, however, I tried to keep it professional. Despite my lewd sense of humour, I actually do want to be respected for my high standards and trustworthiness.

And she didn't just want a bit of sexual banter. She actually wanted more. She suggested we should go to bed together and have some fun. She was aware I was single from our conversation, and she confessed to me she hadn't been happy with her husband for years. It just goes to show the fantasy is not all it's cracked up to be. Hastily, I said I had another job to go on to. If I'm honest, I was a little naïve. I was inexperienced and thought, if this lady was on a Indian restaurant menu she'd have three chillies after her name – not just because she was hot, but also because she made me shit myself.

After I turned down her advances, she got upset and said that her marriage was loveless. I gave her a shoulder to cry on, and stayed listening to her longer than I should have. My dad always told me we have two ears and one mouth so we need to listen twice as much as we talk. I tried to give her friendly advice; it was basically if you're not happy, leave him. God! If only life was that simple! Sometimes, when relationships don't work out, it's so painful and complicated.

I gave her my invoice, which she paid straight away, and I left.

I actually felt a bit sorry for her. But I was also thinking, *Christ! I turned down a guaranteed shag!* Looking back, it was one of the smartest things I have ever done.

Over the next few weeks, she bombarded me with texts and calls suggesting we meet up to talk. She even turned up on my doorstep with a Valentine's Day card. I think she was a bit of a bunny-boiler. She even threatened me; she threatened to tell her husband that I tried it on with her if I didn't meet her. Thankfully, not long after that I moved to a new house; I blocked her number and never heard anything else from her ever again.

I had another scary moment which I will never forget while carpet-cleaning; clearly, dirty carpets inspire dirtiness all round. This time it was at a bloke's house in my hometown. His wife had gone to work and he was home alone. It happened to be a Wednesday. How do I know that so many years later? Well...

We got chatting, talking about our hobbies and interests. He said he was always home alone on a Wednesday. I don't know how the conversation became so personal, however, it turned out he was a cross-dresser. I did suspect he was a little light on his feet to be fair and his lady name was Ruby-May. He asked me if I minded if he put on a dress, as that was his normal custom on a Wednesday. He wanted to be himself. I politely said it was his house and he could do what he liked. On the inside, I was shitting myself. I didn't mind the dress, but I wondered why he was comfortable with me but not to wear a dress when his family was home. When he disappeared to get changed, I sneaked outside and called another cleaner to join me at the house.

There were a few moments between the other cleaner turning up and when Ruby-May re-entered the room in full dress and makeup. What is it they say? You can't polish a turd! God! He looked like some kind of drag act! He evidently wasn't used to walking in heels as he was stumbling around like some drunk person. I said to him, "You're staggering." He replied, "Thanks very much." He soooooo took that comment the wrong way!

"It's good to be yourself!" he said, while wobbling on his stilettoes. He then asked me outright whether I thought he was attractive as a lady. How do you reply to that? I replied I imagined some people would find him attractive, however, as I had a girlfriend, and was very happy, I couldn't comment!

Thankfully, the other cleaner turned up, we both finished the job together and made a quick getaway.

We laugh about it now. Coincidentally, a few weeks later we were cleaning some public toilets, and written on the cubicle wall was a message: 'Looking for other cross-dressers for discreet fun. Call Ruby-May on this number.' It was the same person as I still had the number stored on my phone – and no, not because I was tempted!

Sometimes though, offers are tempting, and I have consented on occasion. The most unusual request I ever had while being a cleaner was being asked to be a strip-a-gram. The staff at a factory where I cleaned were having a retirement party for a member of staff at a local Chinese restaurant that evening. They had booked a surprise strip-a-gram; however, he had pulled out at the last minute, and they were trying to find a replacement. The lady who was retiring had worked at the factory for the best part of thirty years, so I got guilt-tripped into it. She was certainly surprised when I got my kit off, that's for sure!

It was a cold winter's evening; their meal was booked for around 7pm – they wanted me to arrive at 8pm. The plan was to usher the lady outside the back into the courtyard for a cigarette. While they were all out there they would cue the music and in I would walk, wearing a disposable boiler suit with a zip down the front for easy access. Underneath, all I had on was a novelty, reindeer thong – and my love-dragon fitted nicely into the reindeer nose. It was a cold night, so I had trouble finding my bits, and I was feeling a bit insecure – especially since this was my first stripping gig. I found my manhood hiding behind one of my pubes, so I shoved a banana down my pants too for good measure.

It got to 7:45pm; I was parked outside the Chinese restaurant, nervously questioning what the hell I was doing, and how the hell I got roped into it. Was I panicky? You bet I was! Some of these ladies were as rough as rats, and hadn't seen action for a while. I was scared they would tear me to pieces. What if they grabbed at my reindeer? Those 15 minutes sat in the car were the longest 15 minutes of my life! The clock ticked in 8pm, and I walked through into the restaurant. I looked like a right berk. People were staring at me; then I realised I hadn't done the zip up on the front of the boiler suit, so I was showing about three quarters of an acre of chest hair and part of an antler sticking out. I made my way round to the courtyard, and waited for the music to start my grand appearance. There were about 20 ladies and one man in the yard. They were all smoking and acting normally; the retiree had no blooming idea what was about to happen to her! To be fair neither did I…

Suddenly, the music of Donna Summer's 'Hot stuff' came on; this was my cue… I guess there is always one song that brings out the inner stripper inside each of us. I strutted out into the courtyard. It was like a scene from Stars in their Eyes; there was smoke everywhere! I made my entrance memorable by tripping on the door frame and nearly going ass over tit – not sexy at all! However, I was there to put on a show, and boy I didn't disappoint! I shouted out, "It is I, The

Randy Reindeer! Are you ready for some cream-horn?"

The ladies were laughing riotously before I even started stripping. The one man in the crowd had his head in his hands. I slowly and teasingly pulled the zip on the boiler suit, wiggling my hips and dancing to the tune. But it was stuck; the zip wouldn't go down! I struggled a bit, trying to conceal that I was having an issue, but I looked as though I was having some kind of fit. Eventually, I managed to rip the suit off, revealing me in my little novelty thong. I dry-humped the retiring lady. She had a face like Jabba the Hutt, but everyone loves Jabba! Part of me thought, *Thank God for the banana*, because it might have been a struggle to look aroused! Anyway, I seductively went to spray squirty cream on my chest for her to lick off. However, I got carried away in the moment and ended up spraying the cream on her face by accident. Thinking quickly, I decided to make it look as though it was part of the act, so I proceeded to lick the cream from her face. Christ! I thought I was hairy! After licking the last bit from her chin-hair, I almost felt like I needed to be sick. Thankfully, the music was coming to an end. With that, I gave a shake of my ass and headed towards the door, while pulling down my thong so they could see my bare bum. With that, the bloody banana fell out of my pouch, which resulted in roars of laughter!

It was a night I will never forget. And to be fair, I secretly enjoyed it! I think the crowd will also remember it for the rest of their lives, but perhaps for all the wrong reasons. I was like some reject-stripper. But hey! It made her night! I don't think the Chippendales will be calling me anytime soon. Perhaps the Crippendales will though! Or maybe I could be a reverse stripper where customers pay me to put my clothes back on.

As I mentioned earlier, nothing really surprises me these days. But there have been a couple of times when I have seen things perhaps I shouldn't have. Window cleaners are a prime example of people who have this happen. Especially in the old days when all windows were cleaned by ladder and hand. We have a view into your home and can see what goes on. This means we notice things, even when we don't want to.

I remember cleaning windows for a posh lady who lived out in the sticks in a lovely, big country house. She was a senior partner in a solicitors' firm. By all accounts, despite her being stuck up her own ass, and despite her being a bit older than me, I'd be lying if I said I didn't find her attractive. She was a powerful and elegant.

Once every few months, I would clean her windows. On this one particular occasion, I went a day earlier than planned, as I saw the weather forecast was bad for the day I originally booked to do the work.

When I pulled up to her house, I noticed a couple of cars in the driveway. She was obviously home, and I was keen to not disturb her. I decided to just crack on with cleaning the windows. I started off on the windows at the rear of the house; resting my ladder up against the wall, I proceeded to climb up ready to bring the glass to a sparkle. I reached the bedroom window and peeked in; there didn't appear to be any sign of life, so I cleaned it and moved onto the next window. I think it was the guest bedroom of the house. I carried on the same around the many windows.

I got to the master bedroom, and climbed back up the ladder. Please bear in mind it was mid-afternoon. I noticed the curtains were not fully open, but I didn't think anything of it. I started to wipe the glass and noticed the owner and a bloke in bed. They were clearly doing rudies; she was on top and bouncing up and down like Tigger, and it wasn't with her husband. I tried to duck down and get away without being noticed, however, it was too late: the metal part of my squeegee knocked against the glass – she spotted me!

I dived down the ladder and acted as though nothing had happened, carrying on cleaning the windows on the ground floor of the house. She came charging out the front door to confront me. "I wasn't expecting you today!" she blustered. I explained that I was early due to the bad weather forecast. She then said it wasn't a good time for her as her doctor was with her at the moment. I thought, yeah it looked like he had his thermometer up you, checking your vital stats. She asked me to leave and to come back for the planned appointment. We never spoke about this ever again! She is still married, and God knows if her doctor still pops around these days! I forgot to tell her I used to be in the Red Cross too.

Another funny window cleaning story I heard was from a friend who took on a 16-year-old school-leaver to assist him with his window cleaning round; the lad was an apprentice. He treated this lad to breakfast every day at the local café. I say treated; that's what the lad thought at the time, however, at the end of the week he would give this boy his wages and knock off all the breakfasts he had bought him. But that isn't the story.

One day, they were in town working, and he asked the young lad to start cleaning the upstairs windows of this two-bedroom house. He joked beforehand that the lady who lived there was a bit naughty, and she frequently walked around the house naked.

The young lad just thought his boss was winding him up.

He went up the ladder, peeked in, and nearly fell off! The woman was in bed with another woman! One woman was going down on the other. He stayed very quiet and slowly climbed down the ladder, going over to his boss who was cleaning another house. He said he couldn't do that house at the moment as the woman was a lesbian and she had someone over. The boss replied, "Don't be so stupid," and that the woman was an exhibitionist and wouldn't mind if he saw her or not. He'd been cleaning her house for years, and she always put on a show.

He went back up the ladder and started cleaning the windows. He could see that the ladies were still at it. The one lying on the bed had spotted that she was being watched, however she didn't seem to mind, and the 16-year-old lad certainly didn't.

Then the woman who was on her knees suddenly turned around and clocked the 16-year-old watching her. The lad nearly fell of the ladder again – it was his mum! I guess that's one way to come out. I'm not sure he went home and told his dad what he saw that day. Part of me thinks this is a dirty urban myth, but...

It makes me think we should all keep our curtains closed if we indulge in an afternooney, that's for sure!

Some of the mad sex was less to do with my work, and more something that impacted on my livelihood. About ten years ago, I became single after a long relationship, and went a little wild. I probably did a few things during that time which I probably shouldn't have when it comes to women. Having sex with three different women in 24 hours is not something to be proud of. Don't they say the quickest way to get over someone is to get under someone? Just not sure triple dipping is the way forward! However, I was out for a bit of fun and it's not as though I was hurting anyone. I was brutally honest that I wasn't looking for a relationship, and the women felt the same. It's also important to note these were not casual sex buddies; they were ladies I had known for years and we just thought we could cross the threshold into friendship and sex-buddy thing. If I had a pound for every woman I have satisfied in my life... I'd probably have £1.50!

Talking of sex, about 15 years ago, I slept with a married lady a few times from Bridgewater – in my defence at the time she told me she was going through a divorce. She was a lovely girl who wasn't the brightest. Let's just say she'd have trouble blowing the skin off a rice pudding, but when it came to blowing other things, she had no problem at all. Again, not something to be proud of, what with her being married still, but he had moved out. I assumed he was out of the picture completely, but it turns out that wasn't the case. I mean, this does blow open the argument that cleaners don't have affairs!

Now I'm pretty sure this indiscretion came back to haunt me though! I still don't fully know to this day what or who was behind what happened next. However, every week for about eight weeks, one of my cleaning-van tyres got slashed. It was so frequent, I had to install CCTV on my drive. After I did this, the problem seemed to stop, and it also just happened to be the same time I stopped shagging her. They say love doesn't cost a thing. Well, flip me! I think me shagging a married lady cost me eight tyres... and she even joked she felt deflated after I binned her off!

CHAPTER 6

Damaged Goods

All jobs have occupational hazards; cleaning has a few of them. And breaking things is one we try to avoid, but occasional bloopers are inevitable. It's a difficult thing, because breakages can be expensive – but also, especially when in people's homes, they can be personal, sentimental, and irreplaceable!

Over the years, despite our best efforts, cleaners have accidentally broken things, and the worst things to break are always when we are in people's homes – I mean, these things happen, and that's what insurance is for, but apologising for a personal loss is a difficult thing. In most cases, we have informed the owners, and have either replaced or refunded them for the item we have damaged. I'm sure this is what you would expect for a respectable (cough, cough) cleaning company. We wouldn't want to do it any other way…

However, on the odd occasion, we have kept the incident to ourselves… This could be due to multiple justifiable circumstances, and occasionally it was because the customer was a knob! No? Not a good enough reason?

Well, let me explain…

Every now and then an accident occurs, and the planets align to just move us away from the scene of the ~~crime~~ grime. You might have done it when breaking something in a shop or restaurant. Perhaps you have been on the receiving end of such a frustration, finding something broken and the breaker has long since moved on. I haven't ever taken these things lightly, so I only have one major confession for you in this area. But the man and the house were memorable. And boy! Had he been just a little friendlier, the whole matter would have ended so differently.

We were once cleaning at an old country house; you know the kind of place – imposing architecture and millions of windows. It was the kind of place that would suit being a set for a film based on a Jane Austen novel, or perhaps some sort of gothic horror where the male owner locked up anyone who disappointed him in the cellars to wither away out of sight... The owner of the property was an old fuddy-duddy (does anyone still use that phrase?). Well, he was one of them – he might have been the original fuddy-duddy. He was gruff, old-fashioned, pompous, and rude. He also owned a boat and lived nowhere near water. Now, in my eyes people who own boats who don't live near water are either frigging idiots or they have been on Bullseye. And he certainly didn't look like a darts player.

When we were on site, he spoke to us like we were equivalent to the dirt we were cleaning up for him. It was like we were contaminated, and he thought we were lesser beings. His manners were awful; he moaned when we were hoovering that we were making too much noise – even though he had booked us to do the hoovering, and had agreed to the time and day. When we asked if we could hoover in his office, he complained he was busy and said we should use our common sense and hoover around him. Oh! And an age-old issue for cleaners, if we wanted to use the toilet, we were not allowed to use the ones in his house (any of them – even the ones he had long since forgotten existed). To be fair, he was also having work done on an outside barn, so he informed us we could use the port-a-loo which the builders were using. How generous, since it was a 10-minute walk away.

I don't know what it is about old people getting confused with timings, but he totally expected more work than he was happy to pay for. Before we started, I agreed we would do as much as we could in four hours – that means two cleaners working for two hours each. He argued he was expecting two cleaners doing four hours each, and that I was overcharging him. Now, you might think this is an easy mistake to make – and perhaps it is if you think just about the time – but not when you break down the price. I had quoted £40 for a total of four hours work – fair and reasonable. Yet he was expecting eight hours work for £40 – essentially something for nothing. Well, as you can no doubt imagine, we got off to a bad start; he was adamant I was overcharging him! I mean, does he think cleaners don't deserve to earn a living?

His house was rammed with antiques; there was a grandfather clock in the vast foyer, and various expensive and ancient-looking paintings and tapestries hanging from the walls. The place dripped with money, heritage… and dust.

Anyway, while dusting, one of the cleaners knocked an ornament off the mantlepiece. In an instant, we heard the clang and tinkle as it hit the stone and broke. We surveyed the damage. It was a naked, white, male figurine, and thankfully, mostly intact. But when it crashed to the floor, the arm had fallen off. It looked expensive. Luckily, the owner hadn't heard the break.

Now, normally we would report this. However, in a panic to avoid this gruff old man's indignation, we colluded to cover our tracks. We didn't even discuss this plan. It was inspired by mutual fear and dislike. We managed to find some glue and stick the arm back on. However, in her haste, the cleaner managed to stick the arm on back to front. By the time we noticed, it was too late – the glue held fast! To this day, I don't know if the owner has ever spotted it; we haven't been back since – perhaps that's a sign.

You might ask whether I feel guilty we didn't tell him. If I am honest, I don't. Does that make me a bad person? I really don't think so – even now, I feel the same. As the cleaning came to an end, and we had completed the job, the old codger was still moaning we hadn't done eight hours' work. We worked our asses off at his place, cleaning heritage dust and working our way round a home the size of a museum. Quite how he thought we were going to be working for £5 per hour, well below the minimum wage even at the time, was beyond me. Where did he think the money would come from to pay the employee? I think he thought he was doing us a favour by booking our company to work for him. Some people's sense of entitlement is astounding. I guess some people are just never happy – you give them the world and they still want the sun, moon, and the other seven planets!

Well, if he ever takes that figurine to The Antiques Roadshow, he'll be in for a shock.

CHAPTER 7

Blow Your Moan Trumpet

Fanfare, please! Now, I don't want to come across as a grumpy old fart, but no book of confessions is complete without including a good moan. Perhaps the whole book is a rant – and for that I refuse to apologise – I hope you are empathising, and enjoying laughing at the seedy side of your friends and colleagues' dirty habits; they definitely have them! But I want to rant a bit more.

I have covered a few personal gripes already. I am obviously irritated by people looking down on me for being a cleaner, and for having to deal with so many floaters, but so many other things have bugged me in my time as a cleaner. I mean, why is it people just seem to think politeness is optional? Take, for an example, how people act around freshly mopped floors. People see the floor is wet, yet they still walk over it with their dirty feet. Sometimes they grimace a sorry face, while taking exaggeratedly long strides over the floor, as if that makes it better. It always makes me wonder if when the same people spill drinks, do they apologise while walking away without cleaning up the mess? Once, at one job I was on, I even put cardboard on the floor for people to walk on until it was dry. Yet, lo and behold, a smug twat still walked over the floor in his greasy boots. He also happened to be the boss of the plumbing supply firm, and as he stomped his footprints onto the clean floor, he said, "You'll have to do that bit again, won't you?" I nearly shoved my mop up his ass! I'm no cactus expert but I know a prick when I see one!

But I think some of my bugbears are universal. We might all be different, but some things can turn the most rational person into a Raging Karen. Whenever you take on an office cleaning job, one thing that managers always talk about beforehand is how the staff do the washing up of their own cups. And believe me, every single time without exception, the cups are left in mountainous dirty piles. I can't count the number of times I have gone into offices and the kitchen area is just a mass of dirty cups in various states of decay. Instead of washing up, staff just take a new mug out of the cupboard. In each and every one of these kitchens, there is always a sign saying something like, 'Please do your own washing up, washing fairies do not live here.' Funniest sign I have seen said, 'Dishes are like partners, your workmates shouldn't be doing yours.' Oh! And it's not rocket science, if you are going to leave your mugs for the cleaner, it's actually helpful if you leave them soaking. It seems like some kind of cruel joke to leave mugs with caked-on coffee stains and all sorts of cultures and mould growing inside them, like you want our job to be some kind of extreme challenge and survival mission.

Mugs are a central source of office politics, power, and social struggles. They are not simply tea vessels; they represent your humour, biases, and place in the office hierarchy. People are possessive of their mugs; pranks are played with them. Friends become enemies when mugs get broken or lost. Yet some office staff leave mugs on their desk covered in mould, growing new diseases, providing a background whiff of decay to the environment. Sometimes, they even add cups to their collection over time, cluttering their desks further and reducing the opportunity for other staff to get refreshment and hydration. How some staff never get food poisoning is beyond me.

I know the complexities of mugs and refreshments transcends far beyond the issues of the humble cleaner mopping up behind you at the end of the day. We at least miss the political affair of the office tea round. To us, observing from a distance, it all seems complex and often cruel: Who is included? Who is excluded? Whose turn is it to buy the milk? And can anyone even remember the last time Anthony in accounts even made a brew?

But according to a horrifying study there might be even more to worry about when it comes to your lovely morning cuppa at your desk. According to research by TotalJobs, one in five office mugs contains faecal matter because 25 per cent of people don't wash their hands after going to the loo.

In every office kitchen area, you will find an A4 list, often inside a poly-pocket, with staff names and how they like their tea or coffee, how many sugars, and milk preferences. These lists are a good way to see who has been at the firm the longest and who is newest. Sometimes you can even see who is most important, or who are the favourites. Anyway, these lists are a good opportunity for revenge; let me explain. At one office we cleaned, there was an obnoxious twat who always looked down on us and spoke to us like we were floating shits that wouldn't flush away. Anyway, one day while in the kitchen, we amended his sugar preference to eight spoons, and amended his drink order and added the word 'Breast' in front of milk... He was a tit, after all. I just wish we were around when he was served his much-needed cuppa! I would love to have seen his face when he took a sip of that bad boy!

Talking of office mugs, if you ever want to see World War Three in an office, simply use someone else's mug on your tea break. I have seen people go ruddy mental! Some people are pretty possessive of their mug, like a child with their favourite toy. Perhaps they heard about the faecal matter on the rest of the mugs, and want to keep their mug shit-free! I wouldn't blame them! Anyway, they go to lengths to mark their mug-territory, whether it's a picture of their baby on the outside, or their name on the side, or a funny joke that's personal to them. Sometimes, they have already been the victim of ridicule – you might have seen someone like this, where the bottom of their mug has been emblazoned with 'TWAT', so when they drink it, everyone else can have a laugh at them. And Christ! If one of these mugs ever goes missing, major search parties are organised, rewards are offered, and everyone in the entire business is involved in the hunt. I have even seen a mug held for ransom, with photos of it in weird places sent by email to the owner each day.

Well, let me let you in on a secret; the chances are when a mug goes missing, the cleaner probably broke it doing the washing up. In fairness, if you guys hadn't left the mugs in such an enormous and precarious pile, it wouldn't have been vulnerable to disaster in the first place. Besides, cleaners normally get blamed for everything, so when we did actually break something like a mug, we'd never say anything – just bin it and think, *Get a life, you sad TWAT!*

Of course there are some places we clean that staff actually do their own washing up. But it cracks me up when looking at the state of some of the communal kitchen sponges they use. And they worry about people using their mugs! I'd be more worried about what I was using to clean the mug with! It's a well-known fact kitchen sponges frequently contain more active bacteria than anywhere else in the house… including the toilet!

The weird rituals surrounding the office bin are another example of the strangeness of folk. When bins are full in our homes, most normal people empty them. However, normal people become weird once they share an office space; what happens when people morph into staff? In the office, bins overflow, and people just keep piling shit on top. I guess they just see it as not their job to take the rubbish out, and leave it for the cleaner. I think I can safely ~~speak~~ shout for all cleaners the world over, picking rubbish up off the floor and cleaning waste from needlessly overfilled and ripped bin bags is NOT A HOBBY.

And this reminds me of how offices use recycling bins… Christ! Obviously, offices have clear-outs of old paperwork, but despite the fact this happens so often, they rarely have a sensible routine for managing the litter. Instead, they fill the paper recycling bins full with files and paperwork, creating towers of unwanted admin. When full, recycling bins weigh a ton. Unless you happen to be Superman or Mr Incredible, they are impossible to carry when fully loaded. But instead of assisting the cleaner by packing the waste paper sensibly, having multiple bins, or paying for more time when they are doing a spring-clean, they just stack all the rubbish, like a paper Burj Khalifa, and go about their business as if everything is normal and the cleaner can take the bin out in one. One business that kept doing this was on the third floor. We had to walk all the flights of stairs after rebagging their rubbish. There is something a bit humiliating about rebagging someone's rubbish.

Oh! And talking of bags... Why is it at home we have a carrier bag full of other carrier bags, and continue to forget to take them with us when shopping? It really bugs me that I can't get this routine right! I get it's to save the planet, but I end up with multiple bags full of bags, and still forget to take them with me. But then, sometimes I see people struggling out of supermarkets like a circus act trying to juggle all their shopping in their arms for the sake of not spending 10p on a bag. Good lord! Just buy another bag!

Food waste bins are another thing that bugs me. Whoever designed the bags which fit in the bins clearly never ran a test to see if they were up to the job. Most of the time the bags split; the bins always need washing out as they are full of bin juice and it stinks! This is always worse in an office too, as people are always happy to wedge more in and to ignore stickiness, decay, and even maggots. We got called to a council office once where staff were complaining about flies in their office space. Upon inspection, this was because someone had put rotten fruit in the bin and left the lid open. Funnily enough, flies were having a picnic in the bin and were thriving in their disgusting habitat. Nobody had even thought to put the lid on or empty it out.

Oh! Now I have started ranting, I can't stop! Another thing that grates on me like the Cha-Cha-Slide being performed by the Chuckle Brothers is people leaving toilets in a mess. I mean, if you sprinkle when you tinkle, wipe it up or you're a knob! Do people imagine I get some sort of thrill out of cleaning their dried yellow crust off the seat, rim and bowl? I know I am there to clean, but that doesn't mean you have been challenged to make it as stomach churning as possible! And it's not just pee – especially in pub loos. Surely, we all know vomit is easier to clean when it is fresh? As disgusting as that sounds, dried vomit is like cement. You know like dried on Weetabix in a bowl. When we arrive in the morning, being faced with last night's debauchery in the shape of dried chunder is soul-destroying; and it always contains carrots.

And ladies, when you use tampons, is it too much to ask for you to actually wrap them up after you have used them? One office place we cleaned, one member of staff would just place her blood-soaked pipe in the bin. The ruddy smell was rancid!

Another annoying thing that clients do is use Post-It notes to leave messages. Argh! I think people think it's cute – but we are not in a romantic relationship, or in a scene from Alice in Wonderland. Little notes saying 'Clean Me' are just patronising. One estate agent we cleaned for would go around the office prior to us arriving, sticking Post-It notes saying 'Wipe Me' on every surface he wanted cleaned – as if we couldn't work out how to do our job. These notes were literally everywhere, and just created another thing to clean. But he used them as a way to check where we had been, so if we hadn't removed a note, he would phone us the next day and say we had not been thorough enough. I don't want to misrepresent him – at first he had a valid point, as the cleaner didn't wipe the soap dispenser even after his reminders. But after that the notes were everywhere: on computer screens, on the back of toilet door handles, on the base of his chair. I mean – too far! I felt like sticking a Post-It note on his back saying 'Kick Me'!

Another frequent annoyance cleaners face is when companies change their alarm codes and locks, and don't even think to let their cleaning staff know. It just feels like we are second rate and easily forgettable – and this happens so often! The number of times we have turned up to clean only to find ourselves locked out is astonishing. And sometimes it's even worse – as we don't know anything has changed, we accidentally set off the alarms and cause a drama! How do you even forget to inform your cleaners?

The most ridiculous thing is that on many occasions I have managed to guess the new alarm code. You know, like most people used to have the word Password as their password. Well, most offices stick to a similar principle with alarm codes. It's either 1234 or the numbers running down the middle of the alarm code pad. God! I should be a criminal mastermind! I mean, I've watched Oceans Eleven – I know criminal mastermind is a way sexier job than being a cleaner.

Sometimes it isn't the employing client who is the irritant, like bleach on tender skin; instead, it is their customers. When cleaning holiday lets, we always have a set amount of time to clean from when the old guests move out and the new guests arrive. It's a formally agreed amount of time, and it is always published on booking sites under arrival and departure information. Yet, guests frequently arrive hours earlier and get annoyed that their accommodation can't suddenly be available, as if cleaning is a Mary Poppins spell that can happen in an instant! Ruddy hell! It's not my fault you can't read! Just because you have arrived early doesn't mean the rest of the world is on your schedule! One snooty lady tried to employ the denial loophole to get her own way when she arrived two hours early. We were still cleaning the chalet at

1pm when she arrived, and she claimed, "Well, I didn't see it written anywhere!" As if that meant we would just do the work in the past and let her in immediately. I politely pointed out the arrival information on her booking confirmation where it said in BIG, BOLD WRITING, 'Check-in not before 3pm on day of arrival'. Still arguing the point and delaying our ability to complete the work, she retorted it wasn't clear enough.

I joked, "I sometimes don't see things when I close my eyes."

She didn't see the funny side.

When cleaning, certain spaces are more annoying than others. Kitchens in general are the hardest areas to clean. They are more bothersome when they have granite worktops. It's no longer just a cleaning job; granite needs to be wiped, polished and buffed otherwise you get water marks. Who has time to do this? Not me! I have a million other surfaces to clean, and I am cleaning, not prepping your homes for Instagram! Most places that have these worktops tend to be people with money and they always expect blood and sweat for what they pay.

Oh! Another thing that pushes my buttons is people who cancel at the last minute. I know we can't always stop our plans changing, but seriously, it's just rude to cancel with a moment's notice without even an apology. I've even turned up for a job to be told, "Oh! We need to cancel!" When we got there! This kind of thing happened so much when I first started out, I had no choice but to start charging a cancellation fee. I would have my day planned out to accommodate a certain amount of work, having turned work away, and then find myself with no work because of someone else's poor organisation. It felt like I was totally insignificant.

It was as if they thought, *He's only the cleaner, it doesn't matter if we cancel him at short notice* – or perhaps they didn't think about me at all! I mean, ruddy hell! Would any of you be happy to sit around all day losing important income because someone else changed their mind without saying anything?

Wow! Complaining is so cathartic! I'm on a roll now!

There are other things that annoy me about cleaning, even when I am working for one of my best clients. For a while, I really tried to get on board using eco-friendly products; our world is precious, and we should all do what we can to be more ethical. Right? Well, NOPE! Someone needs to put the investment into developing products that work, as these products are crap! They might be better for our planet, however if they don't clean like they are meant to, then I will lose work. They don't cut through grease, clean stains, leave surfaces shiny, and they don't smell nice. Thus, I end up using five times as much of the product, which must make them unethical anyway! And they nearly always come in the same problematic plastic packaging, so if I am using more of them, I am just creating more plastic waste! Plus, they cost three times as much as normal products. When I put together quotes for potential customers these days, if they mention they want us to only use green products I refuse to take on the work. It might seem stubborn, but I think if you want something clean, you need to use the best product for the job. The irony of it is, I normally find the most belligerent customers who demand green-cleaning drive the enormous polluting cars and constantly change their décor, discarding white goods as if they decompose naturally in the environment.

I haven't always felt this way. In the early days, I used to buy green products and tried to be environmentally friendly.

But I couldn't argue that a shoddy job was the price for saving the planet. Then, I would buy eco-friendly products when someone requested them, but frustrated with the expense and poor quality, when they were empty I filled them up with normal products. I know this is a hideous confession, but it happens a lot. Cleaners will often reuse containers and put different, cheaper alternatives in the bottles.

My biggest bugbear though, the King of Pains, is even more annoying than people who take up the entire pavement and dawdle along. I am irritated to a point of high blood pressure by people who look down on cleaners.

So many times, people have spoken to me like I'm dirt, rather than someone who cleans dirt up. Male bosses tend to be the worst; some are just darn right rude, like they want to demonstrate how little they think of you through arrogant belittlement. I think they want to establish their superiority; I mean, sometimes they even ignore you entirely. I remember at one business where I used to clean, I would always knock on the door of the manager's office, and just whizz in to empty his bin. I always said hello, but he never spoke to me at all. He just looked at me, and waited, as if I was a bug that needed to be removed. I was left with the assumption he was an arrogant arse of a man. At the end of the day, we are all the same.

Actually, I take that back – it's not true that we are all the same. I believe we should be nice to everyone; he evidently believed he only had to be nice to people he pre-approved. I think I can sum it up better than that: He was a prick; I have a prick. That's about where the similarities end. Or, to put it another way, he couldn't ever be circumcised as there was no end to this prick!

CHAPTER 8

Dirty Shades of Grey

Being a cleaner is an incredibly intimate profession – especially when domestic cleaning. Now, I don't want to make you feel paranoid; if you employ a cleaner, you do give us a window into your life, however we are not secretly gathering information on you and sharing it mockingly in the pub. I mean, we haven't really been able to go to the pub properly for the last year or so due to COVID restrictions. Besides, it's only really me who is kissing and telling. Though I wouldn't have wanted to kiss most of my clients – no matter how desperate they were.

I also don't want you to turn into one of those mad clients – and we cleaners have a few of them – who clean their homes ready for the cleaner. I always find this bizarre: why bother paying for a service if you are just going to do a lot of the legwork? It's not as if you have a standard to uphold. We don't suddenly assume you don't poop, never have dirty laundry, and apparently never eat or drink anything! No! We just realise you've given everything the once over before we get there, making our job a doddle and you seem like an uptight control freak. It's not like dust just doesn't fall in your house! Although, as you might have noticed already, I do appreciate you washing your cups in advance.

Oh! And I would also appreciate if you picked up your sex

toys – finding a big red vibrator the size of a fire extinguisher on a bedroom floor once wasn't pleasant. To be honest, it made me feel a tad inadequate, and a little confused. But still, what I lack in penis size I compensate for by hammering it in. This sounds much better than saying I was blessed as a child with a large penis and a week later the vicar was sacked! Where was I…

Oh! Yes! Bizarrely, some of the worst houses to clean are the houses that are clean before you arrive as you know the owners are particular about everything – and I mean everything. Often to the point of having OCD, there's no possible way you can just know their idiosyncrasies without there being some tension. And believe me, one thing I hate is when a client follows you around the house while cleaning. There's nothing worse!

There is no getting away from it though – you are inviting a relative stranger into your home to tidy up behind you. We see all your dirty little secrets – and I mean all…

You might think your habits are entirely normal, but when you clean as many homes as we do, we end up noticing little foibles that give your inner freak away. And we have seen them all! There are no personal peculiarities we haven't seen before. We have seen everything, from the person who stores their soups in alphabetical order to the person who hasn't cleaned their grill since it was new over a decade ago. We also know from medication bottles whether you're suffering from piles! There are people who have homes that are coordinated throughout, everything new and perfectly in keeping, and those whose things are part of a collection – down to your guilty pleasures revealed in your old DVD collections. We know what food you like from the contents of your fridge, and we learn about your music tastes when dusting your old CDs you probably should have got rid of years ago. (I mean, who keeps a copy of Crazy Frog or Cha-Cha slide now? Some of you do!) But it's not just your cleaning and tidying habits exposed to us; we see so much more!

The first big tell after the state of the front of your property is the mail pile inside your front door. I always notice whether the pile has been allowed to build up, and whether you have recycled the pointless leaflets that have been imposed upon you. I can tell you, I have been in homes where those leaflets create a second layer of carpet! Plus, we see the pile of bills marked past due and then know you're having money problems. This makes me sad for my clients and cautious to collect payment sharpish.

But we also see the things you don't, and some of these things leave us in an ethical quandary. It's a difficult call between just doing the job well, and being honest – and risking losing the work in future. After all, the truth is sometimes painful to swallow. For example, I have found drugs and condom wrappers in teenagers' bedrooms – what do you do with that? Do you tell, so the parents can protect their child? Or do you tread delicately, believing it's none of your business really and the parents might know anyway?

To be fair I was impressed they were using condoms, as it's a known fact women buy more condoms than men. I personally can't stand them, however, I used to do this joke with partners when putting on a green one. I would stand at the end of the bed and go, "Ho ho ho! Green…"

Before I got to finish the line one ex-girlfriend said, "TWAT!" It made me laugh but apparently it ruined the moment anyway…

Well the same ex dumped me and not long after we split up, she had the coil fitted. Is it bad that I asked for the condoms back? Anyway…

It's also hard when there is clearly someone struggling with alcohol in the family. We can always tell because we find bottles of booze stashed in odd places around the house. We find them in the laundry bin, hidden under dressers and drawers, and even stockpiled in the bathroom. I once knew someone who always had a part-drunk bottle of wine behind the driver's seat in their car. That always made me nervous.

Sadly, I could definitely win some money if infidelity was made into a sport. I can always tell when someone is being unfaithful, not just because they start making an effort in their appearance or put on extra perfume or aftershave but because the cheater always starts hiding laundry. We find items of clothing – shirts with make up on, dirtied underwear, best clothes for an evening out that the partner doesn't know about – hidden in weird places like under the stairs or behind big furniture. But there are other secrets your house can reveal about you. In some cases we can work out how often you have sex with your partner as some couples leave the condom wrappers and tissues shoved underneath the bed.

I learned quickly that just because someone looks polished in how they present themselves, it doesn't mean their home is spotless. Some people put effort into the bits people see and hide the rest. One lady I cleaned for, a divorced recruitment manager, always looked great, and she had a beautiful house in a gated community. But inside it was the filthiest, nastiest place in the world. It made me gag! Her swanky home was just a posh hoarder-hut; it was filled with junk. She always comes to mind when I think of my favourite quote, 'A clean beaver gets more wood'.

This rule can be applied in other scenarios too. There are plenty of people who make the front of their house look great, but inside it is a hovel, unfit for safe human habitation. I always wonder how stressed the resident must be when they finally call us in. Like, have they exhausted themselves working from the outside in, keeping up with their normal life's demands, and just run out of time? Or has the lie got too much, and they want some of that loveliness inside too? Or have they just not been paying attention, but they suddenly have visitors arriving and need to straighten the place out?

Then there are the Bluebeards among us. While it sounds really dramatic, I actually think Bluebearding is an easy habit to fall into. You will recognise it when I explain it: Bluebearding is when the spare room has become a place for secreting everything you don't know what to do with – with a door that closes, becoming secret and forbidden from visitors' eyes. I actually know one woman who has three spare bedrooms, all of which conceal her hoard of unnecessary bargains – even from her husband.

I have another confession. Don't ever ask me to clean your six-bedroom house and then say you need it done in two hours. If you set unrealistic targets, you get unrealistic results. And if I'm honest, I make sure I never rush to get it all done as you'd expect it all the time. The clients who set realistic goals I always go the extra mile for and do something extra they didn't expect like put a triangle at the end of the toilet paper. You guys love that crap!

Oh and another thing: posh people always want to give you their life story when you clean. I really couldn't give a shit to hear how tough you have got it, living in your mansion and that your daughter Harriet is struggling to ride her horse, and that Cuthbert only got an B grade in history which has brought shame on the family. As I understand it, most people have a lot less in life. Stop ruddy complaining – I'm cleaner, not a therapist.

Although, despite all of the habits and secrets you expose to us when we clean inside your home, I would rather give you a good service than clean for one of the cleaning fanatics on Instagram! I feel like they have turned housewifing into something distorted like the families in the colourful houses in Edward Scissorhands. I mock to some extent – being a housewife and proud is amazing – turning home-keeping into a capitalist, perfectionist, elitist game is just as uncomfortable as the hoarders.

And can you believe – some of these also have cleaners behind the scenes anyway!

CHAPTER 9

The Good, the Odd and the Old

You know you are getting old when you get excited about little things, like replacing a mop head, or finding the perfect tog for your duvet. You know the kinds of things I mean – such as the moment you discovered using a certain fabric tea towel makes your glasses pop and dazzle like never before! It's as though being particular about things suddenly brings so much joy.

Funnily enough, the older I get, the more I enjoy talking to older people. Some of them are wise and inspirational and tell the most incredible stories; some of them are the funniest people you could ever wish to meet. But if I'm honest, it's also tragic and regretful to think for some of the old people we clean for, us popping in each week is the only time they see people.

There's one old lady we clean for, to be fair she could win a glamorous granny competition, who breaks my heart every time I see her. She lives alone, as you might have guessed. Every week, she says she's had her life already and she's just waiting to die. I wonder, how do you process that?

Without fail, we hear her TV blasting out every time we enter the cul-de-sac, several houses away from her front door. I never need to ask what she is watching – it's normally easy to work out from the audio – but I always do, to be polite.

She often replies, "I only have the TV on for background noise to make it feel like other people are here."

"Background noise?" I reply. "The whole ruddy street can hear it!"

But really, to think some old people think this way is just unforgivable; as a society, we can do better than that!

Whenever I talk to her, I am struck that despite her miserable outlook, she is hilarious – and she never seems to realise it, she's so deadpan in her delivery. She told me she was a vegetarian for 12 years in her younger days. She always adds, "You know, before being vegetarian was trendy!" Then, she continues, "I was a vegetarian for 12 years, then one day someone left me alone with a salami…"

It cracked me right up!

She said she got a taste for meat again after that, and that she wasn't sure which hole was best to put it in!

I was crying with laughter!

She also told me that on the day Princess Diana died, she had a phone call from a relative informing her of the sad news. She happens to be slightly deaf and didn't quite hear the message. She confessed that for a while she thought Princess Diana was killed by Pavarotti, and not the paparazzi!

I also loved the story she told me about her friend who tried everything to get pregnant but never did. It starts tragically, but it gets better, I promise. And slightly surreal. One day, her husband decided to spice things up in the bedroom. Among all the things he could have done, he replaced the light bulb in the bedroom with a red one. Anyway, the woman went on to have seven kids! It just goes to show, maybe sometimes in life all you need to do is change the hue of things – or get a new job…

I so enjoyed cleaning her house, and I loved her saucy company. She always referred to me as the 'Handsome Cleaner', and flattery is always a good strategy to get me working harder. My gran always called me 'Handsome' too. I used to think she was lying but maybe I misunderstood. I guess a threesome is made up of three people, a twosome is two people, and me being single and hand-some certainly was correct!

Even the way she walked made me laugh! She shuffled along like a lady who had her tights pulled to just above her knees, holding her legs together uncomfortably. You have probably seen someone like it; you know what I mean, where they have a tights-hammock between their legs. I swear she might have kept her fruit bowl between her legs, her tights were so low. She always offered me a grape or two when I attended.

"No thanks!" I would always reply.

She was a proper diamond and goes to prove many old people are not grumpy or miserable. Some of the best lessons we get for life come from old people. One story I heard during COVID was about an old couple going through a McDonald's Drive-Through. It was around the time McDonald's were allowed to reopen, and they were crazily busy. The queues to get a Big Mac were huge, stretching miles! Some people would camp out overnight in their cars just to get a Happy Meal. I mean, after that show of dedication, how happy would you expect that meal to be?

Anyway, the old couple were taking a long time ordering at the Drive-Through self-service speaker. The young people in the car behind were getting fed up with the waiting so they shouted abuse at this old couple.

"Hurry up and order, you old @$!!@*s!" they shouted, adding, "You should be in a care home!" They continued their abuse.

Finally, the couple ordered and proceeded to the paying window. They paid, and then said to the McDonald's staff, "Could we also pay for the car behind as an apology since we took our time ordering."

What an amazing act of kindness this was! Instead of returning hatred or resentment, they showed love.

Then, they drove to the final window where you collect the food. There, they picked up their food – and the food for the young kids from the car behind, and drove off!

I often wonder whether the kids chose to accept their loss and leave with no burgers, or whether they had to rejoin the long queue in order to get their food. Either way, that story catches me in the chuckle zone. Also, the lesson is clear: never underestimate old people; they are wiser than you think. So, get to know old people; they will teach you how to slow down in life. The new old people coming through, i.e. my generation, will be the worst ones we've had! Can you imagine: here is a picture of my dinner… That is old people in 50 years' time! Why do people take pictures of their food and post on social media? Anyway, back to the book.

I'm not sure what I would have done in that situation. I always try to do the decent thing, but sometimes payback just calls too loudly. And often, what is good and what is right are two different things.

I'm being cryptic. Let me tell you about another elderly customer. Each year the clocks change for British Summer Time, going forward at the start of summer and dropping back for the winter. Our older customers would often ask us to change the clocks for them. And my! Old people often own a lot of clocks. I never used to mind, however, this all changed after one of my staff decided to do a good deed and it backfired in spectacular style. Sadly, I paid a heavy price – and it wasn't financial!

We cleaned for this one old lady who lived in a flat, and no word of a lie – in her one-bedroom flat, she had eleven clocks! There was one in the kitchen on the wall, one on the oven, two in the living room, two in the dining room, two in the hallway and three in the bedroom. It took him nearly an hour to change them all, which seemed ironic as the hour she had gained with the clocks going back had been spent changing them to the correct new time!

Anyway, it took a while for me to find out what actually happened that night. While the lady was fast asleep in bed, two of the clocks crashed to the floor, and caused an almighty bang! Being a woman of a certain age, she slept lightly, so the noise startled her. Additionally, as she lived in a block of flats specifically for the elderly, the noise woke up the rest of the tenants too! There was bedlam! Sadly, it also caused to her to shit herself.

So, the next day I was called out to clean shit off the carpet.

All because my employee failed to hang the clocks back up properly.

Going back to when I was called to clean up the shit, we had no idea what had caused the night-time excretions. When I enquired what had happened, she said she didn't know. The woman said she had just heard a couple of bangs which woke her up. Apparently, she shot out of bed and, in her words, had a little accident.

She wasn't very mobile, so at least the shit was just in one room of the flat.

Confused, I had a look around the flat to establish what had happened. That's when I saw that the clocks had fallen off the wall. One had fallen behind the sofa, and the other was lying underneath the dining room table. I quickly put them back up and told her it must have been something outside. I know it was a lie, but I thought there was no point worrying her. She suffered from dementia, so by the time I explained the truth, she would have forgotten anyway.

Another time where we tried to do the right thing and it backfired was when we were asked to clean for a rather large lady who was pretty much bedridden. We called her Pork-Chop Pat as she had a layer of fat around her shoulders, legs and pretty much rest of her body. She lived in a standard two-up, two-down house, and apparently she hadn't left it in years. Judging by the size of her, I wasn't sure how she even made it down the stairs, but somehow she was making it to the kitchen to eat more food each day. She was so big, the type you'd fondle and not touch the same place twice. I kind of think she must have had some kind of eating disorder. And I also think the person providing the food is partly responsible too. Anyhow, did you know, you can make a cow go upstairs but then it can't walk back down? This is because their proportions don't balance on stairs designed for the human two-leg body. I'm not sure how I know this amazing fact – or how someone tested the theory for that matter. However, I think it was safe to say if this woman was ever to make it outside, they would have had to get a crane and maybe take the roof off. She was a large lady, but where was I…?

Oh, yes! While cleaning her place, she asked us if we would let the dog out into the garden. Anyway, we forgot to shut the gate behind us so after I let the dog out, the bloody thing ran off into the housing estate. We had to spend the next hour trying to find the ruddy thing and bring it back. The situation was not helped by the fact that the dog was deaf so it couldn't hear us call his name anyway! The customer said the dog likes treats so I took some from the kitchen to entice her back. I thought, *Ruddy hell! The dog's not the only one who likes food!*

So, there I was chasing around the housing estate looking for this poodle called Winnie (Winnie the Poodle – I promise I am not making this up). Eventually, we tracked her down, enticed her with some dog treats, put the lead on her and took her back home. The first thing the owner said on our return was that it's quite often the dog goes off, but don't worry – she normally finds her way back! Soooo okay... There I was, spending an hour of my life getting this dog back home, who just happens to have a habit of walking itself anyway!

During COVID-19, our cleaning company worked dried up, which is strange as you would have thought it would go the other way with offices and houses needing deep-cleaning and sanitising. So, I decided to use my time productively and undertake some community work and do old people's shopping for them. Blooming heck! That was a big mistake – it would appear buying the wrong item for some people is a criminal act! One morning, this old lady wanted satsumas, however, the supermarket didn't have any, so I bought her clementines. I might as well have murdered someone! She kicked off merry Hell when I dropped her shopping off to her.

But I was a mug and helped again. The next week, she wanted some panty liners amongst other things. Now, I'm a man of a certain age who has never ever had to buy these ruddy things before. She wanted some super-absorbent ones with wings, whatever that meant. Anyway, I searched high and low, but couldn't find any. I explained this to her when I dropped the shopping off, and feeling bad I thought I would cheer her up with my dazzling personality. I said there was good news: "They had Weetabix in stock, and they are super absorbent…"

I'm not sure whether she got my humour or decided to stick Weetabixes inside her panties, however, it made me laugh.

As with everything, I always look for what I learned. It just goes to show, sometimes even when you try and help, some people don't appreciate it. I think Ronald Reagan once said, 'We can't help everyone, but everyone can help themselves.' I appreciate that this woman was stuck at home alone, stinking of piss no doubt, but life is far too short to be ruddy miserable. I later learned I was the third person to do her shopping for her, and the others told her they couldn't do it anymore. I'm pretty sure it was because of the way she treated them.

But this doesn't mean I have lost faith in people. Among the grumps, grinches, and gargoyles, there are the good guys too. There are plenty of people who give back, make you laugh, and brighten the day a little. My gran used to say, if you can't see the sunshine, be the sunshine! And there are plenty of people who are grateful too. So I will keep helping where I can. And I will continue to clean for old people, brightening their homes and providing a little much-needed company.

CHAPTER 10

Can't Get You Outta My Bed

Of all the things we clean, the bed has to be one of the archetypal problem areas. Instagram is littered with influencer-housewives demonstrating ways to fold fitted sheets neatly, and hacks for putting on a king-size duvet cover alone. I call BS on this, but I'll hold that rant in for a moment. There's the age-old debates such as how many pillows is correct, whether decorative pillows are just a waste of time and space, and why putting a blanket across the bottom of the bed has become a fashion statement. And, at the other extreme of bed-lore, there's always a bloke somewhere who hasn't changed his bedding for months.

Sadly I know one bloke who lost his wife and didn't change the bedding for nearly 12 months as it was the last place she slept and it still smelt of her... and on that same flip side, I know a single bloke nicknamed 'Whiffy' who had no excuse not to change his bedding but never did – I don't even want to think about how many tissues are in his bed... or how long they've been there! I even once heard of a teenage lad who slept without bedding, directly on the mattress, under a cover-less duvet, for six months, in a stand-off with his bereft mother who couldn't get him to make the bed.

Just so you know, you should aim to change the sheets once per week. And did you also know your mattress will double in weight in ten years due to dust mites so that's always worth replacing regularly too.

Beds are magical places where time seems to fly. You wake up and it's 6am, then close your eyes for 5 minutes and it's 7:45am. Yet at work its 1:30pm, you close your eyes for 5 minutes and it's 1:31pm.

And beds are also interesting as they are such personal spaces. We find all manner of personal treasures and horrors in the darkness under the bed. From underwear to used condoms, dirty plates and mugs to single lost earrings. Sometimes there's even secrets stashed away, from hidden presents awaiting wrapping, to letters or gifts from a secret lover. Under your bed tells a story, and your cleaner is sometimes the only other person who knows it. Although, never once have we found piles of money under a mattress, so that stereotype is clearly false.

But we don't just clean beds in your homes. We clean beds in all manner of places, from grotty bedsits and tragic refuges to posh houses and five-star holiday lets. But these bring about a host of other issues.

I mean, I will never again take on holiday let cleaning. I say: never! They are a complete pain in the ass, like, a thousand times worse than having piles. The job never runs smoothly. From the moment we arrived on our first day, there has always been something that meant the job could not be completed according to any kind of plan or schedule.

There are always residents who haven't checked out, who argue it's their holiday and they don't want to be rushed. Or they apologise, saying they are just accidentally running late, and sorry to be a pain, but could we give them a few more minutes? But it happens all the time! Then there are the arrivals – it's so frustrating when they arrive while you're still cleaning as mentioned earlier.

"We have paid good money for this!" one posh lady snorted, after arriving three hours before check-in time, denying she had known about and agreed to the arrival time.

I thought, *You should have spent some of that money on reading glasses, love. It's not my fault you can't read!*

This kind of thing happened so many times, the countless stories begin to sound the same.

I always expected people who rent holiday cottages to be respectable. They pay top-end money for these properties, so I thought the customers would be top-end people who would leave the cottages presentable and treat the place with respect. But some were complete and utter dirty rats! On one occasion, we arrived and the sink was full of beard hair. The person staying clearly thought it was okay to leave his beard trimmings all over the sink without even attempting to clear them up.

On several occasions, residents broke furniture and left it for the cleaners to discover, not even mentioning it to the owner, as if the furniture was disposable. Others would not bother using bins and just throw their rubbish on the floor. Frequently, there were used condoms lying around, and cigarette butts in the bottom of mugs, glasses, or just on the ground. It appeared that people on mini-breaks just have no respect at all – as if being on a break meant also having a break from the demands of being decent. Who knew decency was so wearing for some people?

But as you might have guessed, the one thing that didn't vary each week was the dreaded bed-making. Ohhhh Lordy Lord! Before I start my rant, let me give you the background to picture the scene. There were six beds to make up in this holiday cottage: two doubles and four singles; the singles could also double up as two more doubles to give the customers flexibility. So, in effect, four couples could stay there, or a family. It was a lovely place!

And let's face it, everybody loves getting into a freshly made bed. There are few things as pleasing as soft, freshly laundered cotton. However...

Here goes. I don't care what the influencers say on Instagram, fitted sheets are not fitted sheets. They are unfitted sheets at best, or maybe they are non-sexual bedroom torture devices – something that can quell the libido of the most rampant lover. Now, before you say, *Oh, you must have got the wrong size fitted sheets*, you are wrong. And if you continue arguing with me, I might lose respect for you. I think during the first wash, they change size to mess you up. I would no sooner fit one corner on the mattress, go to tuck in the corner on the other side and the ruddy first corner would pop off! Putting a fitted sheet on the bed is like doing a Krypton Factor assault course while simultaneously doing an impossible maths puzzle – and as you know I wasn't the brightest kid at school. I would always find myself running from one side of the bed to other and back again, trying to stretch my arms like some kind of Incredibles character, trying to hold each corner in place, while trying to make something smaller than the bed fit it comfortably. Even when it was finally secure, held in tension like a sheet-shaped drum skin, I always found myself smoothing bubbles and bumps out of it which suddenly appeared. Just as I'd smoothed one side, another bubble appeared on the other. I hate fitted sheets. The women on Instagram showing off how to use and fold these are selling something fake, just like the models who photoshop their bodies to sell makeup. I think they secretly go up a size of sheet to make it seem easier.

But if I am honest, the situation was not helped by the owner of the holiday cottage buying different sized beds and sheets, so the whole thing was a mix-and-match nightmare from the outset, all in plain white cotton.

She always condescended, "Make sure you use the right sheets on the right bed!"

Well, let me tell you, even a king-size fitted sheet never really fits on a standard double bed – especially if it has been put through a hot wash first of all.

Okay, I will move on, and back to confessions. On a more personal matter, before I went on any lads' night out I used to change the bedding on my bed just in case I got lucky. My fastidiousness never seemed to work. The really funny thing is, whenever I was too busy to get round to the task, or if I just accepted I'd be coming home alone so didn't bother, that's when I would end up bringing a lady back at the end of the night. Sod's law, I think they call it. Although who is Sod and how did he get a law? But don't worry – I am a gentleman and don't use and abuse women. Anyway, I couldn't take them to bed… Jeez! The sheets were far too sticky! I was a single bloke back then, after all. Some take up fishing, running, or golf. Masturbation was my preferred hobby for God knows how long. And believe you me, I'm like a sofa bed; give me a pull and I double in size!

As I said, beds are funny places; they are almost magical. And I don't mean because of the sumptuous comfort, I mean they seem to be able to play tricks on your mind. I can be lying there, in my bed, yawning and ready to drop off. And just before I go to sleep, I suddenly remember something I should have done that day that completely skipped my mind over my wakeful hours. But then, I guess that will be the memory foam.

Beds are also magical because they are fortresses. You must have heard the rule that if you put your blanket or duvet over your head, you become invisible to intruders, and the duvet becomes stronger than Batfink's wings. Remember those? Like a shield of steel!

Experts always say you should get eight hours' sleep per night, but I wonder if that is like the five-a-day rule for fruit and vegetables – a noble ambition, but not always achievable. Anyone who runs a business will tell you it is impossible to get that much sleep. I certainly never do! At my busiest, I probably got eight hours spread across four days.

The humble bed is at the heart of many sayings too, isn't it? Some of them are confusing if you pause and think about the words. For example, I've never really understood the phrase, 'You must have got out of bed on the wrong side.' Now, my bed is next to a wall, so it is impossible to get out on the wrong side without injuring myself. But I hate it when people use that saying as why would it matter which side you get out? How did the side of the bed make you angry? 'You must have chosen the wrong queue at the supermarket' would make more sense – you know the moment, you choose the shortest queue but then realise it's short because the assistant doesn't know how to use the till yet, and the person at the front has selected some obscure fruit that doesn't have a bar code, and there's nobody around to verify her age to buy alcohol. Now that can make you feel irritable. A posh lady said this to me once when I was cleaning her house. She commented that I was quiet that morning, and so I must have got out the wrong side of my bed. Thinking back, not only does it not make sense, it is also pretty rude to comment on someone's mood that way. I should have replied, "Have you been hit by an ugly stick?" I'd have mirrored her rudeness and used an equally dumb saying. Whatever is an ugly stick? To her credit, from the neck down she looked lovely; unfortunately from the neck up she looked like a horse.

Another stupid bed saying is, 'You made your bed, you lie in it!" Just pause and think about it. It's meant to be a warning, or a lament that you deserve what you get. But just think a second – it's so ridiculous! I mean, yes I will, thank you! I like my bed – I made it that way deliberately.

But then, people say stupid things sometimes. You know, like when you're on a date, and people ask stupid ice-breaker questions. One I have been asked a few times is, "If you were stuck on a desert island, what book would you want with you?" How stupid. If I'd had chance to pack to be stuck on this island, I'd put in a lot more useful things than one book! I once replied, "I don't read, love." It's such a pointless question as in this day and age, I'm hardly likely to ever be stuck on a desert island without having decided to be there in the first place.

I heard that somebody once replied to this dumbass question with, "How to build a Boat – The Idiot's Guide." There are stupid people out there, but there are some genius people too! (you could always buy a copy of my first book *Baby Pigeon* and take that with you. Never one to miss an advertising opportunity.)

I wonder if they're the ones getting the full recommended eight hours' sleep a night on perfectly fitted sheets...

CHAPTER 11

Virus Recognition

It would be impossible to write a book about cleaning and not talk about Coronavirus. I mean, it's affected our lives for a long time now. But can you remember the early days when we were told to wash our hands more, and to wash them while singing the song 'Happy Birthday To You' twice through? It seems bonkers now, doesn't it? If someone had said back then we would go through three lockdowns, and you wouldn't be able to hug your closest relatives for months at a time, none of us would have believed them. Though I'm sure some of us are thankful for the distance from some relatives. Saying that, I don't want to jest about isolation and loneliness. Personally, I think they're as dangerous and damaging as Coronavirus.

It was a strange time – probably a good time for cold-callers like charities and religious groups such as the Jehovah's Witnesses. After all, everyone was at home! But for the rest of us, it was a challenging time. I mean, life is cruddy when your wheelie bin goes out more than you do! I think most of us turned into dogs roaming the house looking for food, and getting excited about going for walkies. When we did go out, we had to take care not to get to close to strangers!

I'm sure none of us could have predicted the madness which has unfolded like a Jack-In-The-Box filled with Semtex over the last year. The virus certainly brought out the best and worst in people. Back at the beginning of the virus, we really didn't know what to expect, and what changes lay ahead. As a cleaning company, we were ahead of the curve with PPE, because as standard we have some of this stuff in stock. But it was a case of all the gear and no idea. As expected even before the virus, at all jobs we wore disposable gloves, and then at really bad jobs we would wear hazmat suits and masks. It was strange when the whole COVID stuff happened as we had loads of PPE, but there was a shortage elsewhere, and most people didn't know how to use it all effectively.

I must admit, back in the early days of the outbreak, I made a few quid cashing in by selling sanitiser and toilet rolls. The sanitiser was a right result – who knew it could become such a precious commodity! Prior to the shortage, you could buy these things for less than a quid. I sold quite a few for around £35 each! Did I feel bad? Did I heck! I thought, if these idiots want to pay this price on eBay, who am I to stop them? Besides, it has all been normalised and gentrified now. Instead of a bloke on eBay making a few quid, now upmarket stores are stocking sanitiser with botanicals and essential oils and charging through the nose – suddenly, because it is hipster, it is acceptable. Plus What are Essential oils? I confess I'm 45 years old and I have never used them, so not really sure how Essential they actually are. Anyway where was I? In my defence, like with the sanitiser, people were prepared to buy disposable masks for £80 a box when they cost me less than £10 in the first place – and we didn't know what would happen to business in the coming months. It seemed like a no-brainer at the time. Don't judge me – it's not like Boris is my mate and gave me a PPE contract, now is it?

And before you all start shouting at me, I also did several random acts of kindness. At the time, supermarkets were running out of toilet rolls, but I had a few pallets in my lock-up, so I put a post on Facebook offering free toilet rolls and sanitiser to the old and vulnerable. I had to laugh; some care homes got in touch with me requesting the freebies! Bear in mind, these were overpriced private care homes where you need to sell your house so your old mum or dad can spend a month getting care they desperately need. Anyway, they wanted me to drop them some free sanitiser. I asked if they had run out, and she replied no. They apparently wanted to keep some in stock, and they were not willing to pay over the odds on the internet, or to wait for their supplier to restock. I told them to stick it.

And, call me a Grinch if you must, but don't get me started on *Clapping for Key Workers.* That made me laugh! Don't get me wrong – some people who work in care are amazing people. However, when you pay the national minimum wage, you also sadly attract some frigging idiots who don't give a shit. A tenant of mine works in a care home and lived in a shared house. From the moment lockdown started, we agreed the rule that no outsiders were allowed in the house. This key worker decided to take matters into her own hands and hold a house party and invite loads of friends – and strangers! Christ! Then they wonder why all these old people were dying in care homes when you have idiots like that!

Besides the fact, clapping isn't going to put a meal on the table or get car through the MOT for a nurse. So, I'm pretty certain the clapping didn't make much of a difference for the carers, nurses, and medical staff who do have integrity. Someone I know who is a nurse, during the whole clapping debacle, came home from work to find the police waiting for her. It turns out, one of her clapping neighbours had reported her for having people round her house – the people turned out to be her childcare. So much for supporting the NHS. But as long as we clap on a Thursday, it will all be fine! The whole thing stank worse than a loo with a three-day-old floater. But saying that, I did go outside and clap!

Some offices we cleaned for took all the COVID stuff seriously, whereas others couldn't give a toss. For example, one place made us take temperature checks before we cleaned and made sure we had the correct PPE. Another place even made us sanitise the wheels of our Henry vacuum cleaner, which was a bit extreme. I wondered what the difference was between my hoover wheels and me walking into his office with my shoes, but it didn't seem like the right time to challenge their protocols. The biggest thing that bugged me about this arrogant twat was that while cleaning the offices another person came in and he shook their hand! He was such a knob! I thought, *Don't preach what you clearly can't practice!*

During Coronavirus, or at least the first year of Coronavirus, I bent over backwards to help people out – whether it was giving away free toilet rolls or sanitiser to the old or vulnerable, or running errands and collecting shopping for people who were shielding; I feel I did my bit for my community. However, one job stuck with me during this time.

I was contacted by an old couple who live on the outskirts of my hometown. They were in the process of moving house. The first lockdown had just come to an end and the housing market wheels were once again in motion.

"We previously had a cleaner," he said, "however, she stopped coming." But he offered no further explanation. So I popped around to do a cleaning quote on a Saturday morning.

They were pleased to see me, and they looked like a normal old couple. Well, except the husband had gurt ears and what I can only describe as a cockerel's chin – although, years ago, this term was used as a euphemism for a fanny. This chap had a massive gap in his chin just like the opening of a vagina! But panic not! I wasn't tempted to get out the love dragon and shove it in his cockerel's chin!

Their house was very old-fashioned, and a bit dirty. Well, okay, very dirty. They had one of those old four-bar fires which I thought looked a bit dangerous; it creaked and groaned like it had suffered enough. The room was a fire hazard in its filth. Not least, there were heavy, dust-filled cobwebs everywhere, like natural curtains.

"The last cleaner didn't like spiders," the chap said.

I thought, *Your last cleaner didn't like cleaning either, by the looks of things.*

The elderly lady had fallen a few years previously, so she could barely move. She struggled along to show me her house while her husband sat in his chair. I'm pretty sure his legs worked better than his wife's, but he let her do the work anyway. After 35 minutes, she had managed to show me every area of her house and told me what she wanted done.

"The last cleaner just did the floors and bathrooms, and that's all we want done," she instructed.

"No problem," I replied. They were moving soon, so I kind of understood their logic of not wanting furniture polished, despite the fact that most of it had a thick layer of dust on top as well as on the handles and ridges. However, the customer is always right, so who am I to judge? I quoted her specifically for what she wanted and explained I would arrive on Monday between 9:30 and 10am.

That Monday morning, we got ahead of ourselves and ended up arriving early at this particular house. Although, when I say early I mean 9:10am, and not at dawn, so we thought this acceptable.

We pressed the doorbell. There were two of us waiting to complete the job. It took a while for them to answer the door, however, I knew the wife had mobility issues so I waited patiently. Eventually she came to the door still in her dressing gown.

"You're a little early," she commented.

I apologised and said our previous job didn't take as long as planned so instead of waiting in the van for twenty minutes, we thought we would come straight along. As my dad always says, better to arrive early than not at all!

She said, "Not a problem; time is money! If you can start downstairs, I'll go and get changed then you can do upstairs."

All seemed logical and fair.

With that, her husband entered the kitchen, fully clothed and with a walking stick. "I'll take over, Shirley," he said angrily. "Leave this to me!"

With that, he slammed his walking stick on the floor a couple of times and shouted, "THIS IS UNACCEPTABLE! YOU HAVE COME WAY TOO EARLY!"

I thought he was joking. Both of us cleaners had face masks on, which is probably a good thing, as I was smiling away underneath it, oblivious to the fact he was actually being serious.

He then pointed to my member of staff. "And you..." he threatened, holding out his walking stick. "Both of you are out of order coming to my house at this time!" I apologised and explained the reason why we were twenty minutes early. But he wasn't having any of it.

"You have made a very bad first impression!" He scowled, like the impression he was creating was reasonable and justifiable.

I politely said to him, "Do you want us to leave and come back later or another day?" I was trying to console him and rescue the situation, though I had never been in trouble like this for being early.

"No – get on with it. You're here now so you might as well clean."

Someone didn't get any action last night, I thought to myself, *or perhaps we had interrupted his morning loving.* Mind you, he and his wife slept in separate beds anyway. Under my face mask I mouthed, *'F@*king idiot.'* These face masks come in handy sometimes!

Robert Brault once said, 'One key to success is to have lunch when most people are having breakfast.' I've always been an early riser; just ask my former lovers! Don't get me wrong, I appreciate we were early and caught him and his wife off guard, however there was no need for him to yell at us, and hammer his walking stick like a weapon. His manner was completely unacceptable, and if some of my female staff had been there, it could have been quite intimidating.

While we were cleaning, this chap was outside in the garden, popping in occasionally to check what we were doing. The atmosphere wasn't pleasant at any point; he made us feel uncomfortable. This job was rapidly leaping up the charts of worst jobs ever – they were going to make it as a memorable one-hit wonder of the nightmare client charts.

And their house was filthy! There were cobwebs all over the place, like a canopy. Even Lady Havisham would have been ashamed to leave a place like this. However, we stuck to what his wife had asked for, and only cleaned the floors and bathrooms. At the end, we had a bit of time left over so I did a bit of polishing, cleaning up some of the main surfaces.

While we were upstairs, I realised we were being monitored. The landing had a balcony which overlooked the lounge, and I could see him and his wife walking around running their finger over surfaces, checking that we had cleaned. Not that they had wanted any surfaces cleaned.

While cleaning the bathrooms, I noticed a tub of Vaseline in each room. There was one in his bathroom and one in his wife's en suite: what is it with old people and Vaseline? Maybe that generation is kinkier than we think! To be fair, his tub looked more like Marmite so God knows what he had been using it for. Maybe his dirt hole got burgled! Besides, if I am honest, I wanted to shove his walking stick up his ass by the time we got to the bathrooms anyway.

When we finished cleaning, I debriefed his wife on what we had completed; I explained we concentrated on floors and bathrooms as requested, plus undertook cobwebbing and a bit of polishing. She thanked us for what we had done and apologised for her husband's behaviour.

"He's not normally like that," she said with a smile on her face.

After we left, I met with my member of staff, and we both agreed we would not go back to that house for future bookings due to how the man had spoken to us. When I got back to the office, I was about to write him an email and send an invoice when I received an email from him.

This is the actual email:

Subject: *Cleaning*

Regarding your visit this morning, I am extremely disappointed from start to finish.

I have spent the entire afternoon finishing off the cleaning that you missed.

We will no longer require your services.

Please do not call me. The decision has been made.

This email was sent to me at 1:05pm, so his comment about spending all afternoon cleaning cracked me up! By my maths, and I was a retard at school, he spent a whole 1 hour and 5 minutes! Plus, his cleaning was on surfaces they had specifically told us not to do! It's a shame he hadn't done any cleaning before we arrived, potentially for years, as we might have stood a chance of getting everything done! Clearly, he and his wife don't communicate very well as we did exactly what she asked. Or, the man was bonkers.

What made it all even funnier for me was that the man wondered what happened to his last cleaner and questioned why she never came back. He obviously had no self-awareness at all.

You might be wondering what I replied. Did I crack out my best one-liners? Did I send some facetious remark? Other people might have sent an abusive message telling him some home truths. However, there's power in a pen, so I decided to write about him instead! So, Mr Twat, thank you for the material for the book! Besides, I guess the best revenge is love. Some people in life just need a hug; he needed one –

around the neck – with a rope!

Sometimes the problem isn't with your customers, but with managing staff. As I said at the beginning of the book, managing staff is one of the hardest things about running a business, and doing this during a pandemic is a new trial in itself!

I always find, you can see the true character of people when you do really hard, grotty jobs. Some people roll up their sleeves and get on with it, some turn up their noses and moan like buggery, and others don't turn up at all! When Coronavirus first swept our nation, and everyone was scared, some staff wanted to be furloughed, and others didn't. I was always worried about when we finally got back to normal, and companies went back to work, what would happen to all the staff who had been at home for months? Inevitably, some furloughed staff would not be brought back. At the time, they thought it was the best thing ever, being paid to have an extended holiday. However, I don't think they realised, there was a reason they were still on furlough when some of their other workmates had gone back to work. For many companies, this was a case that some were better and more productive at their jobs. I think a lot of businesses learnt how much dead wood they were carrying and how they could be more productive with less staff.

Some pandemic work was actually quite fun. One enjoyable job we picked up was to spray-sanitise the park equipment in a small town just on the outskirts of my hometown. This town had five parks in total, and the people we met varied from park to park. Boy did I meet some characters and have some banter, since all our social lives had taken a massive hit by this point. One park was in a posh area and it definitely had a higher calibre of runners, walkers, and families. Some of the mums were really stunning. Back in the day, I'd have called them MILFs. Another park was smack bang in the middle of a council estate and Oh My God! The park was largely filled with dog poop and litter. But some of the mums we met were as rough as rats fighting over a restaurant bin. Several had missing teeth; they were covered in tattoos, and a few had a speech issues.

At first, I was a bit intimidated to start conversations – in both parks, but for different reasons. However, the women in the council estate park were always friendly. Sadly, the ladies in the posh parks never really spoke to me. We were there for months, and a little chatter makes the day pass easier, but they always just went about their business, aloof towards us. I'm sure they were the type who wouldn't fart in front of their partners, but I bet they did on the quiet.

In the council estate parks, conversations were totally at the other end of the spectrum. Some of the ladies shared a little too much information! One lady, I say lady, but I mean in gender only. I'm not sure you could class her as a *Lady*. She was quite often in the park with her mum and her four kids. She always had a can of energy drink in one hand, a cigarette in the other, and wore jogging bottoms even though she didn't look like a runner to me – unless it was to the fridge and back. Over the months, we got chatting, and she was actually very funny and I liked her a lot. She was a little too open and honest about everything, especially when it came to sex. She had gurt big lips, which she claimed made her a sensual lover. She also joked that she had her mum's lips. I thought, *Flip me! I hope not downstairs!* I had visions of her bits flapping around like flip-flops!

"I suppose I'll have to shag my husband tonight," she would often say. I thought, *Lucky boy. Hold me back!* She continued, "If he's good, I might give him a 'rusty trombone'."

Well, I wasn't sure what that was, so I asked, "What the hell is that? Are you in a brass band or something?"

She said, "It's when I lick his bum hole then place my hand around the front of his body and wank him off!" It was an image that stuck with me – not sure I would want any lady to give me a rusty trombone, that's for sure, however she did open my eyes to a lot of things.

Working in parks was actually a nice part of our job – it got us out and about, chatting to people normally, and we got to enjoy the great summer. But one thing that bugs me massively is dog walkers and the stupid things they do with their poo bags. People go to all that effort to pick the poo up then dump the bag at the side of the path. What is the point of that? During COVID, dog poo became a massive problem where I lived. For some reason, owners felt it was suddenly okay to just to let their dogs crap anywhere they like and not pick it up. Streets became full of dog shit. I know, you could argue it was because kids were walking the dogs for vulnerable people who couldn't go out. However, if they were old enough to walk the dogs surely they were old enough to pick the shit up too.

The strange thing is, back when I was growing up, I never really noticed fly-tipping or dog poo. Did people pick it up more back then or was I too young to care? If I ever found a dog poo back then it was always white. I never see that these days.

One thing that cracked me up with the whole introduction of masks was how hard it was for people to follow simple rules. It was made more complicated by lots of people being given exemptions but having no clear guidance on what classified needing one. In my area, it was really confusing because none of the Polish people wore them. Surely the Polish can't be all exempt from wearing them? Are they prone to asthma? I mean, we are a small town and our Polish community is also small, so hardly representative of the whole country, but it was blatant. They didn't even stick to social distancing rules. I used to see the blokes hang around in big groups near a One Stop shop, smoking and chatting away as if it was normal-times. Then, they would just walk into the shop with no respect for the mask rules. When challenged by a member of staff, the blokes just shrugged their shoulders and pretended to not understand. I read about this a lot in the news, so it seems disregarding rules that were put in place to keep us safe were ignored everywhere. Who was it near you? Was it one social group? Or random people?

Many people were as thick as shit when it came to wearing masks. I drove past one knob who was walking through my hometown with a mask on, yet he had made a hole so he could smoke his cigarette at the same time.

None of this should surprise you if you live in Tiverton, to be fair; it's a very special place. One outsider once asked a local if there was a B&Q in Tiverton. The local boy said, "Oh, that's a tricky one. Let me think… There's definitely a T and a V in Tiverton…" Anyway back to masks… I also see so many people who would wear a mask but not cover their nose, or pull it down to speak. Covidiots!

There might be some positives to come out of the pandemic. I heard some people predict lockdown would start the next baby boom, and who doesn't love a cute baby? I'm not sure if that's turned out to be true, but I have heard more people became alcoholics, which might be more fun, but also alarming. But then, how else do we cope with being trapped inside with the same people other than share a drink or two? I even heard some people completed Netflix! One thing is for sure: if there is a baby boom, by the time 2034 comes around, we will have a whole generation of teenagers known as the 'Quaranteens'.

I shouldn't joke really because thousands of people died; the whole thing is tragic beyond our wildest imaginations. And I still find it hard to believe we started our millennial apocalypse with a toiletries shortage while all wearing pyjamas and loungewear. I know the virus started in China, but I still think Andrex might have sponsored it, because they must have made more money this year than ever before! I suppose, if nothing else, since everyone stockpiled toilet rolls, at least we were a nation with clean asses.

CHAPTER 12

Silly Love Thongs

As I have mentioned, cleaning is an intimate job. In some respects, we are like ghosts. Whether you are in an office, silently aware of secret things, implicitly trusted to see but not see the inner workings of the business, or in people's homes, welcomed into private spaces with access to more areas than most close friends and family, it is a strange job. We often have to suppress normal reactions and clean up messes we simultaneously have to act as though we don't know about. But, if I am honest, at the same time, this privilege can be alluring.

For some cleaners, this privilege is like a power and something that can be misused. It is crazily easy to get into awkward situations with clients where you know something over them (their financial insecurities, secret eating habits, affairs and indiscretions, hidden evidence of misdoings and mistakes, guilty pleasures and clandestine desires) and some cleaners can use this power for their own gain. Even for us normal cleaners, the balance can be hard to manage. I mean, as a red-blooded male, it can be so hard sometimes to manage my feelings when in a home with an attractive client. On the one hand, I'm her cleaner, and invited in to do a job. On the other, all my non-verbal receptors are dancing a jig, noticing I'm in her bedroom. While I'd never do anything to breach that trust, oh man! Sometimes it is hard work managing the embarrassment, or reining in the flirting, which wants to burst out.

Back in the early days, when I was young and on constant heat, I had this one client who had grown-up kids. I mean, ruddy hell! The eldest daughter was super hot, and if I'd met her out in a club, I would definitely have tried it on. Mostly, it was never an issue. She was at university, so lived away. I only cleaned her room to keep the dust down.

But when she was at home, it was another story entirely.

The client wanted me to clean her room each week – she remarked how her daughter was messy. But also failed to mention how her daughter also liked to sleep in until lunchtime.

Before I recount this story, which is embarrassing enough, please remember, I was a young man at the time, and not much older than the student.

Anyway, I set about cleaning her room that day, and it was a mess! There were clothes everywhere. They were all over the floor, the chair, the bed. Drawers were hanging open. The bed was dishevelled, and the curtains were drawn. The room, in fact, was in a worse state than my mate's, who once confessed he only changed his bedding around once a year. So, I failed to notice, among the mess, the piles of clutter, the detritus of student scum, that the young lady lay asleep in the middle of it all. She was like an inverse Princess and the Pea – where the princess is underneath the bedroom.

Totally oblivious, I started to pick up and fold the clothes into piles and put them neatly on the chair in her room. Not to delay telling the story, but that is half the battle with cleaning; you basically just move stuff to less obvious places in tidier piles. Anyway, during this folding session, I also picked up her underwear. Yes, her blue lacy sexy underwear, and added it to the pile of clothing too. Oh, it so gets worse yet.

Anyway, there was this bra. It was lacy, flimsy, and slightly boned – which I wasn't – I promise. But, for some reason, I just held it up and looked at it. Looking back, I could have just been mesmerised. Man! It was sexy underwear! But also, it wasn't obvious how to fold it; plus, it seemed like a ridiculous garment. Aside from slightly titillated, I also felt awkward and weird, and uncertain what to do with it. I was in two minds whether to put it on top of the pile of clothes with everything else, or to just drop it back on the floor and pretend I hadn't seen it. I confess I was holding it up and imagining her wearing it… Anyway, just as I was at my most flustered, and though I had been holding it for no more than a few seconds it felt like minutes, but it was at that particular moment, I heard a surprising sound from the bed. It was the student's voice. I jumped.

"Morning," she murmured, and rolled over.

Mortified, I mumbled some inaudible excuses, and hurried out – only to realise I was still holding the bra, so had to go back and put it on the pile. Inside, I died, inside and deflated faster than an undercooked souffle.

Thankfully, it was never mentioned again, and we continued cleaning for the family. Although I never inquired to find out, I have wondered whether she was half asleep still and didn't really notice who was there – or what I was doing. Perhaps she thought I was a parent in the room, or perhaps she was trying to embarrass me – which I deserved. Whatever the truth of the matter, that day I learned a crucial lesson to always knock loudly before cleaning someone's bedroom. I also had a good lesson in respecting privacy, and my eyes opened into the vast variety in the wonderful world of lingerie!

Blue lacy underwear has always done it for me. One thing I can't stand is picture pants or logo pants. I got with a girl once – stripped her clothes off and her knickers had the words, 'You've got to lick it before you stick it' written on them. It put me right off, and I swear I got a whiff of tuna too.

Talking about underwear, I once heard a funny story where a friend of a friend got caught sniffing his stepmother's thong. Yes, you read that correctly. But the story is so much more revolting than that. Do you really want to hear it?

He must have done it many times, as I heard he made a habit of taking her panties from the laundry basket. He would wait until she showered after work, after which she would normally go out. Alone in the house with his temptation, he would take the pair she had just removed, scurry away to his room, and masturbate with them.

One day he grabbed this sexy black thong that was in the laundry basket. He was in his room cranking away and had the thong wrapped around his very erect penis. He did not hear his step-mother return or call him for dinner.

Suddenly, she opened the bedroom door, and they both had the shocks of their lives. There he was, in all his glory, on his bed watching some anal porn and stroking off. She closed the door really quickly, but he heard her say, "Those better not be my panties!"

They never mentioned the incident ever again. Though many other people have!

Underwear appears in the most bizarre of places. For example, when cleaning public toilets, we always find ladies' underwear in the men's loos. Now, I'm sure this is sometimes after late-night quickies, the remains of a fast and fun bang with a stranger. But most of the time, the underwear is clean. So, there are blokes out there who go to the effort of nicking panties off ladies' washing lines to take them to a public toilet to masturbate over. I mean, it's not the most sensual of fantasies, is it? Besides, I'm not sure the smell of Daz would do it for me. That's if you could smell it over the smell of the men's bogs.

However, sometimes you do find panties left behind after a shag. The worn ones are so obvious compared to the fresh ones. We have even come across some which have thick, glutinous, vaginal fluid discharge in the gusset; one pair even looked like a slug had taken residence!

While I have no way of knowing who these ladies are that end up in the town bogs after a drink at the local, the panties do leave some clues. We have learned women of all sizes love a bit of late-night loo lust! The pants go from one extreme to the other! They are either tiny little thongs or gurt big apple-catchers. Some could easily be mistaken for dropped tooth floss, more likely to cheese-slice a woman's lady parts than offer any comfort, and others could easily be used as tents if the fabric was waterproof. I have even considered washing them and using them as rags… After all, waste not want not…

Despite how revolting many public loos are, it turns out they really are popular spots for sex. I already told you about the dead goat I found in a public toilet on Exmoor. It honestly scared the shit out of me – I almost peed myself; I wasn't sure whether it had been sacrificed in some kind of weird ritual, died in a sex act, or accidentally wandered in by itself. Whichever way, I initially thought I'd found a body.

But public loos are a source of more sexual fun than just animals, sexual call-outs in Sharpie pen, and discarded underwear.

I have found all sorts over the years. There has been lots of drug paraphernalia, from needles to empty Rizla packets and bits of dropped weed, homeless people who are fast asleep in the disabled toilets, pregnancy kits to sex toys and even random vegetables. It's a strange thing to find a carrot which has clearly been inserted into a love-hole. Despite my propensity to waste nothing, there's no chance of taking any of that veg home for my dinner, I can tell you!

On top of all these things, and the random drunk people napping off their excesses, I have found endless porno mags filled with all kinds of stimulation. There are the obvious things like larger ladies, big-tit mags, and orgies. But then there are the weirder ones, like Nazi torture porn – which turned out to be S&M with Swastikas. Or ones based on movies, like The Da Vinci Load, The Porn Identity, Forrest Hump and Smokie and the Ass Bandits!!

Honestly, this industry, as crass or captivating as you might find it, is definitely creative.

Though, I think it should also be said, too much porn can be bad for your health. I heard about this one chap who died after his enormous (ermm – keep your filthy mind in check, please) stash of porn fell on him and crushed him. I am left with a couple of questions. One, how much porn did this man actually have? And two, why hadn't he gone digital? Just saying.

There are times when loo-shagging is preferable to other things we find. This one night, I went into the local toilets to lock up, and heard sobbing coming from a cubicle. Alarmed, I called out, "Are you okay?"

There was more sobbing, and a quiet, breathy, "*No,*" as a response, but no movement to come out. I was aware I needed to lock up, but I was also getting worried about the wellbeing of the woman inside. I encouraged her to come out, offering help, and reassuring her it would be fine. But she refused, saying she wanted me to go. She wouldn't open the door and sounded in a lot of distress.

I explained I had to lock up, hoping that might persuade her to leave, but still nothing. I could hear her rummaging around. I had no idea what to do for the best.

Eventually, she opened the door. When she did, I noticed blood on her jeans. I tried to keep calm to not add to her anguish, but I was rapidly freaking out.

It turned out she had broken up with her boyfriend earlier. She was heartbroken, and had fallen to pieces, as many of us do when grieving a lost love. But, when she got upset, she had taken an unusual turn. She had taken a broken bottle and had carved her lost love's name into her thigh. Looking at the cuts as I tried to help her bandage herself, I think he was called 'BEN'.

Thankfully, she was okay. A little ashamed and certainly in shock, but her injuries were minor. As she wandered home, I thanked God her ex didn't have a long name like 'Christopher'.

Us cleaners, we might be close to invisible to you, but you are not invisible to us. We see and hear it all. Generally though, your secrets are safe with us. It's part of our unwritten contract with you – to be present but also silent. Kids, on the other hand, have no discretion filters whatsoever, and yet they often occupy a similar access to all things personal and private.

A former girlfriend once told me this story. She also

cleaned for me as well for many years and was great at her job. She was a glamorous lady who always took pride in her appearance. She took on cleaning a doctor's surgery each afternoon, but would do after her normal office job each day, so would turn up to clean in high heels and sexy fitted dresses. She was a good cleaner, and personable, so I'm sure the patients and staff smiled as she tottered along cleaning. But this story isn't about something that happened at work.

She has two kids, and this story involves them, and how they see and hear more than you think. One afternoon, she was watching some series on Netflix, and the kids were playing upstairs. It was a good job they were out of the room as what she was watching was pretty erotic, by all accounts. It was just some box set, but there was a blow-job scene which was pretty convincing. Apparently, the nudity was extensive, with full penis exposure, and she was convinced the oral sex was real.

Anyway, time went by. One morning, while dropping off the kids at school, she was chatting to other mums. Her five-year-old daughter suddenly said to her, "Mummy, I saw a willy the other day."

She was mortified! The other school mums found this highly amusing. When she questioned her daughter about where she had seen it, the girl replied, "That's not all. There was a lady sucking the willy."

Again, it brought laughter from the school mums. When the mum questioned where her daughter had seen this, the small child replied, "Mummy, you were watching it on TV."

I don't think any amount of *'it was on Netflix, honest!'* stopped the laughter or teasing after that revelation. I also think she was a lot more careful to check where the kids were playing when watching something adult rated after that!

Plus, I seriously think kids have eyes in the back of their heads! Wherever they keep their eyes, they certainly don't have your back like your cleaner will.

CHAPTER 13

Lost But Not Forgotten

Sometimes, when cleaning, I feel like a twisted version of Mary Poppins. We meet so many amazing characters and stumble over so many weird, wonderful and sometimes worrying things, it's like falling into a surreal land.

I sometimes wonder whether I should start a Museum of the Lost and Found. Think about how fascinating, bizarre, and unsettling this could be! After all, there's a Museum of Smuggling in Devon – with stories of baby corpses being stuffed with drugs, and shoes with false soles on display. In London, there's a Museum of Curiosities, with stuffed animals having dinner parties and all sorts of sex toys everywhere. There's a museum of penises in Reykjavik, with lots of stuffed phalluses on display for you to take a selfie with. So why not a Museum of the Lost and Found. There could be galleries devoted to lost civilisations, treasure troves, and perhaps even to world mysteries, like missing planes, people or places which vanished. But obviously, there would be a gallery of things cleaners have found over the years.

Let me fill you in!

There are obviously the disturbing finds of the ordinary. Honestly, in a high percentage of residential properties I have cleaned over the years, we have found crusty tissues and used condoms under beds. Whether we are cleaning the houses of the rich and famous, or in council houses, sexual detritus lurks in dusty places.

I suppose, in strange way, it's good people don't leave these things out in the open for all to see. However, I always wonder why people don't dispose of them before the cleaner comes round; do they want us to find them? Is it a strange flex to show off they're getting some nookie?

Seriously, I've seen all kinds of condoms. We have found ribbed ones, flavoured ones, covered in shit ones and even once, one stuck to a cat flap!

Once, my mate cracked me up with a condom story. He and his new girlfriend were playing guess the flavour of the condom. He would put one on and she'd go down under the sheets, have a little lick, and shout the answer. But the first time they played, she shouted out, "Cheese and onion!"

He replied, "Give us chance – I haven't put one on yet!"

Anyway, let's get back to the point. We have found some strange things over the years. Cleaning up after office Christmas parties always throws up a few surprises. I remember cleaning at an estate agents' in Taunton the day after their Christmas party. It was 6am, and we didn't expect anyone to be there. I walked in to find four members of staff fast asleep on the floor, and one sat at her desk with her head in a bucket. She was still wearing her Christmas antlers. She told me not to bother cleaning that day.

We cleaned up after a celebrity Christmas party, which turned out to be a hectic affair. She had an artificial snow machine so there were small balls of polystyrene everywhere. And I don't just mean inside her house; they were all down the drive, in the hedges and borders, in the lounge, kitchen, and pretty much everywhere downstairs. It took forever to clean!

The strangest thing though, underneath all the fake snow, we even found a prosthetic arm. Someone went home without it. I mean, you have got to be pretty wasted to not notice your arm is missing.

Many of the most startling finds happen when carpet cleaning. You have to move furniture around the room in order to clean, and often this might be furniture than hasn't been moved in years. We come across all sorts; there's the normal stuff like years of dirt, a Lego brick even though the kids left home twenty years ago, coins – sometimes out of use, the odd vibrator, mice droppings, and false teeth. The list could go on. But one of the strangest things I found when cleaning someone's house was a snakeskin. This freaked the owners right out as they had never owned a snake; there was no plausible explanation for the snakeskin to be under their sofa. It was fairly large too.

I think I'd have moved out and sold up!

Some losses are things we hope to conceal forever, never to be discovered. One day that will stay with me for all eternity started with some more simple carpet cleaning. We were making excellent progress when my mate managed to knock over a jar in the corner of the lounge. It turned out to be urn full of the owner's wife's ashes. Horrifically, the urn wasn't sealed, and as it tumbled to the ground, the ashes fluttered over the carpet.

We stood and looked onto the devastation. Nobody wanted to touch the ashes; nobody knew what to do. Eventually, we put back what we could. As for the rest, we just sucked it up with the machine. However, we did as it respectfully as we could, bowing our heads and saying a few words of apology and farewell while the vacuum returned the room to normal.

It turns out people keep ashes in the oddest places. Plus, it's not always parents and partners in the urns. On one occasion, we cleaned for a lady, and had to move some boxes from underneath the owner's bed to vacuum thoroughly. There was a big wooden box, and it was quite heavy. Later, we found out it contained her horses ashes! I'm not sure why she kept them, and why she kept them under her bed. However, I guess sometimes we are closer to our pets than to people around us. Besides, each to their own, I suppose.

So, at Christmas I am known to be enormously generous to friends and family and normally give them all gift bags full of goodies. After all, it's the thought that counts, and if you can't treat your friends and family it's a sad job. However, I can honestly say, with the exception of my parents, I have never had to pay for a Christmas present at all. All the gifts I have given were freebies from house clearances. Whether it was wine, chocolates, sanitary pads, or a tin of tuna – every family member was treated the same.

Mind you, they used to moan like I'd broken their leg or something at the contents of their gift bags. I am as pleased as a cat with an extra bag of Dreamies with my present-acquiring endeavours. I've only come unstuck a few times. I was not helped one year when I gave my auntie a bag that contained a bottle of wine that I hadn't realised had already been opened and partially consumed. And, to be fair, my gran was a little surprised when her gift bag contained a pair of fluffy handcuffs. In all honesty, I didn't plan to put them in my gran's gift bag, despite her active sex life. God bless her, she'd have probably enjoyed them though – she was always very open about her love of men! She has now sadly passed away, but her memory and zest for life will always live on.

The pink fluffy handcuffs were an amazing find, and ended up being part of Marbles cleaning folklore. They were found during a house clearance and were left in the van as a bit of a staff joke. Anyway, I was in the process of selling my bungalow and had a few viewings on this specific day. One of my staff thought it would be funny to put the fluffy handcuffs through my letterbox so when the estate agent undertook the viewings, they would find them.

Now, I arrived home the exact time the viewings were about to commence, opened my door, saw the handcuffs and threw them in the corner of the office where I had family gift bags all set up preparing for the upcoming holidays. This was how the handcuffs ended up in my gran's bag. She laughed about it, but never said anything to my parents about receiving them.

After she died, family members cleared out her house but the handcuffs were never found. It's a mystery we never solved. I just hoped she didn't use them on a bloke as they didn't have a key with them. That would have been an embarrassing phone call for help! Although, I didn't ever hear about an elderly man being rescued, naked and in fluffy chains. That's the kind of thing that would make headline news around here.

It's always sad when we are asked to clean houses where somebody has died. Some cases were horrific, such as when the body had been there for 18 days before anyone even noticed. How sad is that in this day in age? Somebody dies and nobody in the entire universe notices. Surely, neighbours would notice, even if it's because of flies up against the window – that's a sure sign something is wrong. I guess back in the day, milk would be left on the doorstep for days on end. I suppose most people don't get milk delivered these days. But I still find it sad how some people's absence can go so unnoticed, even when they have family.

We were asked to clear out a property where a lady had sadly passed away. She was still fairly young, in her mid-50s. She was found on the floor next to her bed, and this was 18 days after she had died. I'm not sure how they managed to work out it was exactly 18 days, but you could tell where the body was found due to the markings on the floor where body fluids had leaked out as decomposition began.

At this point, we were asked just to remove the clinical waste, which basically meant cutting the carpet where the body was found and spraying disinfectant/sanitiser around the other areas. While cutting the carpet by the side of the bed, I found the biggest vibrator I have ever seen in my life! It was a big purple one. God! it was massive! It made me smile – she might have lived alone, however, it looked like she enjoyed herself with a bit of DIY! God knows how she fitted the ruddy thing in her; it must have been like some hydraulic drill between her legs while using it. She must have had a massive vagina. I don't wish to speak ill of the dead but you should never tell a lady she has a large vagina. I did once… and I put my foot right in it!

At the end of the day, I went home and told my girlfriend. I commented that it's sad that in this day and age men can be replaced by nine inches of plastic and two batteries. Without missing a beat, she said, "Don't flatter yourself, sweetie. We can replace you with three inches and two batteries."

Some of the funniest porn films we found were at this house in Cullompton. I have never seen so much porn in my life – and this wasn't the pile that fell and crushed the chap I mentioned in the last chapter. For those of you who know Cullompton, I'm sure there is a joke somewhere about tossers from cully… but I can't put my hands on it for now.

Anyway, there were titillating titles included 'Cumalot'. Somehow, I don't think it was written by Shakespeare. Another one was 'Sex Toy Story', and there was also 'Titty Titty Bang Bang'. There were loads with amazing names. Others were, 'Anus and Andy' and 'Saturday Night Beaver'. The list could go on and on!

Once, for a laugh, we placed a DVD on the desk of this prick we didn't like at this particular office. The DVD was 'Womb Raider' as everyone thought he was a c@nt. We left a note saying, 'Thanks for lending it to me'.

I'm pretty sure when he arrived to work that day, he must have hidden it pretty quickly. I don't think anyone saw it. Nothing was ever said of it, and normally cleaners are the first to be blamed. In this case, it would have been rightly so!

Some of the best finds have been in older people's homes. It is well documented that my nan, who sadly passed away in her mid-80s, was still very much active later in life, as I mentioned earlier. So, I wasn't too shocked to find evidence of a sexual nature when cleaning an elderly lady's house. This woman was around 90 years old, but still full of vim and vigour. One day, when cleaning her bedroom, I came across a sexy pair of lacy panties! To be fair, they were right up my street! I looked at her in a whole new light after that day.

That is, until it turned out her granddaughter had been doing her laundry and had got the underwear muddled up.

Another time, we had to clear out a cupboard in this 80-year-old's house and came across all sorts. There were things you just wouldn't expect a sweet old lady to have, like a Twister board game. Okay, she said that was for when the grandchildren came around and not that she was still bendy enough to contort around the Twister board. However, we also found a horse whip and handcuffs which made us laugh!

They weren't fluffy though – sadly, they weren't my gran's missing set!

CHAPTER 14

Much Ado About Hunting

I have always been an animal lover, and I always say you can tell a lot about a person by how they treat animals. I can never fathom how some people are just brutal to animals. Even as a young kid, I treated animals with respect, and all wildlife enthralled me. I always imagined myself as some kind of Devonian David Attenborough. I can just imagine me narrating, "Here is a baboon, such an intelligent primate. Check the ass out on that!" Okay, maybe not.

My parents recently reminded me about the time I took home a wounded crow to nurse. We gave him the name Crowy – I said I loved animals, not that I was good at naming them! My way with words came much later. Anyway, one of poor Crowy's wings was damaged, so we kept him in a cage in the garden and fed and watered him until he was better. We then removed the cage so Crowy was free to fly away, however, he stayed for quite a few weeks after. That is, until one day he flew off, ready to make a new home for himself. Our work was done!

Well, that's what my parents told me. I became a little suspicious when I found some black feathers just outside the back garden gate where the neighbour's cat used to patrol...

Having said that, I am a complete cat lover too, and have my own lovely pussies at home. But they are just so cruel, aren't they? Mine bring in mice and birds – and even rabbits sometimes. Then, they play with them until death seems like a pleasant break. Whenever I mention my cat's delight in bringing in slaughtered birds, people always reply to me that cats bring in their prey as gifts for their masters. I mean, I am not sure I believe this – what kind of gift is that? They normally eat the ruddy best bits and leave me nothing but a sodding kidney and a few inches of intestine to pick up off the floor!

Being a cleaner means driving a lot of miles each year, and in the countryside that inevitably means coming across wildlife in all its forms. I have seen deer in the morning mist, silhouetted against the rising sun. I have seen owls swooping for mice, and a million birds chirruping in the new day.

But one of the worst things about being a cleaner was all the dead animals you come across. Working unsociable hours as I did, I realise I was lucky to see soooo much wildlife around; the dawn hours are filled with a bountiful natural world that actively avoids us in the daylight. But, sadly, I would often be the first to find roadkill as well. It would break my heart to find dead foxes and badgers left in the middle of the road, as well as family pets that had been run over. It used to devastate me to find a cat knocked down by a car and left in the middle of the road for dead. I always stopped, picked them up, and put them to one side out of harm's way. They might have been dead already, but they didn't need the indignity of being repeatedly driven over like a forgotten rag.

Over the years, I have hit a few animals myself, despite my best efforts. Tragically, this includes once hitting a cat. Horrifically, it ran off after I clipped him. I stopped but I couldn't see him anywhere. I still think about it today! I really hope I didn't kill it; I like to imagine it living a happy life, blissful in the knowledge it lost only one of its lives that day.

Sometimes, you just can't avoid hitting an animal or a bird when driving around. Birds especially seem prone to catastrophe; they bomb at cars like kamikaze pilots. They just seem to fly into your windscreen as if it isn't there! I know this is likely because they can't see glass, or because the road actually means nothing to them. But it has left me wondering whether animals or birds ever feel like they have had enough and decide to commit suicide? Is that a thing in nature outside of mankind?

On a side-but-related note, occasionally, when I see a bird of prey eating a dead rabbit, I wonder, are any of them vegetarian? What if they don't like rabbit? Or can birds or animals have food allergies too? Can you imagine a squirrel having a nut allergy!!

Did you know, there is a restaurant in Australia that serves roadkill. Apparently, their menu is an all-you-can-eat buffet charged at a flat rate, and they serve whatever roadkill was found that day! I suppose it's efficient, local, and resourceful. But I'm not sure I'd fancy eating it. I even once came across a cookbook called 'Roadkill Recipes', but I'm not sure how practical it is as a concept. Here in the UK, one of our strangest laws is that if you knock an animal over, like a deer, you're not allowed to pick it up, take it home and eat it. You might say that is fine and to be expected – civilised even. However, the driver in the car behind you is most welcome to pick up the dead beast and have it for dinner.

Though I guess not everyone worries about some of these pedantic rules. Like, one of my mates once had a plentiful feast after he killed a pheasant in his car – he didn't think twice; he likes pheasant and didn't want the bird to go to waste. I suppose the meat is about as fresh as it can be! However, I am still not convinced – I would never take anything home to eat that I had run over. I asked him what it tasted like he replied, "It's stuck in the freezer." He let me have a look; honestly, his freezer looked like a time machine. He had all sorts in there, chicken, fish, a dodo!

Anyway, I have digressed.

Having a job that means moving between sites means seeing wildlife at its best and worst – and seeing mankind at both extremes as well. We were at one point many years ago responsible for cleaning the toilets across Exmoor, and frequently I would come across a fox hunt. Maybe I am naïve, but I thought hunting with dogs was illegal – clearly there's far more to this than I know about. Now, I don't want to get into a political debate, or explore the rights and wrongs of foxhunting... but I can't resist a little seething! In my opinion, chasing foxes or stags with dogs is just cruel and unnecessary. I know, I know. I have heard all the arguments in defence of the sport – I get that population numbers must be kept under control and that foxes cause soooo much devastation of farmers' land and livestock. However, surely, as a civilised society, there is a more humane way to manage populations of animals we consider pests. They're only pests to us! Can we not do this effectively by shooting them? Surely there is an answer that is more tolerable than chasing them until they are exhausted, broken, terrified – and after all that, killing them. We are not cats playing with our prey. Besides which, if it's a sport, then it is not a functional job. It's for fun and for competition, and I don't believe the words fun and competition should be akin to torture and death.

On top of this, the most powerful argument to support enforcing a complete ban on hunting is that all the hunters I have come across are pompous pricks. Of course they like killing things! I even came across a hunt woman once who had that much makeup on I thought she was off to kill Batman. She only stood out, as normally they are covered in mud splatters and not looking glamorous at all.

Now I am ranting I can't stop! I saw one hunt video online once where some hunters had cornered a fox cub and it was surrounded by hounds. You could hear this fox cub cry out in fear. The hunt master then gave the command and the hounds ripped it to pieces. They were saluting the obedience of the hounds!

There are no words sometimes for how cruel humans can be. How is that accepted in today's society?

Like, I also heard a story about a deer that was chased onto a bridge in a village in Dartmoor. There were hounds on either side of the bridge so it had nowhere to go. The deer was desperate to escape, so it jumped off this high bridge and broke both its two front legs. So it had to be shot anyway, but after suffering so much stress and trauma. Again, there are no words to convey the horror I feel at this!

We used to undertake a clean at a pub in the country that was a traditional fox hunt gathering point. There were several portraits and paintings of past hunts, plus several obligatory stag heads or antlers mounted on walls around the pub.

One day, I took a new cleaner with me. She was only a young woman, fresh out of college, and eager to impress. Up to this point, she had worked really hard. When she saw the pictures and a trophy, she had been horrified but kept her feelings to herself. Unknown to me, not only had she left a note to the landlady about how she thought she was an evil, murdering cow, she also walked around the pub and stuck Post-it notes on various pictures saying 'Murderers'.

We always undertook the cleaning early in the morning and never saw anyone, so we left as if it was a normal day. Later, I got a phone call from the landlady explaining to me what she had found. I had to sack the cleaner, despite empathising with her feelings on the matter. The stupid thing is, she didn't say a word to me about it on the journey home. I told her if she was that offended, she should have told me that she didn't want to clean for that place again. I would have understood! But to vandalise property and abuse a client behind my back, even in symbolic ways, was unacceptable. Sadly, it was the first and last time she worked for me.

But she was young, bright, and passionate, and a bit of a rebel. I am sure she will have forged a fiery path that reflects her values.

I guess some people's views are stronger than others'; some people take action and some protest quietly. Some are not phased at all and drift through life peacefully tolerating the world's hypocrisies and inequalities as nothing more than potholes in an unkempt road. But one thing is for certain: I always judge people on how they treat animals. I can turn the other cheek at times, but I have noted my shock and resulting lack of respect. I am an animal lover well mostly … not a huge horse fan if I'm honest, don't trust any animal that can walk and shit at the same time even chickens pull over but if someone tells me they can't stand dogs or cats I genuinely think there's something wrong with them. I mean, pets can give so much love and joy. What is not to like? I think perhaps I need to add an animal-based conundrum to my interview questions; it would be a good way to weed out the wankers! As the saying goes, I'm suspicious of people who don't like cats, but I totally trust my cat when it doesn't like a person!

CHAPTER 15

Failure Is Not a Watson

When your job is to provide a service, it's very easy to feel taken for granted. I guess it is similar in any job where going the extra mile can be misinterpreted for expected effort. But when you are cleaning, the little advantages clients take can be frustrating at best – and demeaning at worst. I mean, there are jobs we all don't want to do; we make a living out of this work! And there are jobs we all don't want to do because they weren't part of the agreement!

Back when I first started out, I wanted to make a good impression. I was doing all the hours under the sun and working like a gherkin. I would bend over backwards to go the extra mile and help people out. However, I soon learned the more you do for people the more they expect. For example, one week at a client's house we found a load of washing up on the side. I just assumed they had run out of time, so I kindly washed it all. It wasn't part of the work the owner had requested, but it seemed like a good gesture. However, from that day forth, they would leave a whole week's worth of washing up for us to do. Annoyingly, our kind act had earned us an additional task.

I was beginning to see how some people end up on the Grinch side.

Then, there was the time we agreed to clean a pub on

Christmas Day morning. This was out of our ordinary agreement, but the owner was anxious to have it ready for what was going to be a busy day for her, and she had always been a good client – I wanted to please her! When I said I would come in the morning, the owner said, "I will sort you out for doing this for us!" I didn't really expect much, but I was encouraged by her attitude of Christmas love and cheer. I turned up, cleaned the pub that had been destroyed by the over-indulgences of the locals, and she gave me a single home-made mince pie for my Christmas tip! There wasn't even a dollop of cream to accompany it!

If I am honest, I didn't even eat it. I slung it across the field when I was loading up the van to leave. She didn't give us a card, a hug, or any extra money for giving up my morning with my family. But I suppose I should be a little grateful; she did have occasional moments of generosity. When her husband died, she offered me a pair of his shoes! I mean, why wouldn't I want some dead husband's shoes?

You might have spotted a pattern emerging, but it took me a while to rein in my natural instinct to help people out if it was in my capacity to do so. I mean, I don't want to be uncharitable! Another time, I was at a different property and noticed the washing machine had finished its cycle. It was a lovely day, and I had a few minutes leftover in the time the clients had booked, so as a gesture of goodwill, I hung it out to dry. As with the dishes at the other house, from that week forward, hanging out the laundry became part of our normal duties. However, the clients never agreed to add on any extra time to do this. Cheekily, they would always set the cycle to finish fifteen minutes after our agreed finish time so we had to wait around before we could hang it out to dry.

This same client then began to take the piss; they would always go out just as we arrived. Suddenly, all these duties were expected without even asking, "Oh, it would be so helpful if you could…" Do you know that saying, 'Some people are like clouds; when they disappear, it's a beautiful day'? I guess there were upsides to their absence! But it wasn't that my heart grew fonder. Anyway, we soon learnt to change the cycle setting on the washing machine. So instead of waiting for a two-and-a-half-hour wash to finish, we changed it to a thirty-minute speed wash. They were never the wiser. It was a valuable lesson to learn in the early days: that I needed to stop doing things for people when it became expected and not appreciated.

I have another funny washing machine story, only this one was entirely my error. This one client asked us to strip the bedding in the kids' room of the house and stick it in the washing machine. Unbeknown to me, as I grabbed the bedding and shoved it in the machine, I had also grabbed a soiled nappy. In fact, I didn't notice the nappy when I set the machine's programme, or indeed at any point before leaving the house. I never once noticed the washing machine window swirling a mass of sheets in a brown, soupy mess! I literally didn't see it at any point – or smell it! I hadn't just thought filled disposable nappies were washable. I just grabbed the washing pile outside each room, and it must have got smuggled away in the sheets!

The owner wasn't best pleased. She had no idea what was in the machine! At first she thought it was chicken *tikka masala*! What a present to come home to! If I'm honest the owner was a little deluded , she would always comment how her kid would look good in a pampers TV commercial, I thought yeah as a turd , it was an ugly looking baby!

Aside from taking advantage, some clients ask the strangest of favours. Once, when cleaning this dear old lady's house, she asked me the most bizarre question ever. She turned to me and said, "I hope you don't mind me asking, however, you see the gollywog on the sofa, would you look after it for me?"

She didn't think she had long to live and was concerned to find the doll, that was evidently sentimentally precious to her, a new home. Her family had all stated that when she passed on, they were going to throw it out with the rubbish.

Now, before anyone starts having a go, I understand how these dolls are an example of past racism, and the name, 'gollywog' is also racist. However, I was concerned by this woman's emotions. She cared for the doll, she had looked after it for a long time, and she saw it as a part of her. I felt sad her family wouldn't look after it, even if it was just to store it in a keepsake box along with other treasured memories.

So, beguiled by the woman's heartfelt question, I replied I would look after him and took him home that same day. As pleased as she was, it felt strange. I was giving this doll a new history rather than continuing hers, and had no idea what to do with it. Unable to use the word 'gollywog', I gave him a new name, Mr Ding-Dong. I'm ashamed to admit, I used to use this name in a chat-up line on ladies back in the day. I'd say things like, "Do you want to come back to my place and meet Mr Ding-Dong?" Well one night, you'll be surprised, a lady did accept the offer, but she was a little disappointed when Mr Ding-Dong turned out to be this adopted toy. She was quite offended that I had such a thing and was surprised I owned it. Once more, my kindness was turning out to be a curse.

As time went by, I still wasn't sure what to do with this golly and became increasingly uncomfortable at owning it myself – people kept reacting badly to Mr Ding-Dong. Yet, I had promised the old lady I would look after it. Shoving it in a box and sticking in the loft felt like I was betraying her wishes. Then, randomly, I got chatting to the owner of a caravan park and explained my dilemma about the toy. He was an older chap and thought the world had gone crazy with all this PC stuff; you know the type – they rant about the snowflake generation who they think are offended too easily by every little thing in society, while simultaneously taking pride in offending people. He said he would happily take the golly and let it sit in his office window and watch the world go by.

We no longer clean this caravan park, and the owner has since sold it. When I caught up with him, he told me the golly sat in his office for years and when he sold the park, he left it there for the new owners to enjoy. To this day, I don't know what happened to Mr Ding-Dong with his new owners, but I hope he continued his adventure and felt loved. And I hope wherever the lady is, looking down on us, she is happy I did my bit in respecting her wishes.

Sometimes, things that go around do come around, but not in the way you are expecting. For example, here's a Devonian tale of karma for you. For a couple of years, we used to clean a house for an arrogant farmer-type bloke whose surname was Watson – like Sherlock Holmes's sidekick, but without the humility or intelligence. He used to talk to us like dirt, and multiple times we considered stopping doing business with him. Really, we only continued to clean as we also cleaned the property next door where the lady was lovely. It was more cost effective to do both as it was out in the middle of nowhere, and I convinced myself the lady's loveliness made up for the arrogance of Crap-Watson.

On a side note, what is it with these farmer-type people? They all dress the same, as though they go to the same shop. (My editor tells me they actually all do go to the same shop – and their clothing range is quite small and unvaried, but with a good array of collar sizes. Who knew?)

Crap-Watson ran a business which was organising shoots of wild animals for posh folk who love guns in a posh way. (The posh way is: we've had this rifle in the family for seven generations and I have been going beating with the spaniels, Tarka and Otter, since I was three.) Well, I assume they were organised shoots and not just a bunch of hillbillies going off shooting things at random. This was something I didn't agree with at all, and always made me feel a little sickened. Scattered around his house were trophy photos of things he had killed. He lived in a house of death!

After a couple of years cleaning for him, his business ran into financial difficulty. While we were cleaning one day, an angry bloke turned up at the door. Crap-Watson cracked out his best disappearing trick and made a quick exit when he saw who was at the door. This bloke and his friends had paid £15k for a shooting trip, but it had been cancelled and they wanted their money back. Quite rightly, so I thought. The fast-moving Crap-Watson clearly had other ideas.

I explained to the angry bloke that I was just the cleaner and would pass the message on. At this point, alarm bells had started to ring as I realised I hadn't been paid for nearly three months. But I rationalised that it was fine as late payments were common with him.

When we finished cleaning that day, the owner was still

not back, so I left a note insisting we be paid soon. He phoned me shortly after and assured me he was about to pay in full. He then booked us for the next three weeks as he was about to put the house on the market and wanted it looking good for viewings. I agreed.

Three weeks passed, and we turned up on the final week to clean, but everything was wrong. The house was abandoned and all furniture had gone. We had a look around, trying to work out what was going on, and I called Crap-Watson. He didn't answer. A bloke turned up and asked what we were doing. I told him we had turned up to clean. He said that he was the new owner and that the house had been repossessed.

The repossession was complete – why on Earth had we been cleaning the house in the previous weeks?

I was annoyed because Crap-Watson promised me I would get all my money, and there was no chance I was getting any of it. It turns out he had lost everything: his business, his car, and his house. We later found out his wife also left him – and she had gone off with another lady! Which, to be fair, made me smile. I kind of get it when someone leaves you for another partner – it sucks but you can try to understand or win them back. When your partner leaves and confesses to being a different sexuality, that's got to hurt, as there is nothing you can do about it. Talking of karma, there was a story of a bloke who left his wife for her sister, not knowing moments earlier his wife had won the lottery. The funny thing is he tried to win his wife back and lost them both and ended up alone!

Anyway, I digress (again). I never heard from this guy again, despite trying to track him down. My detective skills are not as good as Sherlock Holmes's. He always managed to find a missing Watson no matter who had him hostage; no doubt he'd easily find the crap one!

When it comes to why I continued cleaning for Sherlock's reject even after I found out about his debt issues, as always, I was my own worst enemy; I wanted to see the best in him and not kick him when he was down – these things happen to the best of us. But they also happen to the worst of us, to those who deserve some comeuppance.

That said, I would rather continue as I am, giving generously and trying to brighten people's days, than be like Crap-Watson, or any of my clients who happily take advantage of others. After all, the majority of people are wonderful; let's get back to thinking about them!

CHAPTER 16

Teamwork Makes the Dream Work

Over the years, I have become an effective and trustworthy manager. It is important to have clear expectations, and to encourage the best from all the people who work for you. It is also crucial to bring staff together and develop strong relationships. I mean, good teamwork is essential when cleaning big properties; what is it they say? Teamwork makes the dream work. Plus, it allows you to blame someone else when things go wrong...

We used to undertake the cleaning of a large and plush wedding venue. It cost £10k to book the mansion for a weekend and would sleep about 50 guests. This was just the start of the costs; back in the day, this was a huge amount of money. Our job was to clean and make the beds. It was an old-fashioned, posh place, with creaky corridors and uneven stairs. We all thought it was haunted!

One of the biggest tasks was doing all the bedding. By that, I mean washing all the sheets and covers, and then making up new beds; the entire caboodle! And there were beds everywhere!

They only had two old-fashioned washing machines at the property, and I was forever over-filling them to get the linen washed in time – after all, we still had to hang it out to dry and get bedding back on the beds! It was a rush job with inadequate resources. As you might have guessed, it was tempting to find ways to cut corners. Once, I filled the machines up so much, the ruddy things toppled over! The owner wasn't too happy; it was as though I replaced his mattress with trampoline as he hit the roof. And he spoke to me in a serious tone suggestive of a loss of trust in us. When he told me about it, I just said, in the gravest tone I could muster, "Leave this with me, I will speak to my staff about this." I knew full well it was me that caused the catastrophe!

Sadly, the machines survived to spin another day!

Despite the shock of that eventful day, loading up the washing machine wasn't really the biggest problem. Time was gobbled in other parts of the laundry-work – taking it all out and drying it, folding the ruddy stuff and putting it all away. We had to sort it all into king-size, doubles and singles… and everything looked the same! Because of the rush, we never had time to put on a proper wash, so we just used the speedy twenty-minute setting.

Despite them charging so much for hiring out the venue, the owners were complete penny-pinchers when it came to maintaining the property. This doesn't just relate to the cleaning and inadequate equipment; if and when anything ever went wrong, they would always find a way to bodge the repair. They had duct-tape repairs in the most surprising of places! As a result, I no longer feel guilty for tipping over the ancient washing machines.

It was an interesting place to work, to be fair. I swear the place was haunted! Frequently, we would hear strange noises coming from various parts of the mansion while we cleaned. I'm not sure I actually believe in ghosts – even so, I would crap my pants if I ever had to stay there alone! Just like in any good haunted hotel, the lighting was poor, and there were dark corners lurking all over the place. When cleaning in the early evening, the house became gloomy, and in certain quarters of the property, shadows crept around like ghostly hands.

Knowing my thoughts on the matter, my cleaners decided to play a prank on me. Creeping around, they moved a statue into the middle of the hallway. But the prank didn't unfold quite as planned. It was dark, and I walked straight into it! I nearly shat myself in the process though.

But I digress; let's get back to the wrongs I have committed over the years. It is true to say I have always looked at ways of cutting costs, especially overheads – as wise people always say, look after the pennies and the pounds look after themselves! One of my top money-saving strategies was to water down products. Now, if you look up the definition of 'to water down', it means to make things weaker, and I don't always think it's a bad thing to make a strong product go a little further, but there are limits I think I crossed! If a bleach was half empty, I would refill it with water. And if I had one of those crappy eco-products, which don't begin to do the job they're meant to do, I would put a cheaper alternative in it when it was empty. After all, this is still a good thing – I didn't want my plastic going to land fill!

Funnily enough, nobody ever noticed. Once, a lady questioned what I was using to clean her kitchen work top with as she loved the shine. I didn't have the heart to tell her it was 99% water – I just said it was our own secret recipe!

CHAPTER 17

Bug Enforcement Officer

I know this book might make me seem a bit contrary, however, relatively few things truly bug me. I love a good moan, but generally I let things go. I mean, I can probably count the things that get my goat on one hand. Things that I find properly upsetting are things like when you're having sex and your missus coughs – well, flip me! That hurts your willy soooo much! It totally dampens the mood. Oh, and it always hurts when you get a parking ticket.

When you run a business and you are on the road, there is nothing worse than traffic wardens lurking around like uniformed Dementors. Granted, some are better than others, but all too often it feels like they take joy in finding you parkingly-incapacitated. Over the years, I have acquired a few parking tickets where I have parked outside someone's house, and it is permit only. Sometimes we're only inside to get a visitor's permit, or the owner isn't there to give us one. But if we are undertaking work that needs big equipment, something like carpet cleaning, it's imperative to stop directly outside the property at least for long enough to drop off everything. But after dropping off the equipment, we need to drive off in the hope of finding an appropriate car-parking space, and often this isn't possible.

Granted I have put a few notes on the windscreen over

the years saying things like: 'Working at Number 47. Call me.' Or, 'Undertaking work for council – call me'. I always hope that the parking attendants saw me as one of them. I tried to portray myself as just another council worker, struggling against the odds. This mostly didn't work, but occasionally I twitched someone's empathy enough to avoid a fine.

Unfortunately, traffic wardens all have targets to meet, so it's in their best interests to write out as many fines as they can. As such, I get they are only doing their jobs, however, some do come across as complete and utter shit-weasels.

But then, I must admit, I very rarely buy a car-parking ticket wherever I go. Ever. This is especially true in tourist areas like at beaches where car parks overcharge you. I always find a sneaky free place to park, normally like a church or chapel car park: the Lord works in mysterious ways! Mind you, it does help if you put a bible on the dashboard. I always keep one in my glove box; my dad will be so proud.

Admittedly, some people park like dicks and deserve a parking ticket – I wish there was a ticket just for poor-parking wallies in their SUVs who think it's okay to take up two spaces. Ordinary people have the best forms of revenge; I remember once seeing a sign someone had put on a car which was parked outside their house, blocking their driveway. It said, 'Thanks for parking like an asshole. Please don't reproduce'. Attached to the note was a condom – now, I thought that was genius.

But I have another sneaky confession to add among these parking anecdotes. Thankfully where I live, I used to undertake work for the local council who are the ones issuing these parking fines. So whenever I got a ticket, I just passed on the cost the next time I did any council work – I just hid the fine on the next invoice under a different cost. I appreciate not everyone has this luxury, so I can understand how ruddy irritating these fines are! A friend of mine once got one even though she had a permit in her car window. The council justified the fine by saying the entire permit reference number wasn't visible... the windscreen had been covered in ice! But with my Get-Out-Of-Jail-Free card of invoicing the council back for the fine, I suppose I shouldn't really be properly bothered by parking tickets. I mean, Christ! I always laugh when parking attendants say, "It's too late now – I've put it on the system. So if you want to challenge it, the address is on the ticket." I used to think, *If I want to listen to an asshole, I'll fart.*

Talking of bums, doing your business can lead to some shameful actions sometimes. Some customers don't like you using their toilets for a number two while you're working, and rightly so. Mostly, we wouldn't want to. And to be fair, I don't think I've ever done a poo at a client's house, however, I have needed a wee on plenty of occasions. And some clients get proper funny and don't want you using their loo; it creates a little conundrum. If you can't use the loo, where do you go...? Normally, I would take a piss around the back of a customer's house or in a flower pot. I'm sure that's what they'd prefer...

Irritatingly, I would often need to go for a wee when I had just finished mopping the bathroom floor and didn't want to leave footprints on the shiny floor. This also means you have to get creative! To avoid walking on them, I've found the oddest of places to relieve myself, including refilling an old cleaning fluid bottle. I promise that is NOT part of my secret recipe!

I remember once cleaning the communal area of a block of old people's flats and I was dying for a wee, there were no toilets and it felt like I needed a service station pee. There was no holding it; I was already doing the jig, and my knees were pinching together as if they could turn my stopcock to off. So, in desperation, I went into the bin store where they kept the recycling and relieved myself into an empty milk bottle. Anyway, as I was mid-flow, like a hose, and realising I might need about three bottles, an elderly lady walked in and caught me! She crept up on me like a ninja! Luckily, I had my back to her, however she must have noticed as it sounded like a running tap. Unfazed, she said, "I've just come in to sort the recycling ready for bin day."

I quickly put the bottle of piss back into the right box. I felt a bit of pee trickle down my leg if I'm honest; the problem is it's hard to stop mid-flow: ruddy hard! (And I don't mean me!)

The old lady started sorting the boxes and said, "I keep telling the residents to empty the pots and cartons. Look at this!" She held up my bottle of piss.

I didn't know if she was mocking me or criticising her neighbours! I said, "Some people, eh? We all need to do our bit to save the planet." She then emptied it onto the grass verge.

Another confession has to be my horn-dog years which did indeed get in the way of my best professionalism at times. I have been known over the years to be a bit of a Charlie Charmhead when it comes to beguiling and delighting the customers. I'm sure that's obvious with my wit and charm. However, the truth is my mouth normally gets me in trouble. I remember once chatting up a girl in a sexual health clinic of all places and I asked her, "If she came here often." It didn't go down too well.

Even when I was younger, and going to the pubs of a weekend, I was quite often the one who was sent to talk to the ladies from our group of lads – and typically with mixed results. I guess I was pretty confident, but some might say overconfident. It frequently backfired with spectacular results!

I remember one time I couldn't resist joking instead of flirting; we were in a local pub which has now sadly been replaced by townhouses, but back in the day it was the place to go. I spotted a lady as she walked past our group and went to the toilets. She was stunning. My mates egged me on and said go and chat to her when she comes out the loo. So, I waited near the toilet entrance thinking of a great opening line to use; I could have written a bloody novel she was gone so long! When she finally reappeared, I was so shocked I lost my train of thought and said, "Hi, how are you, did you have a good poo?"

Funnily enough, she wasn't amused. She didn't even stop to chat, and I can't think why. My mates found it mildly amusing though.

Let's get back to how this relates to my cleaning company – and yes, there were many times it was my mouth that needed cleaning out! This one time, we were cleaning a big manor house in a village on the outskirts of Tiverton. A couple had recently bought it and moved in. The lady who owned the house was pretty fit and totally rocking her 50s. Her husband, well, let's just say he was closer to 90, but he still he had a massive wallet. It reminded me of the question Mrs Merton once asked Debbie McGee. "What first attracted you to your millionaire husband, Paul Daniels?" I don't want to be judgemental, but I can't help it. Although, I am also reminded of something Nelle Porter said on Ally McBeal –

something like, why is it shallower to be attracted to a man for his wealth and power than it is just for his looks? Still, I couldn't help thinking, how can this 90-year-old, overweight walrus manage to pull her?

I couldn't resist asking. She told me they met while online dating. I said to her I had done a bit of that but never came across anyone as Earl Grey as her. She said, "What do you mean Earl Grey?" I replied, "Hot tea." She smiled at me and said we were clearly on different sites. She did say though, to my joy, that she would have gone on a date with me if she had met me online. That gave my ego a boost! I then used my classic line on her, "I'm like a twelve-stone stick of dynamite, ready to explode... with a three-inch fuse!" This made her laugh out loud and she said I was funny. I must admit when she asked me if I could sort her curtains out downstairs I nearly came in my pants. Still, it was clear her husband had a bigger wallet than me, and she was already smitten. I was just flirting for the fun of it.

But, unknown to me, he was in the room next to us where we were chatting and probably heard every word I was telling her. He stepped into the kitchen at one point, as if to bring our flirtiness to a close. I took the hint and got back to work. I thought to myself, after all my wooing, he could take her upstairs – she was primed for some loving! If for no other reason than to escape me.

But the story gets worse! While cleaning the house, the removal men were also on site moving a few bits into the house. I went out into the car park to collect some stuff from the van and up pulled a sports car driven by a young blonde lady. It turned out to be the owner's daughter. She was stunning! I am ashamed to admit, all of us stopped what we were doing as she pulled up and got out of the car. I guess it was kind of funny as all our heads moved like meerkats, our mouths wide open as she walked towards the house. The funny thing is I thought I recognised her. Later that day I bumped into her in the house and I said to her discreetly, "I'm sure I've seen you before. Was it in a clinic in Exeter?" As soon as I said it, I realised it wasn't her that I met.

She looked at me in disgust and replied, "I don't think so," and walked off.

There have been a few times when we arrived to do work at clients' houses, and they had forgotten we were coming and failed to leave a key out. This always used to bug me (perhaps I am easily bugged after all) as in many of the cases we would have to drive twenty minutes or more to get there, losing valuable time out of the day; and Time Is Money. If you're being reasonable, you can't invoice the client for work you haven't done; clients tend to get annoyed by this and don't come back. However, after this happened enough times, it was becoming a pattern; I started bringing in cancellation and missed appointments charges.

But, back in the early days, before I evolved into this refined gentleman you see before you now, things began to get crazy. Whenever I got to a client's place, and they were not home or had forgotten to leave a key, I would find a way of getting in their house. One example happened at a farmhouse we had been booked to clean. I found a ladder in the barn and noticed an upstairs window in the bathroom open. So, deciding to fix matters with my own hands, I climbed through. It wasn't as easy as I thought it would be and it hurt my knackers. The window was small, and I literally had to dive headfirst through the opening. I caught my bollocks on the window catch and ended up face first in the bathtub.

On another occasion, I found a novel and less painful entry point at a large country house. The owners were not home, and I had phoned them, but they hadn't answered. In the end I decided to break in and clean up like some kind of manly, Devonian fairy. But there were no windows open. In the end I crawled through the dog flap, but I set the bloody house alarm off. Funnily enough, the owners soon turned up. They didn't seem that impressed, so I said, "You're lucky it was me and not a thief! Bit of a security breach you have there!" I'm not sure that added to my endearment.

Moving on… So, as I'm winding down the cleaning company, I decided I no longer needed two vans. Therefore, I made the decision to part exchange them for a brand new one. Over the years I've gone through twelve vans so it's quite nice to keep things simple now; having one van means only one insurance premium each year to sort out, and one lot of tax, one service etc. It's so much less admin! However, I swear my new van is jinxed!

Over the years, I have very rarely had accidents – although as I say that, I am reaching out to touch some wood. I have not had any speeding tickets, and relatively few parking tickets against those I probably deserved. However, since getting this new van, I have averaged a ticket a month! Plus, I have suffered one crash and dented the side of the van in a hedge, and two speeding tickets. For one of the speeding tickets, I had to attend a Zoom speed awareness course. By God! What a waste of time that was! Yes, I know, I know! I accept I shouldn't have been speeding, however, we all do it! Well, I say everyone; I mean everyone except my dad, that is.

Blimey! He leaves three days early if he needs to be in another town in Devon – bear in mind he lives in Devon, and believe me, it's not a big county! I guess I should learn from him and slow down a bit. What is it some people say? 'If you're always racing to the next moment, what happens to the one you're in?'

But then, when you run a business, you are always busy – if you're not, you're doing something wrong. And it's so easy to get caught up in rushing and then find yourself speeding a little. Plus, if they really wanted us to go slower, technology could be developed to limit speed. It's totally possible. We have a strange world where cars are promoted on their speed and acceleration, while simultaneously shaming you into conforming to overly cautious speed restrictions that change constantly and catch you out. The powers that be want you to be able to slip up so you can be put back in your place. Anyway, that's my rant, mostly inspired by the awfulness of the speed awareness course.

That course destroyed four hours of my life I can never get back – the agonising passing of the hours was not helped by some stupid lady who kept arguing the points. If she had kept her mouth shut and accepted she had been speeding, I'm sure the course would have finished a lot quicker. But oh no! Gob-On-A-Laptop just would not let it drop! I was tempted to have a tug during the Zoom session to help pass the time; I mean, nobody sees what you are wearing down below, and I was that bored. I'm not sure I learnt anything except maybe next time I'll take the points instead of enduring another one of these courses. It's like I said to the course instructor, I know the speed limits – I just didn't see the camera!

I know there will be some of you who will argue it's not

that van that's the issue, it's the driver. I can assure you, no matter the strength of your argument, I still think it's jinxed. For the first time ever in my life I have parking sensors. The first AND the last time I relied on them, I hit a lamp post! The van is cursed! I should have kept the old one, that's for sure; I never had any issues with it at all.

What is it my dad says? 'Every old sock needs and old shoe.' Yeah, I know; I don't get it either!

But not all mistakes, mishaps and misdemeanours are mine. One day, I had a call from a tenant of mine claiming her house was disgusting and she shouldn't be living in the property as it was. She claimed there was mould all over the house and that she was pregnant and it was not doing her health any good.

I decided to go around with another cleaner to treat the mould and make it clean for her. I knew the house had a history of damp issues, however, not to the level she was describing. But I obviously felt responsible. So we packed up our kit and went over.

When we arrived, it was safe to say the house was covered in mould and condensation everywhere – it was a nightmare! It felt like we were in a stinky tropical house at a zoo! She started gobbing off, telling me her tenant's rights, and that I should be ashamed of myself renting out a place in this condition. I walked into the lounge, baffled by just how bad it was, only to identify the cause of the problem. She had only gone and put a HOT TUB in her lounge! She had installed one of those inflatable Layzee Spas!

What a knob! And she wondered why she had mould! I wish to God I had words here to describe the intensity of my eye roll!

Thankfully, in some ways, it was the best thing she could have done as it gave me reason to get rid of her. She had been a problem tenant of mine since the beginning. She was a bit rough. Once on her Birthday her friend bought her a spa voucher, I thought to myself spa voucher, what for Pet's At Home!! She had been passed on to me by the council who had a track record of palming off their problem tenants onto private landlords. Soon, she and her Layzee Spa were a problem for someone else!

All I did was call the council and explain she was pregnant, and they re-housed her!

There was another time it was the client who was embarrassed and not me. I suppose it's an occupational hazard walking into clients' houses when you think no one is home or they are not expecting you. This one time I walked into a house, called out, "Hello!" and got no reply. I then proceeded to walk upstairs then heard groaning noises coming from the bathroom. The owner was doing a Groaner Poo! You know the ones – a poo so huge it couldn't exit without vocal assistance! It's safe to say they were pretty embarrassed when they knew we heard it all!

CHAPTER 18

Be Careful What You Suck

One of the most universal tasks when cleaning is plain old vacuuming. It's a job that has to be done at every site without fail. In fact, hoovering is a task we all have to accept as part of our lives – though I can't imagine the Queen has ever pushed a hoover around. The bloke who invented the hoover was actually called William Henry Hoover, and the verb 'to hoover' comes from his name.

We have gone through around 68 hoovers since I set up the company. Do you know a woman in Kent bought herself an Electrolux vacuum in the 1930s, and she was still using the machine when it finally broke in 2008! They gave her a free upgrade – probably to be able to use her story for marketing purposes. Though I can't imagine 2008 models lasting as long as their sturdy ancestral counterparts! Or if she hoovered as much as we did!

The vacuum cleaner is just a genius device. We even use them on hard surfaces as they're just so much better. Hoovers have one major advantage over an old-school dustpan and brush: you never get a small line of dirt when using a hoover; you know that annoying last little bit that won't sweep up! I've never found a dustpan that can triumph over this last little bit.

I can safely say I've never used a hoover for anything other than what it's designed for: i.e. sucking up dirt. But this is not the case for everyone! I saw this one video that went viral showing a drunk man putting the end of his hoover around his knob and trying to suck himself off. I mean, it makes my willy wince to think about it. Worse still, I heard about this bloke who went to A&E with a hoover pole sticking out his arse. I'm not sure why you would ever do this... Surely the edges are too sharp? There are better ways to do a colonic – I can tell you! And you should have seen the look on Henry Hoover's face! He'd only just come out the closet! (For more information, please read my other book, *Baby Pigeon*). The whole thing sounded excruciating to say the least!

Hoovering is just such a standard part of our lives. Did you know a hoover joke actually won 'Joke of the Year' many years ago? It went, 'Well, I decided to sell my hoover: it was just collecting dust.' I personally enjoy the old Frank Carson joke from back in the day: 'A man goes to the hospital with a hoover stuck up his backside. Later, his wife phones up the hospital to enquire how he's doing. "He's picking up nicely." Came the reply!'

As a company, we always use Henry Hoovers. Dysons always seemed overrated to me – they are expensive and heavy, despite their suction power. Contrastingly, Henrys are quite light and easier to get around; they are cheaper to buy, and easy to maintain and clean.

Being easy to clean and maintain is a good thing, as those poor Henrys were given a hard time! My cleaners were forever sucking up things they shouldn't. One day, one of my cleaners was sucking up what he thought was leaves... but it turned out to be dog poo! How the hell he got that wrong, I do not know! The situation was not helped by the fact he had used the actual hoover-head, and not just the pipe. As he continued the job, he rubbed the poo around all over the carpets, giving the house a brand-new fragrance. Now, that's not the kind of perfume you want to last for days, is it?

Sucking up things we shouldn't is just par for the course in cleaning. When hoovering residential houses, we forever sucked up Lego bricks and coins, but some things were more disastrous than others. Once, the owner of a house lost her wedding ring. We spent hours emptying out the hoover bags to see if we could find it; we never did! The funny thing is they divorced shortly afterwards; maybe it was a sign.

But the world is a crazy place, and some people have crazy habits. There was another office we used to clean where the staff would always stay on late, so we had to clean around them. This was a pain, but something we got used to. For some reason, the boss of the firm would always turn the hoover off as he walked past us. The first few times, we thought he was just being a dick and having a laugh. However, it later transpired he has a phobia of walking past hoovers when they're on. Some phobias are bizarre to me. What did he think? Was it the noise that unsettled him? Or did he think he was about to be sucked up by the hoover?

Perhaps he was actually the dude who had been to hospital with the pipe up his butt… surely, that would make any man afraid!

I also saw it reported that Molly-Mae of Love Island fame has taken to hoovering patterns into her carpet. I am not sure if that sounds fun or whether I am damn glad I am getting out of cleaning before it becomes a trend! Can you imagine being booked to style a carpet? Perhaps I need another secret recipe… one that is like hairspray for carpets, maintaining the pattern for days!

CHAPTER 19

Jim'll Chimps It!

Over the years, we have done a lot of relief cleaning for the various councils and other public sector agencies; among our duties, we covered staff's sickness and holiday time at various locations including offices, leisure centres, public toilets, and other public buildings. Some of the absent staff were all on old-school contracts, meaning these people were paid full sick pay as they had been working in the public sector for years – and God! Didn't some of them abuse it!

One cleaner we used to cover for must have only worked 24 weeks of the year if we added up the time she took off for her holidays plus her sick days! She was employed 15 hours a week but only turned up on average 7.5 hours per week! Perhaps she had it right... I guess having paid time off is the Utopian ideal. I mean – I can't deny, it was good for us, but cripes, she barely did any work at all!

I discovered that many years ago some firms used to give staff 28 days' holiday plus 21 days' sick pay each year. That seems crazy! It's almost two months off a year! And we think we have got it better today. Blimey! I am sure you can imagine, staff used to take sick days even when they were not ill as they saw this as their entitlement! As a result, it's safe to say some of the cleaners we covered for were crap. Honestly, this rule does not apply to all public sector cleaners, but as far as I could tell some of the council cleaners we covered for were lazy and didn't give a shit.

One of the cleaners we used to come across we nicknamed Elvis. Why? Well, she looked like him a little, but that wasn't the main reason. This woman would always moan like buggery about cleaning, but never looked for a different job. Every week, it was the same old stories, on and on. How she never got sacked was beyond any of us. She was always talking, as if the hot air from her mouth was doing the work. Well, I say talking; it was more like gossiping. We knew everyone's private lives without even meeting them. So, we said, 'A little less conversation, a little more action needed'!

On many occasions, one council asked if I wanted to take over the cleaning contract, and for a millisecond I was tempted. However, in order to do this, they wanted me to employ their cleaning staff, taking over their existing contracts. I thought, *Not a blooming chance!* And it's not like they wanted to pass on awesome staff. Even the council managers were constantly moaning about their cleaners – and never dealt with them. I swear, if they worked for any other business, they would have been sacked. But then, as I mentioned before with the tenant who had the hot tub in her sitting room, I always found the council were very good at passing on their problems to others rather than dealing with them themselves.

Taking on the problematic buck the council wanted to lose became a regular habit of working for them. I mean, if you had a box of bad eggs, would you hand them on to a friend so you didn't get the stink in your own bin? That's what taking work for some councils was like! They have stitched me up soooo many times with dodgy tenants over the years, that's for sure. I only deal with a couple of trusted council staff now when it comes to housing council tenants.

I remember another shitty council tenant they palmed off on me as a private landlord. They told me a tenant was having a relationship breakdown and needed somewhere to stay. They used the sob story to engage my empathy, but conveniently forgot to mention the drug addiction and random violence. Like if you were asked to adopt a lion and they told you it had been kicked out of its pride – but not that it had a propensity to attack humans with its massive jaws! A few weeks after this person moved in, they stabbed someone!

Another time they told me a young girl had just come out of a bad relationship and needed somewhere to escape her abusive partner. It turned out she was a ruddy prostitute and drug dealer taking advantage of others. Despite their inability to cope with these tenants, they then have no time or support for you to manage them. They just wash their hands of it, and leave you picking up the pieces – sometimes literally if they smashed up the place. I mean, do they expect a private landlord to have better access to social services and police than the ruddy council?

Some chimps at the council should really have a lot to answer for. The way I see it is they waste sooooo much public money. It's as if they see it as not their money so it doesn't matter. I think if all councils were run by business people, this country would run so much better. But then, that was Trump's selling point, so I had also better be careful to not sound like a fat, skin tone like Irn-Bru pervert.

Dealing with inefficiency for the current government has amounted to cut-backs in areas we need staff and people –

like in our schools and hospitals. Yet, I still got paid to drive eighty-plus miles in a round trip to hoover one brand new carpet they had put down in an empty council bungalow; could the carpet fitter not do this? You might think I am exaggerating, but I swear I am not. For that same property, they paid someone else to travel down separately to put in a lightbulb. No wonder there's so many shit jokes about lightbulbs – only I think they must have been written by council workers who evidently think it's a massive job!

Besides, I also never said no to the work, soooooo…

I have to admit, I also learnt public sector contracts were often easy money. Even a low amount of effort was still better than what they were doing. They never seemed to care what we charged as long as we got the work done. We would have call-outs for small, insignificant things we could charge as a proper job. We actually got booked to pick up dog poo from communal blocks of flats. Another time, we were booked to pressure wash off abusive graffiti from around the streets, only to find it painted back later. In effect, we were paid to prep the site for the artist-vandals to entertain themselves the next night!

Another time that made me laugh was when we got called to the council offices one afternoon as a member of the public had suffered an accident in the ladies' toilet… You know, the number two kind of accident… So, instead of asking one of their cleaners, who were already on site or asking another member of staff if they could clean the loo, they called us in to do the job cleaning up *the job*. They justified the expense and the extraordinary effort by saying it was specialist cleaning. But bollocks was it! It was a little bit of poo on a toilet seat. I'm not convinced the call-out charge was warranted from their perspective, but there was no way I was going to take on a random job in the middle of our already busy day without charging for it. I guess everything was done to cover their own asses – so the shit didn't literally cover their asses!

Some of the work was hard-going though. Such as when we were booked to clean up after dead bodies. That never gets easier. Although, sometimes our laughs come from a dark place. Remember the whole Jimmy Saville scandal? Well, we made a few quid off of that, believe it or not. Someone in our area was writing his name all over the place and we got paid to pressure wash it all off! Who wakes up one morning and, having a moment of inspiration, thinks: I know! I was worried I would be bored today, but I know what I will do! I will go round my town with paint and sign Jimmy Saville's signature in as many places as I can! What a great idea! I'm just glad Jimmy never fixed it for me when I wrote to him as a kid.

Please note, we didn't spray the graffiti ourselves just to get extra work. However, the thought did cross my mind for if we ever had a quiet spell!

One of the perks of being the boss is picking and choosing what jobs you undertake, and which ones to avoid. Don't get me wrong – I always lead by example and would never get staff to clean up shit unless I was willing to do it myself. I mean, I have always managed to steer my company towards jobs I enjoy, and some of the council jobs were fantastically enjoyable! However, when it comes to cleaning up shit, I'm lucky I have a strong gag reflex and have handled any job I have walked into – and believe me, I have seen it all over the years. Having a strong stomach is a must when you're a cleaner. That reminds me of my friend's partner who likes to give him a blowy while he is having a poo sat on the toilet! Her gag reflex must be pretty impressive, that's for sure! I'm not sure about her proclivities, but I've already told you about how I feel about poo particles in the bathroom…

Anyway, where was I? Oh yes, the fantastic side of working for the council. One of my favourite contracts occurred during the summer months when we would take care of the maintenance of the various paddling pools in the local parks. We would undertake the cleaning, checking pH levels and so on. We did this for quite a few summers, and it was a laugh!

Despite the fun, council ineffectiveness was still an issue. We were never really given any training in how to keep the pools clean and safe. We had a ten-minute lesson one day in chemical control, and that was it. Boom! We were apparently trained enough to manage dangerous chemicals around small children. When the council asked me one day to sign a document to say I had received full training, I refused to sign it. Well, I took it home and didn't sign it and they never chased me for it – they had no doubt forgotten about it. But, having been stung a few times, I thought, typical council trying to pass the buck and make anyone but them accountable. I realised all it would take is one mother to complain about her child being burnt by the chlorine levels and the council would point their finger in my direction. Although to be fair, the biggest risks were likely verruca outbreaks or a floating poop in the pool.

As it happens, despite the lack of training, we cleaned and maintained the pools successfully without any major incidents. And if I was ever worried about the chemical levels being high I would just close the pool and call the council. I can't say we avoided all minor incidents – kids are disgusting in pools.

Cleaning vomit floating around is not a delightful sight.

The days were all relatively routine. We would open up the pool in the morning, litter pick around the pool. Fish out any leaves and debris that had dropped in, and then take readings of the pH levels. We would then return at lunch time to do the same thing. You might think the work was boring, but I love working with people, and the people enjoying the pool are out having fun.

On hot, sunny days, the paddling pool was rammed full of MILFs! Okay, I'm joking... There was the odd fat bird in a bikini too! Actually, I am joking – but it was noticeable how many women were there with the children, rather than the fathers.

And I do love to flirt!

I also noticed how unforgiving women's swimwear can be. Swimwear seems to be designed for model figures only. Saying that, the bigger women seemed to have sooooo much confidence and didn't give a monkey's if they looked like a Monster Munch in a swimsuit. Ruddy hell, one lady's bikini bottoms were so tight I thought Pac-Man was coming to eat me. I wish I had that kind of confidence; but knowing me, I'd find a way to bottle it and sell it!

Frequently, I would take the lunchtime shift. During this time, I was normally the only man in the pool area. I can only assume the MILFs took their kids for a swim while their husbands were at work. Perhaps our country is still far more traditional than we would like to believe – or at least it seems to be in my home county.

Anyway, it was a shame I had to wear a high-viz vest as it really curtailed my swagger; I swear some of the ladies must have thought I was doing community service (AGAIN) or something… More about that later.

I did try to talk to one or two of the ladies who were there. However, my efforts were scuppered when their children asked, "Mummy, what is that man doing?"

The mums replied, "That Nice Man is a cleaner and is cleaning the pool."

Firstly, NICE is never a good word to use; it is so bland and really just politely stands in place of what you are actually thinking. And, secondly, the ladies saw me as a *just* a cleaner – I think this should be a source of pride, but being a cleaner appears to render any man immediately unattractive. I thought I was doing alright: I was carrying a briefcase, and I was the boss of the company! Plus, in my head I was a pool technician – almost like a scientist. But no! My efforts to engage in summertime banter were deflated faster than a punctured pool float. I guess carrying a litter picker grab with me ruined my poolside scientist image.

I always thought banter at the pool was a funny thing. It was a bit like trying to chat with the mums in the different parks. Even though I had many failed attempts of talking to the pretty mums, I had no such trouble when it came to the Monster Munches. I was just being friendly and trying to pass the day with some fun, but some people just don't want any chatter at all. I remember talking with one large lady who informed me that she was single; she was really positive though, as she used that line, "There's plenty of fish in the sea." I thought, *Flip me. Looks like you ate most of them with chips!!*

Then there was this group of single mums who blooming terrified me! Some of them were so predatory, I would see them licking their lips when I entered the pool area. They were a gang of friends, probably met at Weight Watchers or something, and they egged each other on to create mischief for me and my staff. It started out as fun, but it quickly got out of hand. Gentle flirting and saucy banter suddenly became very sexual and somewhat violating – even though we were the ones in all our clothing! There was this one mum who was a proper big-mama who pursued me with determination, she was fat as a house, wart on her chin and bugs up her nose. I was scared for my life! She was a bigger lady, buxom and full of sass. She was so voracious, it got to the point I didn't know if she wanted to shag me or eat me! They say you can see three things from space, The Great Wall of China, The Grand Canyon and, no doubt, her Fat Ass! Anyway, she wore the skimpiest bikini ever – she looked a little like a human-sized joint of pork tied up in string. I really hope she never forgot her sun-cream or she might have turned into crackling by the end of the day! Joking with her was fun but a dangerous game – I felt like if I let the jokes get going too much she'd end up consuming me like a praying mantis. And I didn't know where to put my eyes, she just let everything hang out. I'm not saying I could see her camel toe – it was more of a camel hoof! Her vagina was like Bridgwater; men know it's there, they just don't want to visit. Anyway, I resisted her charms; I was terrified that if I entered her, it would be like going into the Bermuda Triangle, and I'd never be seen again!

But all joking aside, before anyone thinks I'm a fattist, beauty doesn't have a weight limit and I'd rather be with a big girl with a personality than be with a thin girl who's stuck up her own ass. The summer pool job was one of the most enjoyable we undertook, and it was easy, to be fair. It was guaranteed work over the summer months too; we got paid seven days a week. We had to undertake the work whatever the weather; rain or shine, it was a blast!

Not all the council's problems come from their ridiculous inadequacy. Over the years, while driving around, it is apparent fly-tipping has become a growing issue. To be fair, I'm not surprised, as for a while the local recycling centre has been a freaking nightmare! We have been stopped at the tip on quite a few occasions for one thing or another, or been charged for just disposing of waste appropriately. Or we got stuck in massive queues – no doubt while the people in front of us argued about being refused to drop their *refuse* or as they tried to avoid being charged. No wonder people end up just chucking their crap away in a hedge somewhere.

Back in the day, when doing house clearances, we would put aside some of the decent furniture and let the recycling centre have it to the sell in exchange for us getting rid of the rest of the crap. Then, new contractors took over and anyone who had a sign-written van was stopped and had grief about using the site. There were new rules about businesses dropping waste, and charges started to go up. More and more things were classified as commercial waste. So, when this happened, I just removed all the signage from my vans. This stopped me getting grief for a while, however, they eventually questioned why I was there so often. I used to say I was just having a clear-out at my house… but we did a fair amount of house clearances. They must have thought I lived in a right shit-hole! I mean, who finds two surplus three-piece suites a week lying around? I must have got rid of about nine broken kettles in one month alone! But if I had told them it was someone else's rubbish it would have been classed as commercial waste and I would have had to pay a fee. These charges make doing these clearances less viable. At one stage, there were a lot of back-handers going on regarding chargeable waste, but inevitably quite a few people got sacked for sticking the cash in their back pockets.

Have I ever fly-tipped? No! Well… I'm not sure you would call it fly-tipping, however I have resorted to sneaky strategies to offload rubbish without paying for it. For example, I have had a few tenants over the years who have left loads of crap behind at various properties, and let's just say most of it gets returned to their new front garden in the dead of the night. You might think it petty, but why should I have to pay to get rid of a tenant's rubbish when they are too bloody lazy to do it themselves?

In seriousness, fly-tipping costs our councils millions each year. With that in mind, why don't they just let people use the recycling centres for free? And they should organise collections for lower fees. After all, we all pay council tax to cover these costs, and surely supporting people to get rid of waste effectively has got to be a better option than organising to clean up areas after a mess has been made. Although, I suppose they recoup a fair amount of money in fines.

The amount of mattresses I come across down country lanes and fridges shoved into hedges is unreal. Farmers must get soooooo annoyed when it's dumped on their private land – land they use for business. I know one farmer who this happened to. He said he phoned the council to report it. But they turned around and said to him that as it was on private land there was nothing they could do about it. *Typical council,* I thought to myself. Anyway, not one to admit defeat, he picked up all the rubbish and dumped it on a public highway.

The really bad thing is, once one person has fly-tipped other people continue to add to the pile. But then, I guess that is a bit like having a skip by the side of your house and finding some people think it is acceptable to bung their crap in too.

I've noticed lots of people are so weird with their rubbish. We used to clean a lot of council houses, and I discovered for some reason some tenants think it's acceptable to use their gardens as landfill sites. Why would you want waste decomposing in your own garden? Who wants their kids to go outside and play next to rusting metal and bags of food and bathroom waste? I know a person who was trying to sell his house but his next-door neighbour was proper cruddy. In their garden, visible – and smellable – their bins were overfilled; there were fridges in the garden, and all sorts of other mess. It put people off buying his house completely. The main feedback from the estate agent was that potential buyers couldn't live next door to that mess!

You find the same thing at bottle banks and clothes banks. For some reason, some people always stack other waste next to these bins. I wonder, why? Why if you've got that far would you not dispose of the rest of your waste properly? I once saw a sofa that was dumped next to one of these bottle banks. Lordy Lord! The cheek of some people! Although I suppose if someone was combining drinking their drink comfortably and getting rid of their bottles at the same time, it was a convenient set-up.

I learned a few tricks over the years while doing house clearances. When I undertook really bad houses, I always found out what day bin day was for that area as it saved a few tip runs. I would just schedule the job the day before bin day and next day go back early in the morning and stick the rubbish out: job done.

I suppose my motto is work smarter not harder. Something the council and government could do with learning, that's for sure!

CHAPTER 20

Pull the Wool Over Your Wise

You could say I am smarter than I look. I'm frequently surprised that with my lack of education I didn't end up working in a supermarket as a janitor. I think a lot of my old teachers are surprised too – but there we go. Education isn't the only way to be successful.

Cleaners get a raw deal in terms of social status. It's something that bugs me greatly, however sometimes I meet cleaners and realise there are plenty of us that give us a bad name. But this wasn't always the case. Back in the olden days, in a time when people would answer landline phones by reading out their place name followed by phone number (i.e. "Tiverton, 2-5-4-blah blah blah"), a whole army of old ladies existed who kept the country clean. They were tough as old boots and had skin hardened by toxic cleaning chemicals. You know the kind of old ladies: they are the sort of old ladies who would eat shit desserts like blancmange, sago, and tapioca. They would scrub floors with hard brushes in a way that would wear through the knuckles of the young. Anyway, they are all dead now, and keeping the halls of Heaven shining the tiling. Sadly, it's been left to the next generation to carry the baton of Mr Muscle, and we just don't make that kind of elbow grease anymore. It's probably bad for the environment. Anyway, it might be an oxymoron that although we live in extraordinarily hygienic times, young cleaners don't even come close to the high standards set by these little old ladies who genuinely cared about the places they cleaned. I think many bacteria were too scared of these women to hang around. But they are all gone now, and there aren't many books written about people like them. They are gone and forgotten, turning to dust in the Cleaners' Cemetery. We are now left with a new tribe of cleaners who think keeping a room clean means buying new furniture when the old stuff gets dusty and that a spritz of Febreze actually disinfects a space.

If I'm honest, I miss these women. And always remember to listen to the wisdom of old people. One old lady once said to me, "Do you know how to keep a clean house? Never let your kids or husband in." She also commented how her and her husband were both in their 80s and recently he'd lost interest in sex. "Thank God!" she said!

But even in our strange modern times, some cleaners are better than others. Out of all the cleaning personnel I have met, for some reason the ones that clean for supermarkets are normally the thickest bunch of people you could find anywhere.

I was in Tesco a while ago and a shrill voice called out on the tannoy, "Janitor in aisle seven; janitor in aisle seven."

A harassed shopper had dropped a jar of pickled beetroot. The janitor turned up a few minutes later, looked at it for a few minutes, not blinking – actually, he was barely moving. He then walked off. I was beginning to think he had forgotten about the mess that needed cleaning. But then, five minutes later, he came back with a wet floor sign, and then disappeared again. God knows how much time passed before he returned; I'd pretty much finished shopping and began to think he'd just marked off the pink puddle and broken glass with a sign – job done! But then, he slowly trundled back with a cleaning trolley to sort out the spillage.

I'm not sure why he didn't turn up the first time with the cleaning trolley, prepared to clean up whatever mess he found. His first appraisal of the mishap is beyond me – what was he thinking about as he looked down at the beetroot so blankly? Was he hoping he could clean it up with his eyes like some kind of Jedi-Janitor? Did he have a secret phobia of pickled root vegetables? Blimey! Janitors in supermarkets don't tend to be the brightest, that's for sure; and I should know since that's where I started out! For some reason, their clothes never seem to fit them either. I sometimes wonder whether that makes up a selection criteria at interview. Like, the interviewer sees someone in well-fitted pants, and says, "No. Put him on the tills – he knows how to do up a belt! Take that chap over there – he's wearing trousers two sizes too big and they're on backwards! He'll make a perfect cleaner!" Most of them walk as though they have just pooped their panties, and they always wear high-viz to ensure everyone can identify them as the janitor – as if we didn't have enough clues with the vacant expression and the wrong trousers. I mean – it's ridiculous! On top of these things, they are also normally missing some part of their anatomy too. Sometimes it's teeth, other times it's an arm – probably lost in some kind of accident with a forklift. Always, and I mean always, they are missing many brain cells.

I often wonder whether cleaning brings out the dunce in all of us. Intelligent, interesting people become zombies when they zone into their chores. Pay attention to the people cleaning around you – they separate from their conscious mind, and will just say yes to anything. Kids the world over get permission to do all sorts of things if they ask a parent in the middle of vacuuming.

"Mum! Can I have seven pizzas made of Haribo and the blood of my youngest sibling?"

And there's mum, staring ahead, moving the hoover in neat patterns over the carpet, "Yeeessss, just take your sister with you."

A real example of this comes from doing my own laundry. Once a week, I would use the laundrette to wash my clothes. God! That was another experience in itself. If you are ever having an ugly day, feel free to go to a laundrette as you will feel so much better about yourself. It's a zoo of the apathetic, bored and the downtrodden. I'm sure the people who use these are people who have given up on life. But then, I wonder what they thought of me in there. But I liked to get in and out quickly – and I don't mean sexually. I used to bung my clothes in and leave. I'd then go back twenty minutes later and stick them in the tumble dryer. Some of the people in there would turn into unblinking idiots sitting there watching their washing go round and round and round! Although, I suppose watching the washing is preferable to watching Made In Chelsea.

Anyway, where was I? Oh yes! Talking about cleaning-mesmerisation. I think that makes me resistant to the soporific powers of domestic chores. But there's a chance resistance has made me cunning. For example, I used to buy all my cleaning products from Tesco as they were always so much cheaper than going to a cleaning supplier. Often, commercial suppliers are not the best place for any of our supplies – they just can't compete with online stores and supermarkets. I guess that's a sad fact. But I liked Tesco. The staff very kindly used to leave boxes of stock out for me so I could buy in bulk without any hassle or leaving their shelves empty. So, in the morning I would just come along, load up, head to a checkout where a lady would just scan one of each item and tap in the amount. Easy peasy. I used to buy the Tesco Value toilet cleaner as it was like 28p per bottle at the time. However, the Value toilet cleaner came in the same colour boxes as their own brand cleaner which was 55p per bottle – around double the price. I typically bought six boxes a week. Conveniently, when I got to the till, the Value box was always on the top of the pile, so when check out operator scanned that one, she would put all the others through at the same price. Unknown to her, underneath this box, the rest of the stack were products worth twice as much. I know, I know. You could say this was fraud, however, the first time it happened it was an accident. I just forgot to say anything… Is that really so bad? They should have checked! Plus, every little helps!

CHAPTER 21

Dirty, Filthy Cash!

I guess you could say, where there's muck there's money. I mean this truly: there's cash to be found in your festering filth. You could say, we love the dirty jobs!

For years, donkeys' years (did you know donkeys' years as a saying comes from rhyming slang as years rhymes with ears. It doesn't mean donkeys live a long time, or that they have big ears – although both of these things are also true), anyway – for a long old time, people have found their fortunes processing rubbish and waste material. The saying one man's trash is another man's treasure is completely true when it comes to the cleaning business. But this is true in more ways than you might imagine…

For a good example, let me take you back. One day while emptying a property we came across a bag of foreign coins… although, on reflection, I'll tell you more about them in a moment – after all, I don't want to tell you the juiciest story right at the start of the chapter. Instead, I will tell you about how I learned different ways to make money out of cleaning – and not all of them turned out to be as clean as I would have liked. As you may have noticed from previous 20 or so chapters, undertaking house clearances meant we came across all sorts. So far in this book, I have concentrated on the ridiculous and alarming – remember the mummified cat? But there is so much more to house clearances than the grotesque. At the other end of the scale, I must admit, I have probably thrown out antiques I didn't even know were valuable, especially in the early days. However, as I got older and wiser, I learned that there is hidden worth to be found in old and dusty things. It soon became apparent that there was good money to be made doing house clearances.

On the odd occasion, we pick up jobs to clear houses for people who want us to organise a lifetime of gathered things. The owner maintains ownership of everything and we just sort it out. These jobs are rare. Mostly, we were brought in to do house clearances when someone had died with no next of kin, or when someone had been evicted from a council property. In these instances, our job was to remove everything from the property and dispose of it all. Because of the nature of the work, I just assumed everything was rubbish. Naively, I just thought we were emptying the house of junk. Nobody mentioned whether we could keep or sell any of the stuff in the property. So, to begin with, we just disposed of everything as quickly as we could. Fortunately, in time, we learnt that everything has a value. After all, that clutter used to be money.

Therefore, this kind of work became lucrative – it's always nice to have a job that has opportunities to keep monetising work. We were being paid to remove the items, but I was also able to make a few quid selling on furniture and various bits and pieces at various auction sites. We even struck it lucky on a few occasions: once, I came across over 250 pounds worth of euros which came in handy for an upcoming holiday! Another time, we found an old teddy bear which sold for over £300 on eBay! Another great find was a gold sovereign coin which sold for over £200. As I said earlier, one man's garbage is another man's gold! And I'm quite happy to be a domestic treasure hunter! Or as my staff used to affectionately call me a 'Skip Diver'.

So, now I'll get back to my huge confession... back to the foreign coins we found one day. I mean, before I say what happened, I'm going to blame this incident on my dad, to some extent. He once said to me, "Money is like muck – it's only good if it's spread." My dad is normally pretty wise, so I bore this advice in mind when we found a trove... of sorts.

Back to this one day. I came across a bag of what looked to be a collection of old Turkish money. Funnily enough, I noticed one of the coins looked like a British two-pound coin. Well, I say one of the coins; let's just say the bag was full of these look-a-likes. I put a couple in my wallet and to be honest forgot they were there, but I'm sure you can see where this is going.

A short while later, while out in Sidmouth, I purchased some ice creams. Unknown to me on that day, I had used one of these Turkish coins as part of the cash payment. When I realised what I had done, I remarked how I hadn't noticed. I also noticed the lady behind the counter didn't question it either. She had just taken my money and served me. But the story continues...

Buoyed up by this event, I shared out these coins with my staff! I just thought sharing is caring, and had my dad's words at the back of my mind (see, I told you it was his fault really). After all, why keep the wealth to just me? I wanted to be a good son and a generous boss! Okay, okay! I encouraged everyone to use money fraudulently, but hey! I was just thinking about how I had found a use for this hoard! Buuuut

I did tell them to only use them at a certain pub where a client had cancelled the contract at short notice and decided not to pay me the money she owed. She was a right miserable cow with a fair set of udders on her. You could have probably breast fed a crèche on her tits! But I did have the last laugh.

The story continues…

Let's just say, there was an article in the local paper a few months later, well after we depleted our stash to nothing, A pub land lady was warning people to beware of foreign coins in circulation.

It might not have been our doing, but…

Funnily enough, I don't have any of these coins anymore! And there's still more to this story in the next chapter.

Not all jobs work out as well when it comes to thinking about money. Time Is Money, as they say, and it's so true. As with any business, running a cleaning firm generates tons of moments where you can see your profits disappearing down the drain. I just wish I could invoice people sometimes for wasting my time.

One of the most time-consuming jobs I found was quoting for work and writing up the necessary risk assessments which came into force in the last few years. A quote used to take a couple of hours; by the time you went to the customer's house, talked about what they were looking for, got back to the office and wrote it all up, so much time rushed by. If the job didn't pan out, this time was utterly wasted.

More recently, I have mostly stopped visiting customers at their house prior to undertaking the work. I have switched to estimating quotes, and adjusting the price accordingly when the work is confirmed. Not everyone likes working with an estimate, however, and I can understand why – there are a lot of cowboy outfits out there. But when it comes to inefficient and unnecessary meetings, COVID has helped change people's minds – believe me! A lot of companies and customers have been forced to examine how to do things differently.

Switching to a pricing model based on estimation was fraught work! It sounds simple – I would give the customer a rough price on the phone and when I turned up on the day, if the job was bigger or smaller, I would adjust the price and inform them of the amendment. But in truth, how often would I over-estimate? Rarely! And how often are customers happy to pay more than expected? Also rarely. The truth is, you have to get good at estimating so changes are minimal.

That said, it saved so much time it made me more profitable and productive after all. Time is such a valuable resource, and you have to spend it carefully. This is true for everyone, but not all businesses have switched to a pricing by estimate policy. I know some people who still go out and do the quoting in person, but they now build their time quoting into the end price. I am not sure as a customer I would prefer this method, but I can totally understand why they might do this.

Back in the 80s and 90s, my friend's dad worked for a double-glazing firm, and he was always paid in commission. His job was to go out and do the quotes and if they were successful and they got the work, he'd get paid. If his efforts fell through, he wouldn't get a penny.

He told me a story once when he had to do a quote in the middle of nowhere. Apparently, it took two hours to get there, and he spent a couple of hours with the customer before agreeing a rock-bottom price for them. He knew for a fact they were cheaper than all the other firms that had quoted. However, it became apparent the customer was wasting his time and wasn't going to take him up on the offer. To say he was disappointed is an understatement. This was almost a day's work that would turn into no income. So, he decided to take matters into his own hands!

Upon leaving the customer's house, he asked if he could use the toilet as he had a two-hour drive back home. It sounds reasonable enough, you say? Well, when he was in the toilet, he took the customer's toothbrush and wiped it around the toilet bowl!

"Teach them for wasting my day!" he said with a grin on his face.

But then, he might have been a little over-vengeful. He also joked that just before he split up with his wife, he decided to get back at her for all the things he found annoying. Stressed out, he had a bath after a long day at work. While he was relaxing, he found himself in need of a wee, and being a decent fella, he obviously wouldn't piss in the bath. But hey, where there's a wee there's a way! Instead, he took his partner's face sponge, pissed on it and rung it out in the sink. Then, he put it back.

Did he feel bad about his actions? I'm fairly convinced he thought his actions were justified! He finished the story by jumping ahead in time to a few weeks after they spilt up. He remembered a night he bumped into her out in town. He said she was looking well. He jibed, "Christ! That sponge did wonders for her spots!"

I've done things in life I regret, but I can honestly say I've never gone to that length. However, after a while in business, you soon know just by talking to a customer on the phone if they are going to be a pain in the ass or not. I know, I shouldn't judge too quickly. Sometimes I still get it wrong – but very rarely.

The buzz phrase to look out for is when a customer says, "We're not that fussy and I'm never one to complain!" Believe me, I immediately run for cover. If I can, I avoid these customers; they always expect the ruddy world and pay very little for it.

One thing that annoys me is when you do a job then you have to wait ages for payment. I know lots of companies use a 90-day policy and have all sorts of loopholes to release payment – but this is all ruddy bull, if you ask me. Policies like these can make small businesses unviable.

On one such time, I undertook a carpet cleaning job for a lady I actually knew. I gave her a discounted price of only £20 to clean one room but she just didn't want to pay it. I enquired soooo many times about whether she was okay; I asked if she having money problems, and tried to be friendly. If she had said she couldn't afford it, I would have let it go. The money itself didn't matter; it was the lack of communication and respect that bothered me. Instead, she would either ignore my messages or fob me off, saying, "Don't worry; I'll pay this weekend when I do my banking." Then, the weekend would come and lo and behold, no payment! And no message!

This went on for nearly three months until I lost my rag. I know they, the wise of the world, say the best revenge is love... however, I decided love wasn't going to make this world go round far enough. So, I was prepared to teach this particular lady a lesson. I was planning on driving past her house and pouring a load of dirty carpet machine water through her letterbox. However, en route to doing this she suddenly paid.

Would it have been the right thing to do? Well… Would it have made me feel good? You bet it bloody would have! However, it was a long time ago and I'm not sure I would be tempted to do it now for non-payment. I guess it's not as bad as the builder who demolished his client's conservatory after she refused to pay for it.

I ended up blocking her on social media as I don't need people like that in my life.

It turns out, it's a dirty job doing the dirty jobs. You see people at their best, worst, and most vulnerable; yet you are there to earn a wage. It may be true that love makes the world go around, but money does grease the wheels. As the wise people say, it's a necessary evil. Money could solve all the problems in the world, but it also causes all the problems in the world. Thank God for cleaners: dirty hands really do make clean money.

CHAPTER 22

Barry on Camping!

You know when people meet their idols or people considered really important like the Queen, they say things like they try to remember that their idol's poops don't smell like roses, or they imagined the idol naked to help them act normal. Well, cleaning brings you up close and ugly with this kind of cliché. Over the years, I have encountered many celebrities during my cleaning career. I mean, they don't want to clean up their own messes any more than anyone else. One of the most famous in my humble, Devonian opinion, was Barry from EastEnders; not least because of the ordinary circumstances in which I found him.

We were cleaning the communal shower and toilet block of a caravan park and who happened to rock up for the weekend? None other than Shaun Williamson, aka Barry from EastEnders! He was the last person we expected to find in a Devon camp site. There I was, face to face with a geezer from London. There I was, cleaning the toilets; I had a toilet duck in one hand, bog brush in the other, and Barry had walked in to use the toilet.

I remember it to this day: he chose the end cubicle, the choice of champions. I'm not sure why, but the end cubicle in a toilet block is by far the most popular. I tried to remain cool and professional; it wasn't the right moment to crack out my autograph book and I hadn't even heard of selfies back then. But stories don't become memorable when people remain calm and collected.

After what felt like days of slow-moving time, awkwardness ensued: it became obvious he was having a number two. I lingered far longer than I should have waiting for him to come out; I had just assumed he'd be fast and I'd finish cleaning the loos in no time. But the seconds ticked on and somehow I was still there. To be fair to him, it wasn't a stinky or noisy poo. I'm normally out of a toilet block quicker than diarrhoea if I get a whiff of last night's beers or someone starts making pooping noises, including the relief groans as the poo leaves the departure lounge on its final journey to the bottom of the pan. It's a personal moment I don't need to share with anyone, let alone a stranger.

Anyway, I heard the toilet flush, the door opened and out he stepped. Feeling uncomfortable and not knowing what to say, I uttered the phrase, "Do you feel better now, Barry?"

I could have been cooler. I could have been more professional. But sometimes my mouth just steps in to try to make things better, and it doesn't always know best.

Barry looked at me and said, "I've never been asked that before when leaving a toilet. And my name is Shaun."

I didn't think I knew what it was like to be a fangirl, but…

Ignoring my embarrassment as best I could, we exchanged a brief conversation about the weather, and then he washed his hands and left.

Afterwards, I went in and cleaned the toilet he had just used. At first, still starstruck, I was reluctant. I thought I could leave it as a shrine to him! However, someone else entered the toilet and obviously wanted to use this particular cubicle as it was the choice of champions. I explained to them that Barry from EastEnders had just used this toilet and they looked at me as though I was a bit special. You know, the expression a dog gives you when it turns its head to one side and looks at you in disbelief – well, that was the look I got.

To this day, I still tell people the story of the day I met Barry from EastEnders in a toilet block – sorry, the day I met Shaun the actor in a toilet block. Thankfully he didn't have Well-Hard with him as people would have talked!

To be fair, it's rare for a celebrity to bring out the fan in me. They are normal people, after all, and I'm generally observing their lives from the outside, seeing all the messiness and reality.

One celebrity was a prime example of this. She was a good musician and very successful, but she kept throwing me surprise curveballs throughout my time working for her.

Initially, I wasn't particularly aware of who she was. To be honest with you, when I first met her, I didn't think she was that attractive, not that attractiveness is a sum of her skills, personality or politeness. But she was a bit hippy-like, and that's just not my thing. Don't get me wrong, she is very talented, but I just thought what a down-to-earth girl she was. This was a breath of fresh air; she was like Listerine mouthwash in comparison to the turgidness of other mega-rich customers. Then one day, while cleaning her bedroom, she happened to walk out of the shower in just a small towel. She was naturally stunning, and I fought off the biggest boner while trying not to look at her.

Joking aside, I ended up feeling a bit sorry for her, to be fair. Whenever we cleaned her house she was always surrounded by drop-outs and hangers-on. Most of them looked like they had never done a day's work in their lives; they lounged around and talked twaddle. All of them looked like they needed a wash. One even told me he was a "child of the cosmos," and that he always "carried moon-dust" around with him for "good luck". I promise these are directly quoted, but I still don't know what these phrases actually mean. You might call me old-fashioned, but I just thought, *Go and get some shampoo, son, or spray a bit of Lynx about.* He was distinctly ruining the fragrant ambience we were creating with our cleaning!

In terms of friendliness and treating cleaners like human beings, this celebrity was amazing. Despite her fame and fortune, she was a sound-as-a-pound human being. However, that was not always the case – people with status and money are normally the worst behaved and the dirtiest customers.

We used to clean for a posh lady who always looked down on us and treated us like dirt. One memory stands out above all. Her kids went to private school, and while this is fine, her way of pushing education peed me off to my core. While cleaning her house during school holidays, we met her delightful children. They were pretty lazy, spoilt and entitled. On that day, they all had homework to do, and like all kids, they were reluctant to do it. Normal to this point? Please continue reading.

Anyway, she turned around and said to one of her kids, "If you don't get a proper education, you'll end up being a cleaner."

This was said right in front of me and one of my staff! I nearly choked her with a duster and a bottle of Mr Muscle! I don't use the C word… but what a Conceited Snob!

It turns out all that expensive education and entitled arrogance didn't pay off for him. The last I heard, he was crack addict and part-time rent boy to pay for his addiction. I know, that's also sad in its own way, but I still fume at that statement. It's also funny to me how life goes on and people turn out despite education and background. Class and education don't mean exactly what we think they do. We now live in a world where cleaners can own Aston Martins and big houses, kids from council estates can be among the biggest tax-payers, and aristocrats can end up nothing more than spongers living off their dying names.

Anyway, let's get back to something more light hearted: something else that hacks me off...

Another thing I don't have time for in life is moaners. Obviously, I make an exception for myself! But for everyone else, I don't discriminate. Whether it's staff or customers, I don't have time for people who just moan for the sake of it. To me, the world is a bad place sometimes, and nobody gets everything they want. I just think, if your mindset is always negative the whole world will be negative; so in a way, the world is however your mind is. We should take the world as it is and not as we want it to be.

I have had to deal with various moaning clients over the years. Some were genuine while others were just taking the mick. One example comes from when we cleaned a lady's carpet and she just had to take out her disappointment on someone. To clean the carpet, we had to move an old wooden table which had brass legs. When we moved it we saw it had left metallic stains behind where the feet used to sit.

We pointed this out to her and that it was doubtful they would come out, but otherwise the carpet came up well.

A few weeks afterwards, I received a letter from her claiming I owed her a new carpet for putting the table leg stains on the carpet. As if cleaners go about making things worse than how we found it!

Thankfully, I had access to legal advice, and her ridiculous complaint soon went away! Anyone who runs a business and doesn't have something like this in place really should do some research. Believe me, you only have to phone the helpline once and it's worth every penny. Over the years, good legal counsel has saved me a fortune. They can even draft a letter for you to send to customers who are taking the mick! You might think this sounds over the top, but I promise it soon becomes essential.

Another client who I could not stand was a lady who ran a pub. For the purposes of discretion, let's change her name to Kim Cowdashian. She was a complete an utter cow – if cows are also dicks. It was a contract we undertook in the early days when I was still keen and green.

What she expected us to achieve in 1.5 hours a day, 7 days a week, was unbelievable! The pub was exceptionally busy at the weekend which really skewed what we could do. At the start of the week, 1.5 hours daily was enough. However, at the end of the week, when we had to mop all the alcohol-stained wooden floors, wipe down all the alcohol-stained table tops, clear up all the rubbish, food, and party debris, and clear up the sick and shit left in the toilets, 1.5 hours was not anything like enough.

I tried to address this. When I pointed out to her we needed an extra 30 minutes to clean on a Saturday and Sunday morning, I might as well have murdered a kid of hers.

"You do not need more time!" she shouted, slamming her drink down in rage.

I suggested as a compromise we might do 30 minutes less

on a Monday and a Tuesday and to save the extra time for the weekends, especially if money was tight. In no uncertain terms, she told me that she was the boss and the previous cleaner never moaned and asked for more time, so we had to stick rigidly to 1.5 hours a day. I think this is what people call a clash of personalities; well, if she had one that was – she might have been demonic.

I could see full well why she had such a high turnover of bar and cleaning staff.

I gave her two months' notice as that is what she wanted at the time. I handed my notice in at the start of October, but I was still a little green and naive. I knew Christmas was her busy time, so feeling like I was letting her down, I said to her that I was happy to carry on until end of January in order to give her time to find someone to take over. She thanked me, which was the first time she ever did, to be fair.

We got Christmas out the way; it was tough going in during that busy time when even 30 minutes extra wouldn't have been enough. It was a difficult call every day whether she got free time from us or a shoddy job. We even cleaned on Christmas Day morning. Again, we didn't charge her any extra for this. But then, out of the blue, we got to the second week of January and she turned up at 7am just as we were starting work. It was a Wednesday morning, cold and bright.

"We don't need you anymore," she said. "I have found someone to start tomorrow."

I replied it was no problem; to be fair, I was pretty relieved. Working 7 days a week there was a pretty big tie. I gave her the final invoice, and expected that to be that. But bear in mind she still hadn't paid December's invoice at that point.

A few weeks passed and no payment came. I contacted

her to ask about the delay. She spoke to me on the phone and said she was only going to pay a few hundred pounds as she wasn't happy with the service. She paid just enough to take the remaining balance under £500 knowing that would mean I couldn't take her to court.

On reflection, she never said anything about the standard of the cleaning when we were working for her or when we handed back the keys. Rather, she thanked me for working all over Christmas. Yet, this was how I was rewarded. Some people just take the piss.

How's this for Karma though? Not long after the new cleaners started cleaning her pub they up and left without notice. Then, a few months later, her pub went bust.

Prior to that though, my mates and I were drinking in her pub one night, and disgruntled to be there, I told my mates what she had done to me. One of my friends thought she was bang out of order. Before leaving the pub that night he went downstairs to the toilets and decided to kick off one of the toilet pipes in the men's toilet.

He came back to the table and said, "I think we should leave. It looks like they have a flood downstairs."

I know I shouldn't be gleeful, however, part of me found it funny. Well, at least she then had something real to moan about! My dad always said to me that the worst people to be around are the ones who always complain and appreciate nothing. I wonder if Kim Cowdashian was the type of person to enjoy a rainy day? I hope you enjoyed your wet feet, Kim!

Random vandalism aside, I guess laughing is a good way to deal with bad situations. Plus, there is a positive in every negative... At least with those foreign coins, she had spending money if she ever visited Turkey!

Not all difficult customers are selfish and mean, though. Some genuinely cannot help their circumstances. There was another time we turned up to clean a house and had a terrifying surprise. It was a warden-assisted property, which means the tenants lived independently, however, they all had issues which meant they needed a warden on call. This particular lady was in her 40s. She seemed quite normal most of the time, then other times you would go and she would be stabbing the walls with knives.

"Don't worry!" the warden said. "She's never stabbed anyone yet…"

I thought, *Christ! That's reassuring!* She had anger issues! Didn't she just! So when I walked in one day and saw her stabbing the wall, the first thing I said to her was, "Someone's having a bad day. Shall I put the kettle on?" Then I thought, *What a dick! She'll probably throw the tea over me!* But as my gran used to say, a cup of tea helps most situations. Personally, I think alcohol helps more, but we are all different! I certainly wasn't about to get her shit faced on Fosters!

Eventually, she calmed down. When I asked her what triggered it, she said a voice in her head told her to do it! I've made a lot of mistakes in my life; maybe I should use that line next time.

Tin-Foil Man was another interesting character we undertook work for. We were contacted by social services to help this person as he was a bit of a hoarder. Well, I say bit of a hoarder: you couldn't move in his house. Plus, he covered all his windows with tin foil as he was paranoid that people were watching him and listening – like some sort of paranormal activity or secret spy work.

When I arrived with staff to do the work, he took ages to

answer his door. When he finally did, he answered his door in his Y-fronts and vest top. When he turned around, he had a massive skid mark up the back of him. My cleaners had to walk away as they were laughing too much; the whole thing was both tragic and ridiculous.

It was made worse as he apologised for taking ages to answer the door as he was in the shower! It was impossible to believe him considering how he was dressed, however, when we got upstairs, we couldn't get in the bathroom due to the amount of crap he stored in it. This guy was just odd all round.

We were told to clear and clean. The problem with hoarders is they never want to throw anything out, so we constantly had to distract him and take rubbish out to the vans. After that day, we said we would never clean a hoarder's house again unless they went out. He was a bloody nightmare, giving us every excuse why we couldn't throw away stuff. We even had to argue over some old plastic bottles which he claimed he wanted to keep just in case there was an invasion of some kind and he needed to bottle up water. I just thought, *Ruddy hell! If there ever was an alien invasion and the first person they came across was him, I think they would soon leave the planet!*

We are all different in life, and yes, I probably shouldn't judge this bloke for being different. However, I can't take anyone seriously when they answer the door in skid-marked pants. Some people I guess are not just missing a screw; they are missing the whole frigging tool box!

We got a fair amount of work from the social services. Another case was a guy who lived on his own; how social services thought he could live on his own is beyond me completely. If anything, these people are sorely let down by our welfare state. This guy had serious mental issues and believe me I'm not making fun of that. Every week it was a battle just to get him to let us into his house. Again, when we finally persuaded him to open the door, he was always just in his pants.

Apparently, he used to walk around the streets in just his pants, however I've never seen this to be fair. He was a keen decorator, however his idea of decorating was basically just throwing a tin of paint over the walls. I know some artists have made a living out of doing abstract art, but this bloke took it to another level. Our job each week was to basically clean the bathroom and the kitchen. Social services removed all the carpets from house due to his decorating skills. I asked him once whether he had ever thought about using a brush when he decorates. He just grunted at me.

Apparently, he came from a wealthy family who basically just washed their hands of him. They bought him a house and in their eyes that was enough to deal with this problem member of the family. The sad thing is, he probably just needed love and company. Throwing money at him was definitely not the answer because all he wanted to do was destroy everything material he owned.

We only cleaned his place a handful of times before I decided it was more hassle than it was worth. Most of the time staff couldn't get in to clean which wasted our time. Once my cleaners were negotiating with him for 30 minutes to get in! When I said to the family we would start charging for non-visits unless they gave us a key, they kicked off. At that, I just thought, *I don't need this.* You soon learn when you run a cleaning business which jobs to cherish and which ones are a waste of time and money!

A social worker said to me when we decided to leave the job, "We are not in it for the income; we are in it for the outcome!" I'm sure that's great when you're salaried and your survival depends on outcomes. I thought, *Well, I'm a cleaner: I'm paid to clean, not to stand knocking on doors. Maybe you should do your job better!*

I asked him once where he got his inspiration from when it came to painting and choosing room colours. Of course, I was taking the piss and passing the time. However, it made conversation. He responded by saying that sometimes you just need a splash of colour in your life. I guess, to be fair to him, that is very true. He was just at his happiest when he was throwing tins of paint over the walls! I must admit I did laugh once when I arrived, and he had pretty much covered his face and body in paint. I pointed out to him he had missed a bit on the wall; he didn't see the funny side.

Another time I laughed inappropriately was one Christmas when some of my tenants I have in bedsits were given hampers by a charity which contained food and other essential products. Bear in mind some of my tenants live on the bread line and most were homeless on the streets before I housed them. One tenant showed me his parcel: it contained lots of food, toothpaste and brush, and some fake tan! I had to walk out the room; I couldn't stop laughing! Nothing makes a homeless person feel better about themselves than giving them a healthy tan to look like they have been on holiday! I'm pretty sure this was put in by mistake, but it did make me smile loudly.

I realise I have written about customers in many of my chapters. If anything, this job, like many others is as much about the people as it is about cleaning. For the most part, I have enjoyed meeting my customers, their colleagues, friends and families. The world is a rich tapestry of people; it would be so dull and forgettable without all the misfits, mavericks, masters and menaces. That said, it would still be nice if they opened their doors promptly in freshly laundered pants – it's a small ask!

CHAPTER 23

Cleaner Launders Money

Before I get into the nitty-gritty, first read the article that appeared online and inspired this chapter. I'm not about to tell you about my life of crime – after all, I've merely led a life of grime. I am going to discuss crap bureaucratic security, poor press reporting, and the ineffectiveness of our justice system. Just a quick one then…

Anyway, here's the first article:

Cleaner guilty of processing money from stolen library books

Matthew Burd has pleaded guilty to two counts of money laundering.

A cleaning company boss has appeared in court accused of handling cash from the sale of books which were stolen from Tiverton Library and Mid Devon District Council.

The 113 books were stolen by an unknown thief from the council offices and library which are both situated at Phoenix House in the months leading up to May last year.

Burd has admitted two offences under the Proceeds of Crime Act of concealing, converting, transferring or removing criminal property on or before May 4, 2019. Judge David Evans adjourned sentence until October 30 to enable

Burd to arrange repayment to the council and library.

Mr Gareth Evans, prosecuting, said the full cost is estimated at £4,300 but Mr William Parkhill, defending, said Burd had only received £200.

The case was sent to the Crown Court because of the application under the Proceeds of Crime Act, but the maximum possible sentence remains the six months which could have been imposed by magistrates.

There was me thinking my toilet and I had been through sooooo much shit together; this was nothing compared to the crap I had to deal with in court and in the many months running up to it.

We have all heard it said that there are two sides to every story. Humbly, I disagree; there are three sides to every story: your version, their version, and The Truth. Sadly, the three never fully match, and often for good reason. And I can't promise to tell the whole truth here – it's not just my story wrapped up in it.

Their version, the press and the legal system's version, is as recorded above – simple, factual, but lacking detail and not representative of what really happened. In this chapter, I want to finally have my say: my version. This is about how dreadfully we treat people.

But first – the article. Wise people say there is no such thing as bad publicity unless it involves children or animals – although perhaps they aren't wise, perhaps they are just PR execs trying to convince everyone of their best spin. However, when all this came to light it was probably the lowest point of my life. Okay, who am I trying to kid? Finding out my dad had prostate cancer was the lowest point, but this came fairly close. As I will show you later in this chapter, the press were a joke! And truth had very little to do with their work.

Before I get too much into my story, there are a couple of things I want to mention about the article. Firstly, I'm no journalist but as far as I'm concerned, they missed a trick with the headline. Surely 'Cleaner Launders Money' would have been a better title. Of course, if I had been sent to jail, they could have gone with the headline 'Jail Burd'. Alternatively, they could have gone with, 'Not A Clean Getaway'. So many missed opportunities! They should be ashamed!

Secondly, someone asked whether it annoyed me when the newspaper printed my age. I thought this was brilliant! The reader was more concerned about the violation of the paper revealing personal information than the actual contents of the article. It was as if they thought people would judge me more for being in my mid-forties than for my alleged criminal offences!

Having now lived a tabloid reality, however local and small-scale, I believe more than ever it is sad that journalists don't print the actual truth, instead leaning heavily on a version of events that scandalises and sensationalises people's lives. The miserable thing is, since this went online, everyone who read it has told other people about it and added bits to the story. Since we are all part of a relatively small community, these rumours and embellishments eventually get back to me. And worse – when the gossip doesn't make it back, and the whispers remain and reverberate in hushed tones among the community, they really damage reputations and trust. What starts as an apparently factual article (and sometimes it is false facts), carefully selected to be the most evocative and enigmatic, it grows into salacious beliefs like toxic weeds.

I've heard so many different versions of events now; but I guess that's how gossip works. I still don't understand fully how people reading the same article can have so many different interpretations of it – especially when they become everything from the sublime to the ridiculous. They say artwork is subjective and that people can look at the same picture and see it differently; well, it turns out short editorial copy is the same.

I suppose it's amusing that with all the rumours going around, I found out soooooo much about myself that I didn't already know. I have worked hard to see the funny side and to be grateful for the good that comes from adversity. So, I want to say a BIG thank you to everyone who gossiped for making me the centre of their worlds. If nothing else, it brought friends out into the light and weeded foes out of the shadows. Plus, I was centre of attention for a while – who doesn't love that? (Well, I don't really. That's why I had my willy reduction. More about that later...)

It's a strange truth that the people who know you least always have the most to say during times of controversy and trial. It was definitely true during this time for me. But the people who mattered to me knew the truth and didn't judge or chastise – instead, they reached out with love. I received a few lovely messages of support, especially from my girlfriend who was amazing!

As always, my parents were my rock. My dad says people are always quick to believe the bad things they hear about good people. I guess Dad was always going to have my back. When he saw the article online, he sent me this amazing text message: 'Let it go! Just like the weather storm today, once they get it out of their system, it will blow over. We love you.' His words helped get me through the stress and anguish.

In many ways, the article pushed me hard, and I had to dig deep to find the good over the bad. With determination, I faced the turbulence head on, held my head up high, and carried on cleaning. I had meetings with the majority of my clients face to face, told them what happened, and offered them transparency and honesty. Thankfully, they accepted it, and continued to use my company. You see, cleaners are in a position of trust. For many places, I am a key holder, and I have access to all sorts of valuable and confidential things, so this could have ruined my business completely.

Aside from destroying a business and livelihoods, there are other ways rumour-mongering devastates lives. So, the next time you hear gossip, don't repeat it unless you know the truth. And even then, think first whether there is anything to be gained from passing on the details. Your comments could ruin someone's wellbeing and could even push them to have suicidal thoughts. The worry people suffer when going through events like these is enormous – and the courts are paid to judge so you don't have to! Thankfully this didn't happen to me, but that was because I was surrounded by good people who cared about me. I always had someone to turn to in my darkest moments.

Plus, I always have my humour. Laughter really is the best medicine and joking about the most traumatic things helps break the tension. The first thing I thought when I read the article was, *It looks like I won't be doing my next book signing at the library!*

However, this was not a laughing matter. So, before I share with you as much as I can about this case, I just want to thank the article for getting one bit right: "The books were stolen by an unknown thief." Despite what some of the gossips would have you believe, I did not steal these books. The police and the courts accepted this, and that's why I was never charged with theft. I've never been a thief. Aside from not wanting or needing to steal – doing so would be stupid – it would be far riskier for the reputation of a cleaning company; even just a hint of light-fingeredness would lose me clients. I mean, we have cleaned sooooo many places over the years, and if anything had gone missing from these places, I'm pretty sure people would have quickly pointed the finger. The sad thing is, if anything ever goes missing at any place of work, suspicion always falls on the cleaners first!

But I'm rambling, and I can hear you asking, what happened? And why did you plead guilty? Well, let me tell you about it…

I pleaded guilty against my legal advice. I will explain why shortly, but here's a section of the email from my solicitor outlining their viewpoint after the first magistrates' hearing:

Dear Matthew

Exeter Magistrates' Court – concealing criminal property

I was very pleased to be able to represent you at court. You were adamant with me that you wanted to plead guilty to the offences in order to put this matter behind you. I had previously emailed you my concerns about whether a guilty plea was appropriate, but you wanted to get the maximum credit and you entered your guilty pleas to the two charges.

So, let me take you back to beginning of the story. This all began when we undertook some relief cleaning for the council. I became aware of books going missing when we were asked about them. Apparently, lots of legal books had gone missing and I was asked if I knew anything about it. I replied that I didn't, but the truth is, later on, I had my suspicions.

The person on the phone then claimed they were asking a limited number of people who had access to this secure legal department, and that my cooperation helped with the investigation. I laughed out loud when she said that it was a secure area; the area in question was accessed by a four-digit door code written on a Post-it note just inside the cleaning cupboard door which was always left open. Let's just say 'secure' was a misnomer! In reality, it could have been accessed by anyone, especially when the Post-it note clearly stated, 'solicitor door code'.

I don't want to slag the council off as it makes me look bitter and twisted, which I'm not at all! I'm very thankful to the council for giving me so much work over the years. There are a lot of good people who work there, however, like most public sector places in my experience, there are too many coaches and not enough players. This means mistakes happen and everyone tries to slide the blame elsewhere, like dirty grease off a Tefal pan.

Anyway, moving on... About ten days later, I had another call from the same council lady informing me that a few books had turned up and asking if I was sure I didn't know anything about the other missing books. Again, I answered no. Then, the very next day I got a call from a different person asking me to return all the keys I held for the council and that there was going to be a criminal investigation into the missing books. Shocked, I thanked him for the work he had given me and returned all the keys promptly.

For context, as a cleaning company, we undertook a lot of

house clearances and office removals, and we would frequently be asked to take stuff either to land fill or a recycling centre. As previously mentioned, we would sell anything of value either online or at auctions. This seemed to be sensible – we would make a few quid and the things would be reused instead of being dumped. At the time all of this was happening, I was also in the process of moving house and was having a major clear-out of CDs, books, and other items which I didn't want to take to my new home. This meant I was selling a lot of stuff online. It also meant other people were selling stuff for me, and putting their own stuff on my active accounts. It also meant I wasn't as secure with my account information as I should have been. I mean, not council-insecure, but still. I wasn't monitoring any of this and I should have been.

So, I moved house. Due to the loss of the council contract, I downsized the cleaning company and unfortunately had to lay off some staff. The council was quite a big contract for me, so at the time it felt like an enormous blow. It seemed ridiculous to think I would jeopardise this work for a few books. However, in hindsight, losing the council contract has been the best thing to happen to me as I have such a better quality of life now.

Eight more months passed after handing back the keys to the council and life settled into a new rhythm. So, I was a little surprised when the police knocked on my door. They wanted to ask me some questions about the books! They informed me that 17 books were missing from the council, and it appeared 13 of them were sold among a batch of books by an account linked to me and the cleaning company. They wanted to check my house to see if I had the missing 4 books – which I didn't. And I didn't say anything I was thinking, either. I didn't know anything for sure, and I didn't want to speculate when I thought it was just a few books.

They informed me that they were doing an investigation and they thought I had sold 300-odd books. They thought the 13 stolen books from the council offices were among them, and they asked me if I could come to the station for an 'informal' chat.

Now, this is the bit where I should have been honest about how the books appeared to have come into my possession and were sold via an account linked to me – but the reality is I panicked and was worried about my company's reputation. I thought I could be clever and outwit the police! Ruddy idiot that I was! So, I gave them a receipt from an auction I had attended where I purchased five shelves full of books which came as a job lot with other stuff I wanted. I thought, stupidly, *It's only 13 books which have been apparently stolen… surely this is nothing?* I just wanted it all to go away! In hindsight, honesty would have been the best policy, and this is something I deeply regret.

I didn't hear any more from the police, and as far as I was concerned it was over and done with. I had given them an explanation and I thought I wouldn't hear any more from them.

While all this was going on, my dad was diagnosed with prostate cancer. I'm not a deeply religious man, however, I said a prayer at the time that if any more came from the police I would plead guilty to any charges brought in exchange for dad's recovery. A further seven months passed, Dad had just finished his cancer treatment, and the same day he got the all-clear, I had a letter from the courts informing me I was being charged with selling 17 books stolen from the council and 98 library books. It was such a bittersweet day; I was overjoyed my dad had the all-clear, but inside I was crying my eyes out.

I confided in my best friend. I was shocked to find out about the 98 library books as I knew nothing about these, not even a small suspicion – and nothing had been said when the police questioned me about the missing legal books. Some will question why I pleaded guilty. I never stole any books, hence I never got charged with this. There was, however, a paper trail which led to one of my bank accounts which made it look like I had sold some, and I could not argue with this. I certainly couldn't prove my innocence without incriminating others. The books were sold via one of my sites and I had to take responsibility for them. Apparently, the books made me £200 quid. Out of the 263 books sold on my accounts, 113 were apparently stolen.

At this point, I had two months before my court hearing. Harbouring a well of worries, I kept it to myself, my best friend, and my girlfriend. I felt like I was living on death row, mired in the calm before the storm. But I learned it's true what people say: worrying never helps any situation. Two weeks before my court hearing, I finally confided in my parents; they were amazing! They supported me and told a few others close to me to ensure I was surrounded by love and care. So, it also taught me not to keep these worries in – it gives the worries far more power than they deserve.

I've never been more nervous in my life than the day of my court appearance. I dressed up in a suit and thought it was a good thing to look smart. God! I was overdressed! While I waited outside the courtroom, I felt like I was in the holding pen of a Jeremy Kyle show. The other people going into court looked like smackheads; it was upsettingly tragic! One couple were outside drinking from a bottle of whiskey! Judging by the smell, it was obvious some of the people were homeless. I could smell them, and I was wearing a face mask! I can't imagine how bad it would have been without a mask! It turns out there are some upsides to Coronavirus! I sometimes think this when someone farts in an enclosed space – thank God for face masks!

An hour before my court hearing, my solicitor had a final meeting. After it, he informed me that if I was willing to pay back the estimated value for the stolen books and plead guilty, it would be over quickly. The estimated price was £4,300! As extortionate as this was, particularly as they had estimated my gains at £200, I agreed to this. As far as I was concerned, I just wanted the matter to go away. And I wanted to honour the promise I had made for my father's health. At that moment, I did not care about the money, truth, or justice – just completion.

I entered the court, gave my name and address, and pleaded guilty to the two charges. However, the magistrates could not deal with me that day as the prosecution wouldn't drop the accusation related to the Proceeds of Crime Act. They thought I had gained my wealth through immoral earnings and wanted to investigate further. They would not accept that I had worked my ass off! Plus, I am pretty good at Monopoly! Just saying!

So, four weeks passed, and another court date came round, only to then be told the case couldn't be heard as there had been a cock-up. Probation had not been informed of my hearing, and in this country, people cannot be sentenced without a meeting with a probation officer first. I was also made aware that the council and the library had received all the books back from the online retailer, so at this point, we were expecting my fine to be minimal – everything had been recovered. They had all the books back. At this stage, I was annoyed as the process was dragging on and on. Christ! I had pleaded guilty months ago and I was willing to pay the full compensation – I couldn't understand why this couldn't be dealt with immediately!

That evening I had a text from a girl who works for me. Before any resolution to the case, before any chance of telling the truth, the story had been reported and was all over social media and the press release at start of this chapter. It wasn't a great feeling, to be fair; I felt like I was being treated as guilty regardless and speculation ruled. My heart sank when I first read the article through. Luckily, I wasn't on Facebook, so I didn't have to see it unfold myself. But I was told it was shared a few times – that would have been mortifying to see. I couldn't let it affect me; I just had to dust myself down and face the music. It's a horrible feeling though when you know people are talking about you, especially when you can't do or say anything to defend yourself.

Despite the rumbling negativity in my wider community, most people I dealt with day to day were supportive. Out of all my customers, I only lost one contract because of the incident. Plus, I had loads of messages of support for which I was truly grateful. Since my dad is a community and pastoral worker, he knows the neighbourhood well. He had loads of people from the church phone him and say they were praying for me and offering money towards my fine. My dad obviously declined their offers, but it meant a lot to know kindness was so close by. Part of me thought, *Let's not look a gift-horse in the mouth here… The Lord works in mysterious ways!*

But not all of my family responded with generosity; some of them responded with wry humour instead. My brothers unleashed their joking in different ways: my younger brother offered to take the blame if I bunged him some cash. The older one, well, once he got his head around it, with his dry sense of humour, said, "Well, at least I won't get a book for Christmas this year!"

So, after four more stressful weeks, the final court appearance came round. While walking to court, I passed a Big Issue seller who had two pigeons on his arm which he was stroking and feeding. I found this fascinating and it kind of put things into perspective for me. No matter what is going on, there are so many people worse off than you. This guy had nothing; he was homeless, but he still gave his food away to feed the birds. He reminded me that love and joy can be found in the smallest of moments. I made a mental note to draw out some money and give it to him when I came out of the courthouse.

I got to the courthouse at 8:30am expecting an early start, but it got to 9:15am and I still hadn't been called in for my meeting. I sat watching the judges casually strolling into work as if they had all the time in the world to catch up on their apparent backlog of cases that were mounting up because of COVID-19. God! I don't know what time they were meant to start work, but believe me, most of them didn't walk in until way past nine – and they were casual about it. I couldn't see them rushing or going the extra mile to help out the country! They are a law unto themselves, that's for sure!

Finally, I had my probation meeting. Ruddy hell! The lady

taking it was stunning – I had the most inappropriate erection ever! It was as though someone had poured boiling water on my willy as it ballooned in size. I am joking, but after watching all those old, stuffy men saunter around, it was great to see someone young and normal! She wore a white blouse with a pair of tight trousers and believe me her ass cheeks looked as tight as the skin of a tambourine! Bang it, baby!

But panic not, I didn't slip into Charlie Charmhead mode (or Sleazy Sam mode, as my editor says). I remembered what my barrister told me: look remorseful and engage your brain before you speak. That said, I had to hold my hands in front of me to hide my boner. Sleazing aside, she was lovely, professional, and kind – she put me at ease. She said she would recommend to the judge for my sentence to be community service.

After my probation meeting, I had a quick chat with my barrister and solicitor who both told me it would be sorted that day. They hoped we would avoid going down the POCA route (Proceeds of Crime Act) as this would mean it would drag on for several more months while they completed an audit of my accounts. But then they shared a bit of bad news… My case was being heard by a part-time judge due to the backlog of cases. I thought, *Oh shit!* I remembered what it was like at school when supply teachers took lessons when your normal teacher was off; they didn't have a ruddy clue what they were doing! I thought this would likely be the same, but they told me not to worry as he was a good judge. I didn't feel reassured since they had felt the need to raise it as an issue… But there was nothing I could do, so I tried to put my growing sense of doom to the back of my mind.

The time came, and I entered my court hearing. It was

strange because of COVID; the prosecution attended via Zoom, and there were only nine of us in the room. This included me, the judge, his assistant, my barrister and solicitor, my fit-assed probation officer, two security guards, and one reporter. What a motley crew!

I stood to give my name and plea then sat down to hear the prosecution give their evidence to the judge. It was a bizarre feeling not being able to say anything. It was as though I was some kind of ghost, present but not present. I was in the room, but these people were deciding my fate, appearing to disregard anything I had said. The fact is, I had made the prosecution's case easy for them since I had already pleaded guilty at the earlier court hearing. But it was interesting to hear how they made the evidence point to me; they even fabricated some of it to make it fit their version of events!

The judge praised a council official who apparently did most of the investigation on behalf of the police. I couldn't hold back a smile at that point; I just thought, *Christ! Some investigation! She didn't even catch the thief!* She would probably be good at Cluedo… It was Mr Peacock, with a candlestick in the library! Well, at least she got the location right!

So after about fifteen minutes, the prosecution and my barrister chatted with the judge, and then the judge gave his verdict: "You have stolen from the public!" he announced emphatically!

My Barrister interrupted him and said, "No, he's not been charged with stealing the books…"

But the judge carried on, "I am going to make an example of you. You are in a position of trust which you have breached. Therefore, I am giving you 300 community hours which is the most I can give you." My heart sank, and he continued. "However, I can't set a compensation figure due to the CPS putting POCA on file, so that will be settled in due course."

Ruddy hell! 300 hours! I renamed the Judge Pepsi Max since he gave me the maximum. What annoyed me most was that there was no reason to go down the Proceeds of Crime Act route as I had offered to pay the money back – even the money I wasn't responsible for. This meant it would drag on for another six months for them to do a forensic report on my accounts. This is obviously what then happened, and surprise, surprise! They found nothing other than a successful business. I had told them repeatedly I had earned my wealth through hard work and smart decision making, but they were convinced a cleaner couldn't be rich without immoral actions.

The whole thing was a farce, particularly since the books were recovered and I had pleaded guilty and offered to pay compensation to the value of the books. It wasted sooooooo much public money and took up sooooo much court time when it could have been an open-and-shut case and the council ended up with less money than was first offered.

When the judge said he was giving me 300 hours of community service, my initial thought was that I wouldn't let it bother me – I was used to working eighty hours a week so I thought I'd bash it out in no time. Sadly, I then found out later community service is as crap as the court system!

The general feeling was that I had been treated heavy-handedly. My barrister thought my sentence was harsh, especially considering I didn't steal the books. But that's life; sometimes you're the pigeon and sometimes you're the statue. And it was my own fault. I should have been honest from the outset. I tried to cover the crime, thereby incriminating myself. Sentence given, I had to do the time: simples!

Of course, the burning question you want to ask me is, who did steal the books? Were the books even stolen in the first place? The truth is I might know more than I let on … but if I did know, do you think I'd be stupid enough to put it in a book? Theft is a serious crime, so I'm not going to make light of that, but I have my reasons for keeping quiet. Not everyone makes their decisions from the same place, and I had made a promise to God for the health of my father. Granted, it's not as simple as that, but this is my book, and the theft is not my story.

The bit that is my story is that it was a serious event, harrowing to experience, and surprising in the ineptitude and idiocy of bureaucracy. Additionally, by keeping quiet, I risked going to prison for money laundering. However, sometimes, saying nothing is the best answer. Silence means you can't be misquoted, and I've never been one to shift the responsibility onto others – even if they should have shouldered it. The burden fell to me, so I carried it. Plus, I love the fact that I'm old and wise enough to know staying silent is far more powerful than having the last word. Of course, the flip side of the argument is people with things to hide never have much to say! You might side with the gossips and assume I was more involved than I admitted. I hope not. If I'm guilty of anything, it's not saying what I thought at the beginning; I'm not guilty of being light-fingered.

But the anguish didn't end there. I had a few days of reprieve, and I started to believe it was all over. But then, a few days later, it all began to kick off again. On the Monday afternoon after my court hearing, I was browsing online and went onto the Devonlive website. Up flashed a picture of me coming out of the courthouse with a massive headline: "Library cleaner caught selling stolen library books". My heart sank like a rock. After reading the article, I genuinely thought that was the end of the cleaning business. Not only did the reporter publish a picture of me (thankfully he got my good side), but he had also written in the article that I was the one who stole the books. I was incensed! How dare he write this! I was never charged with theft! I called my solicitor straight away and told him what I had seen on the internet. He told me to contact the editor directly. At 10pm that night the editor sent me an email to say he was sorry and that he would drop the story. This happened, but the damage was already done – the story had been out there for some time anyway. But then, I found I had bigger things to worry about…

Every Tuesday my local paper, the Mid Devon Gazette, is distributed. Lo and behold, my story was in there. The very same day, it was printed in the Western Morning News, and both articles were written by the same reporter as on the Devonlive site. It turns out the Mid Devon Gazette, the Western Morning News, and Devonlive are all part of the same news group. And, to add insult to the injury, someone at the gazette had edited the original story and changed it from 'Burd SOLD the books' to 'Burd STOLE the books'. Whereas the Western morning news kept to SOLD the books. I mean, I know both are crimes, but these are different things! And now it was in print and being posted through letterboxes all over the county.

Yet again, bureaucracy was about to make everything complicated and allow everyone to cover their arses but mine. This was a serious case of false reporting, and I believed someone at the Gazette had altered this on purpose. I guess it's a small town and they need news stories, but I wasn't happy for it to be at my expense, or indeed jeopardise any more of my staff's jobs if trust in me waned further. Firstly, I contacted the editor of the Gazette a few times but had no answer or reply – it's typical really; being unavailable is the predictable first line of defence; it's just a shame he was a coward. In the end I reported the paper to IPSO, the Independent Press Standards Organisation. You'd think this would be straight forward, and the papers would have to retract the articles and offer an apology – even if it was in small print on page 27. But I didn't get anywhere because in summing up the judge had used the words, "You stole from the public." We could all see in the records that my barrister corrected him, but since the statement was there, they could print it. This was their justification for using the verb 'stole' in their articles. Apparently, they didn't give a shit about accuracy, just about printing the most dramatic story. Print press is dying a death and they don't seem to care anymore who they harm in their failing attempts to save themselves. It's just another example of people not giving a damn about other people.

But then, there's no point me being bitter and angry about this: life is too short. Although I must admit, I have never bought the Gazette since, and I won't again – not just out of petty revenge, but I know for sure there's no truth or integrity in their journalism, plus the paper is crap and just full of adverts. Furthermore, I have encouraged a few places we clean, especially communal places like elderly people's homes, to just buy one copy instead of buying residents one each. So far, I have probably cost them £11.20 per week in lost sales! But then, every penny counts!

I'm not bitter at all, honest!

Thankfully, even after all the bad press, I didn't lose any more work. If anything, I gained quite a bit – so the old adage of all publicity is good publicity works to some extent, no matter how uncomfortable the process. I guess it meant people heard about me, and if they asked around, they would have heard good reviews. I got some bad comments on various sites, however, there were some pretty funny ones too which were entertaining. Plus, when my brother posted both the Western Morning News and the Gazette's articles on social media, a lot of people were disgusted by the false reporting. So, I guess we helped open some people's eyes about the bad practise of the press.

As I am sure you can imagine, not everyone was gracious. Some of the worst comments people added when the post went live are a bit too rude to publish here, however they were along the lines of me being a greedy bastard. Crazily, some were extremely personal attacks from people who didn't even know me! But there were some funny ones too, such as, 'Did he forget his library card?' But my favourite one was, 'Never let the facts get in the way of a good story', which could be the motto I take from this whole experience.

I must admit, I hit rock bottom once this was in the press. People kept telling me it would all blow over, but it felt like time was moving at a glacial pace. At every turn, there was more judgement and negativity. My dad reminded me there's only sixty minutes in the darkest hour, and it is so true. I try to hold this saying in mind now; however bad things feel at the time, it will pass.

Whatever you think of my actions, I didn't deserve this. I felt ridiculed wherever I turned, and everyone felt they had a right to comment. Regardless of my actions, I had paid my dues – more than my dues. I didn't need a trial by public, with the whole of Devon out with their digital pitchforks. I had only ever wanted to get into cleaning to sex up the industry – I wanted to earn a penny or two, and they clearly needed a hunky bloke like me about. I never craved fame, and especially not notoriety. In my eyes, people should only be in the newspaper three times in their lives: when they are born, when they marry, and when they die. And here I was, a petty celebrity that everyone thought they could gossip about and deride.

My friends and family think someone had it in for me. This could be true; maybe someone was a little jealous or vengeful for a reason I don't know about. I don't know about this. As far as I'm concerned, I'm nothing special. Well, I'm not now I have had my willy reduction operation; I only have the one now! Ah! Well! Laughter is the best way of dealing with most things.

After another week passed, I had a call from my probation officer to arrange my community service. He was a little shocked with the number of hours I got. "300 hours for selling 200 quid's worth of books!" he exclaimed. Something didn't sound right to him, but there was nothing we could do. Besides, I know I am moaning about the legal system, and I don't want to indulge that too far if I can help it.

Due to COVID, my first probation meeting was on the phone. It lasted over an hour, and it was basically to take all my details so I could book in my sessions and start working off my hours. I got 300 hours for selling 200 quid's worth of books! I'm not sure if I mentioned that before! The funny thing is, at first, he thought I must have been done for dealing! I can only assume he meant drugs as I'm not sure anyone has ever been done for being a book dealer!

"Roll up! Roll up! Come 'ere and see! I have some great literature! Originals, honest!" To be fair, my editor-cum-English-teacher would be well up for that! Anyway, moving on...

After going over the basic stuff like name and address details, he asked about my education and what sort of qualifications I had. He asked if I have any GCSEs. I told him I had an A in music. He then asked if there was anything else. I explained I was thick as shit at school. Then he asked if I had any skills like carpentry or bricklaying. I thought, *Christ! What does he want me to do? Does he want me to build a new library or something with my hours?* I said sorry, my skills were limited, but was a dab-hand with a bog brush and a mop.

Then the questions got weird, and I had no idea where he was going with them. He asked me what I thought about diversity. I said what, the group? I can't dance for toffee! However, if he wanted me to learn some street dancing to pay the community back, I was game. He said no, he meant working with people who are a different race or religion. I said I didn't have a problem, but I couldn't promise to always make PC jokes. To be honest, I thought he meant whether I would drop a rucksack joke around a Muslim, or if I would make a gangster joke to a black man. And in all honesty, I couldn't promise I wouldn't. I love a dodgy joke that crosses the line – and I love them in return too. There's plenty of jokes to make about Devonians and cleaners. But it turned out some of the people I met were an entirely different species of mankind.

Community service was certainly an eye-opener, and I

certainly met some interesting characters. During the induction, we were told the rules: no alcohol to be consumed before or during community service, the same went for drugs, nobody could bring weapons with them, and no violence. I thought this was all stuff which was common sense, but I discovered lots of people need this spelled out. One dick on the induction, who I will name Dopehead-Dave, asked, "Is carrying a machete classed as a weapon?" I just rolled my eyes!

The instructor then ran through the expectations of service. He said most people had between 40 and 300 hours of community service, and nobody needed to tell anyone why they got the hours or how many they got. Obviously, Dopehead-Dave piped up again, "Well, I've got 80 hours for nicking some cars!"

Fabulous news, Dopehead.

After the induction, we went for a taster session of litter picking in the afternoon. Why we needed a taster session, I don't know. It's not like we could dislike it and decide not to participate further. But we went along anyway, and it was in walking distance of the office.

"Where are we going?" Dopehead-Dave asked the probation officer who replied we were off to such-and-such church. "Oh! I know where that is! There's two expensive lawn mowers locked up in a cage outside, and my mate nicked the lead once on a nearby church!"

I just thought, *Ruddy hell! Dopehead-Dave has already cased the joint!* Perhaps the taster session was to whet the appetite for future criminal endeavours.

I then got talking to Drink-driver-Dave; he was only a young lad, and to be fair he was sound. I quite liked him. It turned out the advice to not share our crimes and punishments didn't last long. Drink-driver-Dave got 120 hours for driving while drunk, smashing into two cars, and running away from the scene. He was quite open about it, as Dopehead-Dave had been earlier. In the back of my mind, I thought, *Christ! I would have been better off nicking the mobile library van while drunk, crashing into two cars, and running off. I would have got less hours then!*

Same goes for stealing cars which was worth 220 less hours than selling a few books!

So, we arrived at the graveyard, which was a fitting place for my dignity to crawl away and die, and it also happened to be right next to a college. We were all given a high-viz jackets which had 'Community Payback' written on them. I felt like my career had reached a new high! We teamed up in pairs. Thankfully, Dopehead-Dave was with the probation guard, and I was with the normal lad. Dopehead-Dave piped up, "Shame college are not in today! We could see some fit-ass student girls!" I cringed a little and thought, thank God they weren't in. I'd rather nobody saw me like this, especially not young, hot, up-and-coming women who would not want our attention anyway.

So, we started litter picking around the grounds of the church. We found all sorts: beer cans, bras, needles… It was pretty rough, and sad too to think this is what was happening around the resting places of all these people.

While working, some young lads walked past, shouted at us, and lobbed an apple at us. My humiliation was complete. Thank God I went home to people who cared, a job that was successful, and my own independence – it meant I could bounce back. I could see why some people keep spiralling downwards. Community service is just a way to put you on show to the public and allow them to judge you again – like a freak show. As if all the torture and judgement in court, in the press, online, and in your community wasn't enough. If I hadn't already been made to feel like scum, I did then in that graveyard.

But there were some upsides. Due to COVID, community service options were a little limited so we were told that we could do 30% of our hours via online courses. In my case that meant 90 hours, which was a bonus! I was happy to get some courses in – and I thought I could just half pay attention anyway if they were dull – wink, wink! Let's just say I fully planned to keep my camera off.

When we finally got out into the community, work ranged from working on a farm for the disabled to cutting grass verges in various towns and villages. Unfortunately, they only allowed us to work one day a week, so it took best part of seven months to complete all my hours. I really enjoyed it, to be fair, especially the farm for the disabled – and I don't mean the animals were disabled; it was a farm for disabled people to go and work on. This was rewarding and interesting.

I will remember the characters I met and the stories I heard all my life. Some were poignant, some were funny, many were surprising. One guy turned up two hours late while drinking a can of cider and wondered why he got turned away that day. Another guy couldn't accept he should be doing community service. He was apparently convicted for beating someone up then robbing him; however, he said he didn't rob the bloke, his mate did! He was fuming that he got 80 hours for this! Another guy I met told me he was a florist… It turned out he grew cannabis.

Our probation officer also told us some funny stories.

One community service group were planting bulbs, and someone decided to plant some in the shape of words so the flowers would grow later to spell out 'Fuck Off' in a colourful, floral display. Of course, growing flowers are a slow business, so nobody knew about this until the day the flowers bloomed their expletives. What a lovely welcome for the town of Torquay!

The stupid thing is, in our group I was known as top dog as I had the most hours. I felt like a mafia don! When some of the guys asked me how many hours I had and I said 300, they all took a step back as though they were scared of me! That was until I told them about the books!

Most of all, my experience taught me crime doesn't pay, that's for sure! But as my probation officer said, if you're going to do crime, just don't get caught!

CHAPTER 24

Foot a Sock in It!

It can be said that I consider myself a bit of a comedian. I love making people laugh, and I also believe laughter is a great medicine. I even quite like offensive humour – you know the kind of joke, where you say exactly the thing that is inappropriate or rude, but because it's inappropriate or rude. However, while I might like this kind of humour, I can't promise to always check with my audience first. In fact, sometimes offending people actually makes the joke funnier.

That said, I sometimes manage to put my foot in it totally – I don't just manage to wedge it in my mouth, but sometimes it's covered in poop too: the jokes are just too hard to swallow.

One example where I said the wrong thing was to a customer after addressing a mistake we had made. We used to undertake a regular weekly clean at a posh bungalow; I say used to… There is a chance that my jokes contributed to the end of this customer relationship. However, I didn't make the mistake – that was one of my employees.

All our work for this customer was hunky-dory for ages. That was until one of my cleaners cocked up one day while cleaning the kitchen. He accidentally switched the gas hob on by mistake, and didn't notice, leaving gas filling the home like a balloon ready to burst.

The owner came home from work around five hours after we finished… and nearly blew the bungalow up! You see, the owner smoked, and normally lit up as he arrived home. Thankfully, on that particular day, he smoked in his car on the drive home. Apparently, on his normal return he walks into the house still smoking. Thank God he didn't that day, as all that would have been left of him would be his smoking shoes!

He phoned me and went mental! In fairness, he had a valid point! It was a dangerous mistake to make, and it took the house ages to air. But raging furiously doesn't help as anger just creates an uneasy atmosphere. And in awkward situations, my mouth takes over. And this was prime awkwardness, with lashings of embarrassment to boot. My mouth decided to help me out.

I said, "They do say smoking kills!"

I'm not sure the joke helped break the tension in any way. In fact, there's a chance it just added insult to injury.

But yelling doesn't make things better. I had already accepted responsibility and apologised, so the yelling was just him releasing hot air and hotter emotions. It made it impossible to offer any way to resolve the issue. As he continued ranting, I stopped him mid-bellow with the words, "With all due respect…" which translates to, "Shut up, you dick, and let me talk!"

This reminds me, don't you think the worst thing you can do when someone is ranting full on in your face is to smile at them? It winds them up even more! But sometimes it is hard to resist. I guess I should be thankful this complaint happened over the phone – I was grinning ear to ear after my smoking joke, and I was smiling hard at the ridiculousness of him not listening to me apologise.

The outcome was that we stopped working for him. It was our fault, but I do not feel sorry for the loss.

I still think this old gas-lighting man, who nearly blew his head off in a scene reminiscent of Hot Fuzz because of us and not the greater good, was a bit strange. He told us one of the first things he does every day when he wakes up is check his mouse trap. He had a cat that loved hunting. It kept bringing in mice and releasing them! He used to say to us that nothing made him happier at the start of the day than seeing a dead mouse in the trap! I thought, what a strange thing to say! Out of every possible thing that could bring him happiness, from love to nice food, travelling or spending time with friends, out of every single joyful possibility, his top choice was finding a dead mouse in the trap in the morning. I guess it takes all sorts to make the world go around.

Anyway, back to my gaping trouble hole. My mouth gets me in trouble a fair bit. Another instance happened when we used to undertake the cleaning for a cancer charity. I was already incensed with this client as I regularly saw first-hand how much money they wasted. It really annoyed me. For example, they bought the most expensive paper towels for their toilets. I offered them an alternative at half the price, but they refused. It might seem a little thing, but charities can't really be flash with the cash, surely?

They wasted money on big things too. The chief executive drove a top-of-the-range Mercedes which cost as much to lease as the average monthly take-home wages. I was sure that money would be better used elsewhere! Anyway, I'm ranting... Perhaps to disguise my guilt... Well, here goes!

One day in the warehouse, where volunteers and paid staff worked doing various jobs, I was talking to these two ladies, and we were having a bit of banter. We were talking about carrier bags and how some women were quite hard to get into, almost like a carrier bag where you have to add a bit of spit to gain entry. As I'm sure you can imagine, this conversation was already offensive, funny, and crude. Just randomly, I pointed to one large lady and said, "I imagine you wouldn't have any problems. I bet you are more of a Bag-For-Life... easy access!"

Anyway, she complained, and I lost the contract. It was thoughtless, but I do take the mick out of my dick, and my friends and I insult each other constantly, so I suppose I'm just not always good at knowing other people's boundaries. Rudeness and insults are a fundamental part of my social traditions. I just thought it was funny. She did look a bit tough and rough and probably used a brick as a tampon however I obviously apologised, but I guess there are jokes an apology doesn't make up for. As a joker, this is something I have to accept, and I learn from my mistakes. These days, I definitely hold back on commenting on the moistness of a woman's vagina until I know her better.

However, I also think they were looking for an excuse to get rid of me after I pointed out how much money they could save on various items. I don't think I aligned with their ethos; the chief exec wasn't about to invite me round for dinner with the wife even before bag-gate.

Despite moments like these, I don't always regret crossing the line. I have used a few polite insults over the years when people annoy me, and it can be a good way to diffuse my rage or the incident unfolding. When I disagree with someone, I say things like, "This is what you call a clash of personalities... if you had one!" Incredibly, sometimes it breaks the ice and makes people laugh.

I like adding on something surprising to compliments, such as my response to one member of staff who was celebrating her 40th birthday and was finding it daunting. In an attempt to cheer her up, I said, "Don't worry, you look like a 25-year-old... from behind!" I'm not sure if it worked, but it made me laugh.

Don't get me wrong, I frequently question many of my words and actions, and I often can't explain them. I remember once for a laugh trying to hypnotise one of my girlfriends by swaying my willy in front of her eyes, saying, "Follow my eye. Your eyes are getting heavy, you are feeling sleepy."

She was quite a serious lady and didn't see the funny side. She just told me to grow up as I was acting like a five-year-old kid!

And then there was the time I was on a date with a lady, and she was talking about her happy place. She said, "When I feel sad, I go to my happy place."

I said, "What, Greggs?" It didn't go down too well. In my defence she was a big lady who looked like she enjoyed the odd cake or two – and who doesn't?

And another time, I was on a date and the lady in question asked me how many people I had slept with. Of course, I lied and made it sound less than I actually had. She turned to me and said, "I've slept with 27."

I said, "Flip me! You don't look like a slapper!" The look on her face was priceless. As someone who has slept with a fair number of women, I am in no place to judge – I just thought it was funny!

And there's more. Another time I was about to have sex with a lady. I was pretty much at the point of entry when my phone rang. I decided to answer it and said, "I can't talk – about to go through a tunnel." Apparently I ruined the moment!

But it's not just me who constantly says the offensive thing. Perhaps it's my hometown's humour. My mate was at a funeral once and the vicar was talking about a young lad who died, which is tragic. However, the vicar, in his speech, said, "George died doing something he loved."

My mate whispered to his girlfriend next to him, "Heroin." She couldn't stop laughing! Heroin wasn't the cause – it was drink driving – but apparently George was a car enthusiast who also was partial to the odd recreational drug!

I guess we all say and do funny things; sometimes they are defining, sometimes they are regretful, sometimes they make no sense at all. I once got asked something odd by a client who had multiple pets. She asked me, if I had the choice would I prefer to step in dog or cat shit? I just thought, at the end of the day they are both shit, and I'd prefer to avoid both. Her grass was always covered in both dog and cat shit, and she said she always prefers stepping in cat shit. I just thought, why don't you just pick it up, you lazy cow! It was the oddest menu I have ever been offered, and I wondered if my answer might give me a preferred route through her garden, like some sort of shit-based assault course.

It's safe to say my mouth has gotten me into trouble over the years, but I normally try to joke my way out of it. I suffer from the classic disorder of not thinking before I speak, and I certainly don't have a filter. Thankfully, I have only lost one contract because of it, and that was the cancer charity cleaning contract I mentioned earlier. Generally, I find a way to turn things back to humour, either by making the jokes even more ridiculous, or by turning the humour on myself. I certainly don't mean to upset anyone. However, I also don't like the idea of banning joking just because it's offensive – I think we should just remember it is a joke. If we can't laugh at ourselves and the crappy things going on in the world, we're all destined to be angry and depressed. That said, you might judge me more harshly... Let me continue confessing to you.

I remember going into an office once and a lady who worked there had her hair down which was different to normal. She had long black hair, and it almost looked like a mane on a horse.

I said to her that she looked very horsey today, to which she replied, "What, because of my teeth?"

So, I continued, "Well, no, they are big, but I was more talking about your lovely hair which is almost like Black Beauty's"

Now, I was meaning to talk about the hair, but she looked shocked that I commented her teeth were big. This was a tricky moment. Turning on my fabulous charm, I said she had lovely teeth; however, I wouldn't take her to Africa just in case the poached her for ivory.

Thankfully, she found that funny, but the more I tried to dig myself out of the hole I created, the bigger the hole became. Suddenly, I was on the edge of a massive caldera about to blow!

A worse time was when I was at a petrol station filling up and the lady behind the counter had the ugliest looking pitbull I have ever seen. I told her that I looked like that when I was younger. She responded by telling me everyone normally says her dog is ugly. And this is where I probably should have just smiled and left. But I didn't.

I said, "No, not ugly. I looked more retarded!"

The look on her face was priceless, but not all priceless things are good. Thinking back, I'm not sure that joke was PC. At least it wasn't insulting her; it was about me... and her dog. Although I guess joking that a dog has some sort of disability is not a good start to a conversation with a stranger.

I love to have a laugh with clients and customers as life is too short. They say laughter is the best medicine, and I agree, unless of course you are asthmatic. Some people in life will either laugh with you or at you, and I suppose both are better than no laughter at all.

I have noticed the older the ladies I work for, the more flirtatious I become. Some older people you can have a right laugh with. One lady we cleaned for each week was amazing, and I'm sure we were the highlight of her week. She loved a bit of cheeky banter. I'm also pretty sure I used to give her a lady boner despite the fact she was in her 80s. She was delighted with any kind of sexual innuendo and teasing. But having cleaned her toilet after she had used it, I'm not sure I'd ever dine on her lady sandwich however desperate I become!

She was a vibrant lady, and I learned a lot from her. I guess, you can either accept you are getting old and laugh about it or sit around and be a miserable cow like some other customers I've had. This lady used to have big pillows up one side of her bed to stop her falling out. However, she always had them on the side facing the wall, so she was never going to fall out that side of the bed! When I pointed it out to her, she calmly said, "I thought they might be on the wrong side." As if this was a normal mistake to make. However, she had dementia, so by the time she remembered she had to move them, she forgot again.

She was often the instigator of sexual banter. I was bent over at her place once and she tapped me on the bum with her walking stick. The first time she did it I ignored it, the second time I joked with her and said, "Don't damage my best feature!"

It's funny having people comment on you having a good bum – it's not something you can easily check for yourself. Previous girlfriends commented on my 'perfect' bum being my 'best feature'. I'm not sure I saw it myself; it's not that perfect, it has a gurt crack down the middle of it!

Sometimes, my mouth isn't the problem. Sometimes it's just the rambling thoughts inside my rambling mind and I realise my chuckling is distasteful. This is clear whenever I think about myself ageing. As I approach my 46th year on this planet, I am showing the signs of wear and tear. Don't get me wrong, the bodywork is in not bad condition, however, the greying of my hair is certainly making me look a lot older than I really am. But I love fishing for compliments. I love it when ladies say that grey is distinguished or that everyone loves a silver fox. Some of them then say, "Just look at Philip Schofield!" Well, when I think about it, I don't wish to be like Philip Schofield. He came out the closet after God knows how many years of marriage, and that seems like more stress than it's worth! That's not a compliment; it's a warning!

I mean, I can't help but think about his poor wife, but my thoughts ramble into strange places! What got me was when everyone commended him for what he did, and that's all good, so little attention was paid to his suffering wife. Although, she must have known something wasn't quite right after that many years of marriage, surely? I'm not saying he kept going for the bum hole each time they had sex, but... I did feel sorry for her though, in the same way I feel the pain for Siamese twins who share the same bum and one of them turns out to be gay...

Although I'm not obsessed with anal sex. I promise!

How do thoughts like this get inside my head? And once they're there, why do they continue to grow?

Anyway, where was I? Oh yes, my sprawling offensiveness and my greying hair. My brain decided to help me out and offered me an idea that was clear and smart. I decided to try and dye my hair for the first time ever. I didn't realise how technical this could be! I kept the product in for just 10 minutes. The packet suggested 20 minutes, but as it was my first time, I thought I'd ease myself into it gently. I'm sure many of you can guess where this is going.

The box claimed the dye was medium brown. Well, I placed the product on my hair, waited the required time, and then washed it off, eager to see my newly youthful self. Ruddy hell! Medium brown, my ass! It should have been Hint of Ginger! I had to check the package to make sure I got Just for Men and not Just for Orangutans! I looked like an advert for safe sex.

I guess being a joker and unafraid of cracking out an insult or two means I then have to be ready to take them in return. After a couple of weeks and many washes with blue shampoo, my hair began to look more natural. However, before it settled down, lots of people commented, "Your hair is ginger!" while also laughing at me. Their pointing felt as though they thought I might not have noticed myself. During this couple of weeks, I learned that just as cleaners get branded, so do ginger people. All I could think about was setting up a GoFundMe page: 'Every year, through no fault of their own, millions of kids are born ginger. With your help we can find a cure!'

But wait! I know what you are going to say! I brought this upon myself: I caused my gingerness, and I have spent my years cracking out unsavoury jokes. Plus, I had decided to dye my hair and foolishly only left it on for half the recommended time. Flip me! I had it all going for me! I was a cleaner with ginger hair! Does life get any better? When a few ladies commented, joking at my expense, I quickly hit back, "Red in the head, great in bed!" Having a comeback was my way of dealing with it. To be fair, thanks to people like Ed Sheeran and Prince Harry, being ginger has become cool – but it's not equal rights out there just yet, especially not in deepest Devon.

But, you see, it's not always me who is being offensive. I notice lots of other people are at it too. Lots. This is a truth that is older than me! When I was at school, the ginger kids used to get beaten up and have their dinner money nicked. Remembering this, I consoled myself that at least my gingerness was temporary. But it annoyed me that the facial recognition on my phone didn't even recognise me, and I had to keep tapping in the code. It was like my phone was bullying me! However, as much as I love a joke, especially rude ones, it's sad to think that so many people actually judge others on their appearance or by their job. Just because they are ginger doesn't mean that they are less of a human. One of my staff is a proper gingerist, if there is such a word: she hates ginger people. If she sees one coming towards her while walking, she will cross the road, as if ginger hair is contagious. I think this is shocking, and I mock her for being such a xenophobe.

Then there are the job-snobs who equally annoy me. When I bump into old school friends and they ask what I do for a job, I am always irritated by the look on their faces when I say I am a cleaner. This is especially true when I bump into old school teachers who tilt their heads to one side and give me a sympathetic look with the phrase, "Well it's a job, isn't it?" I'd rather be the man who makes unsuitable vagina jokes than someone who looks down on others for their jobs.

But being ginger didn't help my thought-farting. My brain took over what my mouth didn't have a chance to say to anyone! I began pondering a list of comebacks ready for my next encounter, but while doing so, I happened to notice an upside to being ginger. It's fair to say, while I was temporary ginger, it certainly didn't help my sex life. Flip me! It's an easily marketable form of protection. Parents, if you want your kids to be old-skool, and you don't want them having sex, just dye their hair ginger. They won't get any action at all!

You might want me to zip it now, but as I already said, I can't zip my mouth. It has a life of its own. Safe sex to me when I was a kid was pulling the bed away from the wall and sticking a cushion behind the headboard so my parents wouldn't hear me banging away. My parents are religious and didn't really believe in sex before marriage, so I'm pretty sure if they had known about the ginger thing, they would have forced my younger brother to bathe in ginger hair dye because he was constantly banging away with anyone and everyone!

I think having an unzipped mouth runs in the family. For example, one of my friends cannot help telling me far too much. He told me once he had a three-way with a girl and his mate. One had the vera, the other had the bum hole, and they basically spit roasted her. He said after his mate had taken her up the bum, this girl sucked his mate off. Is this sexy? It can't be hygienic! I'm pretty sure she must have tasted poo.

Sometimes, I actually manage to keep my mouth closed. Thankfully. The threesome story is a prime example of where I managed to keep in the list of things I wanted to say but didn't. The girl is now married, and I bumped into her husband not so long ago after God knows how many years. He told me he was settled down with a local girl and gave me her name. I immediately knew who he was talking about, and I had to bite my top lip to stop myself from recounting the rampant sex event. He was proud she was one of very few girls from my hometown who hadn't been around the block, and he claimed his wife was an angel. I thought, *Bloody hell, she definitely wasn't in her younger days. She's had more rides than a Blackpool donkey, that's for sure!*

But I didn't say it.

That said, as you may have realised, it's safe to say there have been many awkward moments in my working life. Pretty much most of them I have caused myself, and I could have learned to avoid a lot of them. But none of them compare to a mate of mine who came home from work one day and found his wife wearing a strap-on willy!

I'm not sure how I would have reacted in that situation. Apparently she did it for a laugh as he kept going for bum hole and she wanted to show him how it felt, however, I was once having sex with a girl from behind and noticed how hairy her back was. I'd never observed it before, and it put me off if I'm honest. I felt like I was having sex with a chimp, and let's just say she sounded like one at the time. Looking back, hopefully I didn't slip in the wrong hole by mistake… Anyway, moving on! Here are a few of my own personal awkward moments!

Many years ago, we were cleaning a large house. It was a regular job, however I had over-quoted for the work. By that I mean I had quoted more hours than it actually took to do the work. Unfortunately, it was out in the sticks and the owners were always home, so it didn't pay to reduce the hours and charge less. So, we used to kill time. Unfortunately, there was no WiFi in the area at the time, so we had to make our own entertainment. I'm sure you can imagine how this could quickly go wrong!

Quite often, three of us would be on the job, and we would play a game of hide and seek. One day, I decided to hide in an upstairs cupboard, only for the owner to open the door and find me.

"What are you doing in here?" she asked, surprised.

I quickly thought on my feet and said, "I didn't realise you were also playing hide and seek!"

I'm joking – I actually said I had heard a noise, went into the cupboard to investigate, and the door shut on me. I'm not sure she believed me, but I got out of the way before she asked me anything else. Also, we never played hide and seek again.

Another awkward moment came when I was cleaning a house and I found out the owners were expecting an au pair to stay for the summer. I only discovered this as I was cleaning out the guest bedroom and saw a welcome letter and a list of rules they expected the au pair to stick to.

When I was cleaning downstairs, the owners came back and we made polite conversation. I then said, "I see you have an au pair coming to stay?"

"How do you know that?" she asked.

"I saw the welcome letter," I said. "I wasn't being nosey,

but I was wiping the desk and the letter dropped to the floor."

Well, she didn't look too pleased. "I hope you didn't read it!" she said, and I had to work hard to not snigger or snort.

Sheepishly, I lied, "No, I didn't!" However, I don't think she believed me!

Of course I had read it, and it was a fascinating and terrifying read. The poor, unsuspecting au pair lasted a mere two weeks at the house before she went back to her home country. After seeing the list of rules and what they expected from her, it was clear she wasn't there just to look after the kids; they expected her to be more like free labour for the summer! Since when has an au pair been required to help muck out the horses? That was rule number 67!

Another awkward moment came when I was cleaning at an old lady's house, and I decided to put on her dressing gown. She was in the lounge watching TV; myself and another cleaner had finished, and we decided to play a game of 'Guess Who'. Anyway, I got the dressing gown on with ease, however, trying to get the ruddy thing off was another matter altogether. I was stuck and flapping around like a bird with a broken wing.

Suddenly, I heard the old lady get up and start making her way to the bedroom where I was. She was walking with her Zimmer frame; the thud of the frame was getting louder the closer she got, and the drag in between each thud made it sound like some supernatural, hideous demon spirit about to burst in and murder us for our treachery! It totally panicked me as I just couldn't get the gown back over my head!

In the end, and just about in the nick of time, I managed to pull the thing off, but I ripped the sleeve. She walked in and there I was holding her dressing gown where the sleeve had ripped. *Bollocks!* I thought. *Caught in the act!* Desperate to not get into trouble, I told her that while I was cleaning it got stuck under the door and I couldn't free it and that's how it ripped. She said not to worry, it was an old one anyway. The feeling of relief was like a rush from doing an extreme sport.

The other cleaner didn't guess who I was either. Plus, as a token of good will, I bought the old lady a new dressing gown. For those of you wondering who I was pretending to be, it was Super Gran! Do you remember the TV show or the books?

Another occasion that was awkward, I feel a bit of shame for doing. Normally, if I work on Armistice Day, it is always an occasion where we will down tools and join in the two minutes of silence when it falls at 11am. I feel strongly about this remembrance service; it is a small token of a way to show respect at the end of the day, a tiny gesture to remember those who made the ultimate sacrifice. I always think it's the least anyone can do.

However, one Remembrance Day, I was rushed off my feet and totally forgot all about the two minutes' silence. I walked into a kitchen showroom, and I didn't even notice people were stood still and not making a noise. I just burst through the doors, calling out, "Morning, everyone! Ruddy hell, it's like a library in here!"

That's when the manager pointed to the screen on the TV, and it dawned on me: it was Armistice Day. I wanted the ground to suck me up there and then!

Some of these awkward moments are pretty tame compared to what used to happen when I worked in radio years ago. In particular, I enjoyed hearing when radio competitions went wrong. There was one in Australia when they were playing a version of Mr and Mrs on the radio airwaves, and I heard about it as a production warning. The game they played was based on a famous TV game where they basically ask the husband and wife the same questions, and if they give the same answers they win a prize. This one was a biggy – the prize was a holiday.

On the day I am thinking about, the wife was at home on the phone and the husband was at work. The questions were:

How many times do you make love each week?

The wife answered, "Twice."

When was the last time you did it?

The wife answered, "Yesterday."

And finally, where was the last time you made love?

The wife responded, "In the kitchen."

So, they then asked the husband the same three questions. He was a little embarrassed answering them, however, his wife was there encouraging him to be honest to win a trip on the Gold Coast. So, they got to the first question: how many times do you make love each week?

He replied nervously, "Twice."

"Correct!" the presenter said.

When was the last time you did it?

Nervously, the husband said, "Yesterday actually."

By this point, the presenter was excited. The final question: where was the last time you made love?

The husband went quiet; his wife shouted on the other line, "Just tell them! Be honest!"

The husband said, "I'm not sure I should."

His wife said, "I've already told them so you might as well."

He answered, "Up the ass."

They didn't win the trip to the Gold Coast; however, it was a legendary piece of broadcasting!

Another spectacular piece of radio which was the most awkward moment I have ever heard in my life, and it happened on a radio station in the USA where they were giving away Kayne West tickets. So, the concept was, they got a contestant on the phone, and in this case, it was a lady, and she had to complete a kind of dare for a prize. All she had to do was call her husband at work and get him to say, "I love you," without telling him directly. Sorry, I lied, that's not all she had to do…

Now, the twist to it was, she had to first tell her husband some shocking fake news which was fed to her by the radio presenter. In this case, she had to tell her husband that their eight-year-old child wasn't his. I mean, the things people will do for Kanye West tickets baffles me!

As you can imagine, this had disaster written all over it. So, the lady phoned her husband at work and the radio presenter dropped the mics so the husband had no idea he was live on the radio. The wife than casually says to him, "Babe! I really need to tell you something! This secret is eating me up inside! Anyway, our son, Dylan, well, he isn't actually yours!"

As you can imagine, he hit the roof! The wife tried to calm him down, and she kept telling him, "I love you," in the hope he would say the words back and they would win the tickets. But Oh Boy! The call went in completely the opposite direction!

The husband turned around and said, "Well, we both have secrets. I've been shagging your sister for the last few years!"

The radio presenters came back on air, realising that this had backfired, and cut straight to an ad break. I'm not sure what the outcome was as they didn't talk about it again. I am not convinced it was really worth a pair of Kanye West tickets!

But, back to me and my confessions of awkwardness. My girlfriend once asked me what my favourite sexual position was, I replied, "Next Door." Another personally embarrassing moment was when I was pulled over by the police. I went around a roundabout and noticed a blue light flashing in the background, so I pulled over. As it happens, one of the cleaners I had with me that day knew the police lady; she apparently went to school with her.

"Do you know why I've pulled you over?" she asked in a serious tone.

I was going to cheekily answer, was it to get my number? However, she was as fat as a house and looked angry. I didn't think it was worth flirting and making things worse. So, I said, "Yes. Was it because I was on my phone?"

She replied, "No – you're not wearing a seat belt."

I nearly died there and then.

She then said it was lucky for me she hadn't seen me on my phone otherwise it would have been six points and £200 fine! Thankfully, she let me off with just a caution for not wearing a seat belt. I don't even know how I wasn't wearing one, to be fair, as it's just a habit to put it on. I never forget… Well, almost never. However, I nearly talked myself into bigger trouble. Sometimes saying less is more!

But then, that's the story of my life! Perhaps I'm like a Bag-For-Life – easy access into a whole bagful of trouble!

CHAPTER 25

Social Tissues

Throughout my life, I have heard many people use intellectualism to wax philosophical about Mankind. They talk about what they've read, where they've travelled, or use historical name-dropping to make themselves sound insightful, as if the thoughts of a man who has been dead for four centuries can tell us how to cure the ills of man – even though, wise as he might have been, we still suffer from many of the same problems. Well, let me tell you, cleaning generates as deep a philosophical thinking as any books. Using nothing more elitist than bog roll, some innovative cleaning hacks, and a good old-fashioned cuppa, I will show you some of the inner workings of modern people – in all their filthy glory!

Cleaning has long been recognised as important for your state of mind – both representing your current welfare as well as a way to affect your disposition. You might have heard it said that always making your bed in the mornings is a good way to start the day with positivity, or other sayings such as tidy house, tidy mind. That said, it also means you can go home confidently with whoever you pull if you get lucky. Just don't have a golliwog on your bed!

We have already discussed the mental Instagram cleaning influencers, but that is just about showing off how tidy they are as a kind of currency – shouting, 'I am better than you because my home is more coordinated.' But there is one woman who knows the true value of cleaning: Marie Kondo. She has now made a TV and publishing career out of helping people to love their homes through cleaning and organising the things in it. She even talks to the house and thanks it, performing gratitude through domestic chores. I mean, I admire her care but as a simple bloke from Devon, I can't say I talk to my wardrobe often – the mirror on the other hand... Saying that, I once saw an old lady doing this, but I think she was a little barmy and not Kondo-ing her home. Anyway, my point is this is just the beginning – the tip of the cleaning iceberg of wisdom.

For example, I have a theory that you can tell how much a company cares about its employees by the quality of the toiletries in the toilets. In fact, I'd go further – how companies manage rest breaks in general is symptomatic of how we care for our society. And it's not whether they offer yoga after work or send you cute little mantras to get you through your day. No. Just ensure your staff can have a decent dump, and you're onto a winner!

Over the years, we have cleaned a lot of offices and factories and you can work out which companies actually give a shit about their employees by the quality of their toilet paper. Simple.

Do you remember when we were kids at school and we used to have that hard toilet paper? You know the stuff – it had zero absorbency and essentially acted as sandy greaseproof paper to smear your poo up your back! Ruddy hell! That stuff could take the barnacles off a ship's hull! It exfoliated your ass every time you wiped! It was a sure-fire way to terrify kids from taking a dump at school. I wonder if our primary school experiences with loos is what has caused us to be so uptight as a population in adult life! I wonder how many psychologists have run through the thought process. Well, sir, you do have some early developmental repression; did you by chance have to use that sandpaper loo roll when you were small? Perhaps schools were offered a two-for-one deal, as the paper was perfect for our heavy-handed artwork and sanding in DT classes, wasn't it? I wonder how many people now have public-loo-PTSD as a result of a traumatic toilet experience at the age of six.

Perhaps these traumatised kids have grown up into the bosses who inflict crap paper on their staff nowadays.

What always struck me as a crappy touch, at several posh offices we cleaned for, such as solicitors' offices, the managers would put posh toilet paper in the customers' toilets and in the staff toilets there would be a cheaper version. Nice way to let your loyal employee know how little you care when their pants are down. What a way to make your customers think you're better than you are!

Although, there is another side to this story, and I realise I'm being a bit unfair. I don't like unnecessary extravagance, so I've never understood why people spend a lot of money on buying the most luxurious toilet paper. At the end of the day, it wipes up shit and then gets flushed down the loo anyway. It's hardly something to treasure. That said, poor quality paper can ruin someone's day... and their productivity, so think on that!

Going back to the office, and to philosophy from cleaning. I have also contemplated what we can discern about the human condition from other toilet behaviours. I mean, I cannot fathom the reason nobody EVER changes the toilet roll holders in the office. Is it an action expressing the thought, *It's not my job,* or are employees so stressed and pressed for time, they cannot possibly fit in one more humble task? Or are people just too selfish to do something that might benefit others? The number of times I would clean a place and find the cardboard roll on the holder and the new roll on top of the toilet, I honestly came to think I must have been the roll-keeper, the only one with the key to change it. I think if I found a loo roll changed, I'd have probably needed medical attention for shock! But surely it doesn't take brain cells to change a loo roll? Why is it so hard? I guess it's true what they say, everyone wants to change the world but nobody wants to change the loo roll!

Wisdom from loo roll etiquette goes even further. I love the phrase somebody once told me about this necessary little paper bundle. It goes: life is like toilet paper; you're either on a roll or taking shit from some asshole! Flip me! How true is that?

Now I think about it, the humble loo roll is actually the source of so many pertinent observations about the human condition. Cripes – like those cute but destructive Andrex puppies pulling paper all over the house, man's wastefulness is evident in how so many people waste toilet paper. Some people do things like layer it over the seat before they sit on it. It's like they think one layer of paper is going to protect them from a horrible bacteria – that's what you have skin for! And showers, of course. Plus, it's why they pay people like me to come in and keep those germs at bay. I mean, why else would people be so wasteful? Unless they're worried about splash-backs of course, but still, you can wash your arse easier than we can keep producing these toiletries at the pace we use them!

But then, I think people generally use more toilet paper than they need. Don't get me wrong, I understand most of this is down to the quality of the paper; hence why I think it is the responsibility of the employer to look after their staff – and their arses. After all, there is nothing worse than putting your fingers through the paper while you're mid-wipe after a curry poo.

But if everyone used less sheets every time they wiped, they would probably save a tree every year – maybe more. Entire forests might recover off the back of more conservative bog-roll usage. Plus, that would be a considerable reduction in the amount of plastic packaging and transport too. But then, perhaps it is easy for me to comment because I'm pretty consistent: I use six sheets per wipe; it gets you good coverage and poop-clearance. And I always crumple it before throwing into the pan. Can you believe 40% of people fold the toilet paper?

And don't get me started on scented toilet paper! You see it everywhere: lavender, coconut, floral bouquets… What is wrong with people? Are they hoping to conceal that their shit stinks too? I swear, the people who buy these must be the same people who have tidy homes, but everything is wedged into a cupboard that's bursting at the seams. I think I end up house clearing for some of these people! For God's sake: the paper is not where you need fragrance! Do you go into bathrooms and sniff the roll? Really, what is the point of perfumed bum paper? I don't think your bum hole is commenting, "Oh! What joy! This is a lovely scented paper!" while it's being wiped. Saying that, I still think some ladies could do with a plug-in air freshener for their fannies. Febreze Fannay does have a ring to it. Where was I?

Personally, I recommend sticking to mid-range toilet paper; it is soft enough for comfort and cheap enough to use. At the end of the day, you're going to flush it away – and that's the only thing apart from poo and wee that should go down the toilet. Although a reasonably priced bamboo paper is also a good consideration these days – it has a much smaller environmental impact, and it rhymes with poo. Also, so many loo paper companies have given themselves pleasing pun names, such as 'Serious Tissues', 'Who Gives a Crap?' And my personal favourite: 'Bumboo'!

This reminds me... While I am thinking about toilets and loo roll, a female friend of mine once told me how her bloke liked to have sex over a toilet. Wait, it gets more interesting! So, he would take her from behind and while he orgasmed, he would push her head towards the toilet and then flush it! I told her it sounded more like abuse, but she then replied it wasn't the most unusual thing to happen to her during sex...

I know, right? How is that not the most unusual thing to have happened during sex?

I enquired what she meant, and she continued by telling me about one previous bloke who liked her to bark like a dog during sex. I don't know what this tells me about her that she found her head being flushed more acceptable than barking for orgasm! Sometimes there are no words! I suppose for her there were either just woofs or choking sounds. Subsequently, I have been sorry I didn't extend the conversation and ask what sort of barking noise he liked – a high-pitched yap like a Chihuahua or a big deep bark like a Great Dane. I should have asked, is this what he thought dogging meant? Ruddy hell! At the time, I thought the less I said the better. Who knew I had a shy side? And who would have guessed my shyness would be triggered by gruff sex?

Another side of the human condition that has occurred to me through the process of cleaning is our innate propensity to solve problems and create innovative solutions. For example, anyone who knows me, and really knows me, knows I am tighter than a camel's nostrils in a desert storm. So, it won't come as a great surprise to know that we very rarely had loads of cleaning products in the van and quite often they would be watered down anyway. As a result, there has been the odd occasion where we had to improvise – and often with great success. So much so, I wish I'd created an Instagram account to rival the upsurge in extreme housewives.

Earlier in the book I mentioned we used Tipp-Ex on mould in a conservatory, but there have been many occasions this kind of radical, outside-the-box thinking has been useful. For example, one day while cleaning a house, the owner left a note for us to remove the black mould from her shower. Normally, we would just leave bleach on it and go back to it later. However, we didn't have any bleach and nor did the woman who owned the house. We were faced with a conundrum!

I thought, *I can't just leave it.* Obviously, we wanted to do the job well to be professional, but it's also worth noting this owner was a bit of a cow so it wasn't worth the earache to not finish the job whatever the method. This woman had a big gob; let's just say I have a big willy, but even I'd get lost in her mouth! Despite this, we tried all our other cleaning products, and they didn't touch it.

So, stumped for what to do next, I looked on the internet. This was an issue in itself as Devon is far from being the county with the best phone signal. So, first of all, I nicked her WiFi code! Then, I read an article about how vodka can be used to clean mould. I know, I know – that is an expensive solution! But thankfully the woman had some, so we used hers!

For the solution, I mixed 50% water and 50% vodka in a bottle and sprayed it on the mould. Then, I just left it for five minutes, feeling smug the issue was solved. When I went back to it nothing had happened. So, I thought, *Stuff this, let's just put neat vodka on the stains!* Again, I left it for a few minutes; this time, lo and behold, it worked!

I then put the lady's vodka back and she was none the wiser! Unless of course she thought we had enjoyed a quick tipple at work...

I must admit I do love a surprising cleaning hack, and there appears to be no end of the human imagination for solutions. Some have been around forever and are testament to the innovation of our ancestors. Over the years, I have cleaned windows with vinegar and newspaper like they did back in the 1920s only cos I didn't have any window spray in the van. But, in truth, I am probably a little reserved when it comes to experimenting with alternative household products as cleaning materials. Some I have embraced, such as cheap cola to eat away limescale, but others have baffled me. Apparently, Listerine, the popular and intense mouthwash, was previously marketed as a surgical disinfectant and as a great floor cleaner. I'm okay with this so far, but I haven't checked its effectiveness since it was also marketed as a cure for gonorrhoea – and I'm not convinced it's the best choice of substance to put on your most sensitive parts... I can assure you, however, ketchup is great at cleaning many metals, and baking soda is a one-stop-shop of cleaning brilliance. We really need not spend a fortune on a zillion different chemicals for each separate job – we have everything we need in our cupboards already: just add a little human ingenuity!

Humans are a mind-boggling species if you stop and think about it. We are as hard-working as ants, as ingenious as foxes, as skilled as spiders, and as artistic as bees and birds. We can be as cruel as orcas and as playful as dolphins. Then sometimes we just sit down, and watch others do it for us. We are the only species that builds its homes and then finds ways to persuade people from entirely other countries to make things for us or come and clean for us. We are simultaneously industrious and lazy. And as far as my job goes, it's always puzzled me how people work hard to pay for someone to work hard cleaning for them.

But I always think it's interesting to see what ignites a strong work ethic in people, and I find it follows a pattern where work ethic is not intrinsic, but directly related to expected rewards. Cleaners are quite like keen-bean paperboys and girls (or are they known as paper-people these days? Although, that makes them sound like a decorative ornament you can make at home). The expectation of extra tips over the holidays always drove easy recruitment at Christmas. I suppose this is like all of us really – I'm not sure bankers would be so quick to be blood-sucking leeches without their massive bonuses rewarding their savagery.

But the truth of it is quite sad really: cleaners very rarely get tips. This is at once an example of people being greedy, wanting extra pay, and people being selfish, not wanting to give away a single penny more than necessary. It's an example of both these contrasting human qualities existing in one exchange of services like a people-based sweet-and-sour!

Aside from our strange loo roll habits and our resourcefulness, the other simple thing that forms the backbone of our social conduct is the importance of a cup of tea. I know I am renowned for being tight, but the extent of human thoughtlessness and lack of generosity always astounds me, and never more so than with the power of the offer of a cuppa. Oftentimes as cleaners, we don't get offered drinks. Just like with the tiered loo rolls I talked about at the start of this chapter, there's a hierarchy of hospitality too. I bet you as many pounds as you'd like to carry, important clients always get a cup of tea – and a nice biscuit too. I guess the rule isn't about how to treat your guests, but knowing the different ways to treat different guests of varying degrees of importance – apparently, you must never serve your server...

Although, to be frank, at some of the places we cleaned, you would never want to use the cups anyway, that's for sure. I have witnessed mould in various colours and shapes. I have also seen respectable staff members assume a quick rinse is enough to make a mug usable again. The word sticky now evokes harrowing images I'll not scar you with! I hope these people are different at home – but I'd be too terrified to find out.

I remember one of my staff members getting a cup of tea from a client once. My staff member was really looking forward to it, but the milk had clearly gone off – it had turned, and we could see and smell it. This woman still served it to my staff member as if it was fine and dandy. To make matters worse, the tea was basically 90% milk! When the customer wasn't looking, the cleaner ended up pouring it in one of her plant pots.

And this isn't a one-off either. The number of tradesmen

who say they get offered drinks at customers houses but never drink them as they are rank is surprisingly high. Some researchers did a survey recently and it found 60% of tradesmen don't even get offered a drink when working at a customer's house. Over half of those who were offered drinks said it was awful and they ended up throwing it away! Would we offer our grandmas drinks with such little care? What about our bosses? So why is it okay to be slapdash with our cleaners and other tradespeople?

But this might be a good place to stop as I can feel myself getting wound up like a spinning top. So, I won't even get started on the absence of biscuits for cleaners. The social stratification of biscuit offers for guests could be an entire chapter – nay, an entire book – by itself! From whether you give out individually designed shortbread or cheap-assed Rich Tea fingers that can't take a dunking, the biscuit is as political as anything else. You'll have to tune in for my next book: *The World is full of Hobnobs*. Now that really would take the biscuit!

CHAPTER 26

Bin There, Done That

I have learned some lessons along the way in my cleaning career. Some of them have become lifelong learning; others continue to prove to be true, but still make little sense to me.

Something that always catches my attention are the strange habits of older folk. Some are understandable, for example most of the old people we clean for are deaf and therefore have the TV on soooo loud it's deafening. I sometimes wonder if it stops their neighbours from being able to choose anything different on their own TVs. And yet it's always older folk who complain that the youth of today are so noisy! They can't hear Columbo or Coronation Street, but they can make out the sound of teenagers listening to rap music a street away. That said, I don't mind the TV on full when I'm cleaning – it means I can still follow the story even when I am hoovering.

The other thing older people do is have the heating on full blast – even during the summer! Christ! One place we went to was like a sauna! The house had its own weather system, and the BBC gave it a humidity rating! Curly hair frizzed within seconds of entering the hallway. I'm surprised she didn't have tropical parrots flying around the living room – it was that hot. I've sweated less cleaning greenhouses. And of course, old people also bulk buy everything. *You're 97 years old why are you buying 96 jars of mayonnaise?* And they are also soooooo proud of their age - *I'm 97 years old, you know*, yes but you still smell of piss!

At the other end of the age spectrum, I have learned you can't talk to kids in this day and age. I don't mean you can't talk to kids because they're rude or stupid – I mean you can't talk to them because you then look like a weirdo! I was at a women's refuge cleaning a while ago and a lady came into the kitchen with her daughter. As you can imagine, being in a refuge can't be pleasant, so I felt inclined to be friendly. I offered the little girl a sweet and the mum intervened, explaining she didn't allow her to accept sweets from strangers. I totally get this, and I initially felt bad for offering the treat, however, as I left the kitchen the little girl turned to her mum and said, "Mummy, is that a sex offender?"

Another thing I have learned is that every customer is unique regardless of wealth or background. Also, you must treat them all the same no matter how you feel about them – you must treat them as you would like to be treated, even if they are failing to uphold that value in return. Being polite doesn't cost anything and being rude doesn't change the other person – it just means there are two arseholes and not one.

But sometimes it's challenging to do this, and this is why we invented clichés and small talk. It means you can cope with any person at any time. I have come across my fair share of weirdos in the past, like the bloke who wanted to travel to every Wetherspoons pub and take pictures of the carpets. This was a genuine hobby. Apparently, train spotting wasn't niche enough. To cope with this kind of surprise, most staff and clients use the weather as conversation openers when meeting each other. Familiar patterns of conversation such as, "What horrible weather!" and, "What a lovely morning!" go a long way to raise a smile and make people feel comfortable. Typically, everyone says the same thing when it comes to rain: "Oh! I hate the rain. I don't mind if it's cold, I just don't like rain!"

And the weather does make a big difference – in a country with such a variable and often dismal climate, the weather affects our habits, moods, and motivation. Every month has its place in the yearly cycle, and it's inevitably the same. January is a bad month for us cleaners, and this is for several reasons. Firstly, office staff are normally grumpy as hell in January. January blues are a real thing. As are extended hangovers and over-spent bank accounts. Sadly, the brunt of their anger is often directed at the cleaners as they are easy targets. Secondly, a lot of offices have clear-outs, so there's a lot of old files to clear and dusty old furniture to empty and organise, so the work is filthier than usual. Thirdly, everyone is always sad to see the Christmas decorations go; fairy lights do put people in a better mood. Finally, a lot of companies decide to either get rid of or replace cleaning contractors with the new year, so there is normally a lot of change. This is especially true if companies are struggling; the first to get the boot will be the cleaning contractor, and some poor unsuspecting employee is given the cleaning work on top of their normal duties.

This brings me to the next lesson I learned – and it's a sour one. There is no loyalty in business anymore. The little old ladies who cleaned the same offices for 147 years just don't exist these days. They have hung up their fluffies for the final time and gone to the great dust cloud in the sky.

Regardless of how long you have cleaned for a company, when the time comes and your face doesn't fit any more, don't expect a golden handshake. One particular office we cleaned for over five years had the atmosphere of Buffalo Bill's house when Jodie Foster was hiding in the dark. They sacked one female staff member when she told them she was up the duff. Apparently, in her interview she failed to mention she was doing IVF! Anyway, I'm pretty sure that's illegal, but when each staff member feels silenced and alone, what can you do about it? It's the same company who tried to exploit the furlough system until a member of staff walked out and told them he was going to report them. Rightly so, I thought!

It wasn't an enjoyable office to clean, in all fairness. They had such a high turnover of staff we didn't get to know anyone. The ones who were there didn't speak or move; instead, they sat like robots robbed of personality. Whenever we cleaned, we felt like we were in the way – as if the management would have preferred us to be invisible. The tension was high, like an overstretched elastic band about to snap.

Anyway, the office manager was a renowned super-bitch; all the staff would moan about her, and many staff left or walked out due to the way she spoke to people. She was a wannabe tyrant. Thankfully, I personally didn't suffer this side of her for most of the five years, but I was always aware of the sufferings of others. You could see it in their eyes even when they didn't say anything. Granted, she never looked happy and always grunted when I spoke to her. But I am a simple man and when I am uptight, I always have a simple solution: a good shag. So, I thought maybe she just needed finger blasting; it's amazing how a bit of fingering can change the outlook for some people.

Then, out of the blue in a recent December, I received an email from the office manager. Bear in mind we had cleaned for over five years, and I thought we had a solid relationship with the firm. The email just read, 'Take this email as confirmation we will not need your services in the new year.'

That was it. It was short, to the point, and as sharp as Marie Antoinette's guillotine. There was no thank you, no message saying happy Christmas, no best wishes for the new year or the future. I didn't take it personally though. The manager's rudeness was legendary, so I guess I finally saw first-hand what others had been talking about. When I read it, I smiled to myself and simply replied, 'Thanks for email. Have a lovely Christmas!' After all, the best revenge is love; I was not going to stoop to her level of rudeness!

As it happens, she did me a favour as it was a job we had ear-marked to drop off as other contracts were financially better sense, and I was struggling to staff it. But it just goes to show it doesn't matter how much you do for people sometimes, you're just a number and sometimes your number is up. But then, I've always found when one door shuts another one opens. I often believe it's hard to see the crack of light in a new doorway if you're still standing in the light of the door you should let close.

Another lesson I learned is about territory. For example, never advertise your own ironing service in someone else's laundrette – they kick off merry Hell! Ironing was a good hustle to add to my cleaning empire. After a few years of trading, I set up a side business where we would undertake people's ironing. It was always something people asked for, but I wasn't always able to help. Then, I employed a lady who enjoyed ironing – which is weird! But I was grateful for that unique hobby.

Anyway, to drum up enough business, I made up some

flyers and put them in laundrettes. My error was worse than just the location of my promotional material. I didn't put my number on the flyer; for ease, I put the ironing lady's number. So, initially, it was her who received all the abuse for my crossing into someone else's business territory.

The business was a sound idea. The plan was, I set it up for her, gave her an iron and a board, made flyers, and got 25% commission on all work she completed. From memory, we charged £15 for a basket containing a maximum of 5 shirts. We soon learnt if you didn't put a maximum of shirts people would take the piss. The next thing we knew, the poor ironing lady was up all night starching collars and ironing delicate fabrics. But we soon got the perfect system.

Anyway, the business did pretty well... until the owner of a laundrette phoned up and went mental, saying we were taking her work!

That said, it was easy money for me – I suppose you could call me an ironing pimp! I didn't even get involved in drop-offs or pick-ups, but in hindsight that was a massive mistake. Our system was simple; I just got given the money at the end of the month and left her to do the invoicing. After a few months, I noticed that I was getting less money, yet she always seemed to have loads of ironing. I think she soon cottoned on that she didn't really need me. Still, it was good while it lasted. I suppose it's another lesson in why you should never employ family members. After all, you are bound by codes of trust and favour, but actually each of you just wants to make money.

Another lesson I learned was that customers are not always right – sometimes they are crazy and expect the impossible! When you're a cleaner or run a cleaning firm, don't think that nobody will contact you on Christmas Day, because believe me, they will! One client messaged me on Christmas morning wondering what time we would be in! Christmas that year happened to fall on his cleaning day, a Friday, and he had assumed it would be business as normal. Plus, he messaged me at 7:45am, waking me up!

When I replied I didn't work on Christmas Day, he simply replied, 'Oh no! I suppose I'll have to clean myself today!' I suppose there's a second lesson here – there's no pleasing some people! I suppose in his mind, if he didn't want to do his cleaning any other day of the year, why would he want to do it on Christmas Day? But then, it's not just idiots who make this assumption. Did you hear about how the Queen was allegedly upset her staff refused to 'bubble' with her for four weeks over Christmas during COVID? Apparently, she expected her staff to forego any time with their own families to allow her to have a well-tended royal Christmas. God forbid Lizzie having to cook her own sprouts that day!

And a another lesson is more of a warning really. I have learned people collect the strangest things, and it always comes to light when people die suddenly. I mean, someone has to sort through your things, so perhaps get your guilty pleasures in order early to avoid suffering a post-mortem humiliation. Porn was the most common collection we uncovered when clearing out old council houses. It always used to be stacks and stacks of VHS tapes – and I'm talking the old-school stuff. Sometimes it was under the bed, sometimes in dusty heaps in a garage or in a cupboard, sometimes even hoarded all over the house. Generally, there was too much of it to be a healthy thing, bringing to mind images of these people just sitting and watching porn for day upon day on end. I'm sure you can imagine there was also a lot of used tissue paper in these houses – and not the posh stuff! There was lots of Debbie doing everyone across the USA, and a whole lot of deep-throating. But I guess all of that sounds tame when compared to the enormous array of options available online nowadays. Anyway, the lesson I took from this is to clean away anything you don't want your mother finding.

A strange but true thing is I've never really owned any porn; perhaps I'm too much of a modern man after all! The closest I came, pun definitely intended, was a collection I put together when I did a paper round as a kid. Every time Helen Labdon was featured on page three, I would cut her out and stick her into a scrap book. A really sad thing is I still have it somewhere to this day. Does that make me sound like a serial killer? I haven't got locks of her hair in there too.

Talking about porn and lessons, I'm reminded of a personal moment. One of my former girlfriends bought me a porno video once to spice up our sex life. They weren't cheap! Forty-odd quid she paid for it! Mega bucks! This was before porn was free on the internet, back when you had to buy it from special shops with papered out windows, or from a dimly lit section of a film store where everyone looked sleazy or uncomfortable. Anyway, it turned out to be more of an educational video, so we learned a lot of anatomical vocabulary, but it didn't really help get us going. From memory it featured two oriental ladies who were pretty hairy down below, almost as though they stuffed a couple of ferrets down there!

And finally, one final lesson, always use a library card when withdrawing books from a library – you would not believe the grief you get when you don't!

CHAPTER 27

The Cleaning of Life

I know the thank-you section should be for all the people who have helped and supported me along my journey, but I actually want to use this section differently. My friends and family know how much I value them, and I will thank each of them personally – and I might even get them a better Christmas present this year.

Instead, I want to throw the love out to all the people who have helped ignite a fire in my belly. So, I want to say a big thank you to all the people who say, "That's not my job!" or, "I couldn't do what you do for a living!" It's your attitude that has helped me earn a decent living and retire early.

Countless times over the years, we have had call-outs and charged a fortune all because someone has been too proud to get their hands dirty. All too often, someone within their organisation could have cleaned it up in next to no time. It's your squeamish snobbery that has allowed my business to thrive. Whether it's removing dog poo from the entrance to a block of communal flats or cleaning up wee on a toilet seat as someone thought it was below their pay grade to do it, we have pulled up our rubber gloves and mucked in.

So, I owe you a massive thank you. I am proud of the business I built and all I achieved, and I am grateful there was opportunity to do it. It takes all kinds of people to make the world go around, and I hope I've helped to keep it turning – even if it was cleaning the crap off the tracks. There is money in muck, and being someone who was never afraid of hard work or getting my hands dirty really paid off for me.

We are all guilty of judging people on their appearance or for what job they do, so I want to share this true story with you. A vicar I used to know went to take up a position in a new church. On his first Sunday service he dressed up like a tramp and walked into the church and sat down. Some of the congregation moved away from him, others just stared at him, and only one person went over to him and shook his hands to welcome him to the church. With that, he walked to the front of the church, took off his tramp's clothes, and underneath this was his clerical clothing, complete with white dog collar.

There was a gasp from the congregation.

He started his sermon by saying, "Some of you should be ashamed of yourselves. You judged me before you knew who I was."

So the next time you see a cleaner, and you want to walk on by without smiling or saying hello, perhaps think again. They are people too and don't want to be treated as a smelly ghost. You may think they are the lowest of the low, a skid mark on the underskirt of society, but I can assure you, he who laughs last, laughs longest – and I have been laughing my way to the bank all these years. Once I took off my gloves and pinny, of course. But I've also learnt that money really doesn't make you happy. I wasted sooooo much time making money I often forgot about the most important things in life, how human beings treat each other.

So, this thank you is double sided. One side is tart with

bitterness from all the times I have been snubbed, pitied, or jeered at for my profession. Since we all want clean homes, streets and workplaces, it goes without saying we should highly value the people who do this work. So, say hi to a binman and a trolley pusher. Ask after your cleaner's health and family. Put out a tip at Christmas.

The other side of my thank you is truly grateful. I have had a great career. I have met the most amazing and the maddest people, had countless adventures, and my days were filled with laughter and camaraderie. It's been a blast. I have worked hard and for that I have been rewarded.

But it's nearly time for me to hang up my marigolds for the last time. I am passing on my fluffy duster to the next generation of cleaners. God help you all – the youth of today Instagram everything, so if you do something daft or gross, you won't end up as an anecdote in a comedy memoir. No. You'll be a meme for the whole world to see.

So, tidy away your skeletons, pay your cleaners and service staff well, and be polite to everyone. Wishing you the very best: may your homes be clean, your offices tidy, and your mugs ready for the next cup of tea.

And as the saying goes: if you do judge a book by its cover, you might just miss out on an amazing story!

ABOUT THE AUTHOR

After the success of his first book, *Baby Pigeon*, based on his online dating experience – Matt Bird is back, sharing his words of wisdom on the cleaning industry, an industry he knows inside and out.

Matt Bird – a unique, funny, hard-working and successful 40-odd-year-old (anyone would think he wrote this.)

He has run a successful cleaning business for 20-odd years in a small rural town in Devon. It's a special place. Let's just say the marriage counselling service here isn't called Relate, it's called RELATED, and the £3 supermarket meal deal comes with a two-litre bottle of cider as a drinks option.

Let's just say that over the years he has employed the good, the bad, and the stupid, and dealt with customers you would not believe.

Printed in Great Britain
by Amazon

77733087R00174